LOVE
&
MUSIC

Published in Australia by
Magpie Lark Press
PO Box 256
Doreen Victoria 3754

First published in Australia 2021

National Library of Australia Cataloguing–in–Publication entry

 A catalogue record for this book is available from the National Library of Australia

ISBN 978-0-6452194-0-1 (paperback)

Cover layout and design by Betty Martinez
Book layout and design Sophie White

Printed by Kindle Direct Publishing

LOVE & MUSIC

A novel of love, friendship
and forgiveness set in the
colorful world of opera

Patricia Ryan

For Claudia

ACT ONE

- 1 -

Melbourne, October 1990

All week heads had been bobbing up in the nest in the gum tree at the back of the garden, squawking and gobbling. Then, on Leonora's last morning, a feathery bundle emerged and toppled into an ungainly glide, flapping its wings and looking around as if surprised to find itself on the ground.

Watching the small bird Leonora silently urged it on, relieved when it fluttered up to the garden bench where the parent birds perched, waiting. It seemed a good omen. Tomorrow she would be on the other side of the world, spring sunshine exchanged for mist and falling leaves. Unlike the fledgling, she would be spreading her wings alone.

She couldn't remember a time when she hadn't wanted to be a singer, a dream no one but her mother had taken seriously. Listening to old opera LPs as a child she'd heard the voices with a kind of recognition, as if their sound was mysteriously in her bones, deep in her DNA.

She'd held on to her dream through years of exams, competitions and finally the conservatorium, resisting well-meant advice from her mother's friends to do something "more sensible". Now here she was with a scholarship to audition in Germany, on the brink of a whole new life.

She wasn't worried about the journey; she had someone to meet her when she arrived in Munich and a place to stay. Everything had been organized for her. Except the most important thing, the one thing no one else could do. Her audition for Maestro Roberto Mazzone. The scholarship would fund a place in his studio but she had to sing for him in person first. He didn't take everyone they sent him.

A burst of magpie song came from the garden, birds calling and answering from tree to tree until the air was filled with their warbling. Perhaps more chicks had flown.

Leonora turned away from the window and picked up her music case.

What if the Maestro didn't accept her? What if she was going all that way for nothing?

Leonora glanced at her watch, relief at how much time had passed mingled with a pang at the increasing distance from home. With nothing to see but the clouds, the plane hardly seemed to be moving.

She thought of her mother, alone now. It had been just the two of them for so long. Leonora was only seven when her father's cancer was diagnosed and her mother had given up her career as a concert pianist to nurse him, teaching at home after he died. Leonora couldn't remember when she first clambered onto the duet stool next to her, tapping the keys with chubby baby fingers, only that sitting at the piano and singing were as natural as breathing.

They had always known the day would come when Leonora would make her own way. It was what they both wanted. Still, leaving was a wrench. And they didn't know how soon she would be back. The longer she could study with the Maestro, the more great singers she could see perform and learn from, the better.

The thought of the audition loomed again. She would only truly have won if the Maestro accepted her.

She reached up and turned the air vent away from her face. *When*, not *if*, she corrected herself. Singing for the Maestro was the next step towards her dream. There was too much at stake to fail.

- 2 -

Munich, October 1990

In the arrival hall Leonora scanned the signs held up like flags by the waiting taxi drivers, a prickle of nervousness in her stomach. People jostled around her, blocking her view as she tried to find her name. The crowd thinned but there was no sign for her.

Her briefing hadn't included any instructions if no one was there to meet her. Half an hour, she thought. If no one had come by then, she'd make her own way.

"Miss Ford?" The voice behind her was high-pitched and out of breath. "Are you Miss Ford?"

Leonora turned to see a young man gazing at her anxiously, his face flushed and damp with beads of perspiration. "They sent me to the wrong terminal for your flight. Please excuse me." His nose was pink at the tip and quivering, as he tried to catch his breath. Leonora bit her lip to suppress a smile. He was already reaching for her suitcase, too intent on hurrying to the exit to notice.

On each side of the autobahn trees were bright with autumn color, beyond them straw-colored meadows with rolls of silage in neat rows. The arch of the sky felt smaller, more contained, unlike the horizon Leonora knew, where land lay unconfined as far as the eye could see. Changing hemispheres had altered everything. She felt light-headed, disoriented.

Off the autobahn the fields gave way to neat villas painted white; in front gardens towering firs like Christmas trees cast blue-green shadows. In its outer suburbs Munich still lived up to its old nickname *das Millionendorf* – the village of a million people.

Now tall buildings, shops and apartment blocks lined the streets. Would she be staying in an apartment, Leonora wondered? When she'd seen her address – *Lindenstrasse 18* – the romantic in her had hoped for a house with a garden, a linden tree even, like the Schubert song. Mentally she gave herself a pinch – she needed to come down to earth.

And then the taxi turned into a street where a whole row of lindens blazed ochre and gold along one side, and stopped in front of an old-fashioned villa. Bay windows leaned out from the walls, above the porch a stone Madonna and child gazed down and through the open doorway a small figure in black was coming forward to greet her. Like one of those tiny figures on a cuckoo clock that came out if the weather was fine.

"*Willkommen Mädele*. I am Frau Felder. Welcome to my house."

Inside was as old-fashioned as outside: dark wooden doors along a dark paneled hallway; a large hall-stand beside a table with a black telephone on it.

"You'll want to ring home, Mädele." A smile lit up Frau Felder's face and she nodded, as if she had been quietly assessing Leonora and had given her approval. "But we can talk about that later." She turned towards the stairs. "Your room is on the top floor. Leave your case here for now if it's heavy."

It was. As well as her clothes, Leonora had packed as many music scores as she could carry. Clearly not much escaped Frau Felder. In her black dirndl dress and apron, her silver hair plaited and fastened round her head, she trod as lightly on the stairs as a girl; as if she had lived here so long, going up and down these stairs each day, that her footsteps had forgotten to age.

The room was more than Leonora had expected, with a small kitchen area in one corner and a separate bathroom outside on the landing. Back home a real estate agent would have stretched its description into a studio apartment.

The furniture was simple: a bed that could be converted into a couch during the day, a small table and chairs, a wardrobe and a bookshelf. There was a bright cover on the bed and light was streaming in through an open window and a skylight in the sloping roof.

Frau Felder spread her hands, encompassing the room. "I think you'll find everything you need, Mädele. I've put a few things in the cupboard to start you off. And you'll be able to sing as much as you like. No one will hear you." Her eyes sparkled with good humor. "Though I might listen sometimes for the pleasure of it."

Leonora smiled. "There'll be a lot of scales and exercises when I practice, Frau Felder. But I'll be happy to sing for you any time."

"Thank you, Mädele." Frau Felder smoothed an invisible crease from her apron and gave a little curtsey. "I look forward to a command performance. And now I shall leave you to unpack. Come down if there's anything you need."

Leonora crossed to the window and looked out into what must be the back garden: a lawn, a vegetable patch, three small trees. Apple, pear or plum, perhaps. The fallen leaves gave her no clue. It was too cold here for lemons. One more thing she had left behind, the pleasure of picking a lemon straight from the tree.

Two chickens wandered into view, pecking their way through the grass. A knot in her stomach uncurled. She could feel at home here. Who would not, she thought, with a landlady who looked like a grandmother from a picture book and called you "Mädele" – dear girl?

The only thing missing was a piano. Leonora flexed her fingers and ran them along the window sill in an imaginary scale. For the first time in her life she would be without a piano of her own and her budget wouldn't stretch to hiring one. She could make do with her small electronic keyboard for pitching notes when she was singing but she needed a piano if she was to keep her hands flexible. Finding somewhere she could practice regularly would be her first task.

There was so much to do – find a post office, a bank, how to get around. But all she wanted to do now was unpack and sleep.

And in a few days when her voice had recovered from the dryness of the plane journey she would make a time for her audition.

When not *if*, Leonora reminded herself as she went downstairs to fetch her suitcase.

- 3 -

Munich, October 1990

The Maestro wasn't what Leonora expected. She'd imagined someone older, like the picture of Toscanini on the front of her opera scores, white hair and flashing eyes, not this elegant man in a dark suit waiting behind the piano at the end of the long room.

"Come in, Miss Ford." His English was precise, with a slight accent.

Her breath high in her throat, she walked towards him, her footsteps clattering on the wooden floor. She had crossed the world for this moment. She wouldn't get another chance.

She was close enough now to see his face. He smiled at her and gestured towards a chair near the piano. "Put your things there and come and stand where I can see you. We will begin with some exercises."

He played a scale to demonstrate. He must have done this hundreds of times, she thought. But there was no hint of this in his expression. Her knees were trembling but her breathing had steadied. Sheltered in the familiar curve of the piano, she made herself focus on her voice, letting the notes run up and down in a smooth line. He took her higher and higher, then down again, lower and lower. Obediently she followed the chords, like a dancer following a choreographer, a split second behind. At last he paused.

"Now the *messa di voce*." He looked up to see if she had understood. "You are familiar with this?"

Leonora nodded, thankful that her teacher at the conservatorium had insisted on this exercise, so difficult to perfect: singing on one note, from very soft to loud, then back to soft, keeping the sound steady and free. She felt confident enough to look at him now. His expression was pleasant but gave nothing away.

The exercise finished, he made no move to continue, fixing his gaze on her. She shifted her weight from one foot to the other. At least she had lasted this far. If he asked to hear an aria she might have a chance.

He nodded, as if he had come to a decision. "What have you brought to sing?"

"*Mi chiamano Mimi*, from *La Bohème*." She thought she saw a flicker of boredom in his eyes, quickly suppressed. It seemed too obvious now, every soprano's party piece. And what was she thinking of, telling him it was from *La Bohème*, as if he didn't know.

Her cheeks burning, she handed him her score. He glanced at it briefly and put it down, closed.

"Leonora. A most operatic name. Were your parents lovers of opera?"

She swallowed, trying to overcome the dryness in her mouth. She hadn't expected a question like this.

"I was named after my grandmother." It was on the tip of her tongue to add that she only heard about the heroine of *Fidelio* when she went to the conservatorium but she stopped herself in time. Auditions. You could never predict what would happen. That was why people dreaded them. She took a deep breath, straightened her spine and lifted her chin.

"Mimi," he said. "Do you know the whole part?"

Instinctively she knew this was a pass or fail moment.

"Yes," she said, wanting to say more but not finding the words. She was desperate to sing and get it over with.

Quietly he began to play the introduction to Mimi's farewell in Act Three. "Then let me hear this instead. Remember, Puccini has marked this *lento molto, dolce*."

The familiar music calmed her. She had worked on this scene over and over until she had mastered the long phrases sustained on one breath. She had sung it into her body, and now she could let her voice tell the story. It was all there in the music, the bitter cold, Mimi coming through the falling snow to part from her lover; hearing him say he was afraid she was dying; the memory of her happiness when they were first in love, the resignation of her final farewell. *Addio, senza rancor...*

When she had finished, it was quiet in the studio. The Maestro closed the piano lid and stood up.

"You have a feeling for Puccini, Miss Ford. But was that last phrase the *fil di voce*, the wisp of voice that he asked for? One of my first tasks will be to teach you to sing a true pianissimo." He paused. "I will see you twice a week for one hour. But do not underestimate this commitment. I will do my best for you, and I expect nothing less in return. I do not waste my time."

Her breath caught in her throat as she answered him. "Thank you...Maestro...Mazzone."

He smiled. "My pupils just call me Maestro. And I shall call you Leonora. Now go and see my assistant Frau Meyer. She will arrange your times."

Leonora ran down the stairs, her mind in a whirl, the paper with her lesson times still in her hands, like a talisman. She had come out of the studio in a blur of excitement, oblivious to everything but Frau Meyer writing her name in the Maestro's book. She barely noticed the girl with red hair laughing and whispering. It happened sometimes in auditions. You were so out of yourself that afterwards it felt like waking up from a dream.

Outside it was snowing. Leonora pulled the hood of her jacket over her head, tucked her music case under her arm and pushed her hands deep into her pockets. Autumn in Munich was giving way to winter. The snow had begun to settle, blurring the edges of the buildings. She hurried on, the taste of the snowflakes sharp on her tongue, past the National Theatre with its banners and posters. She imagined her name there one day. Why not? She was going to study with the best voice teacher in Germany, some said the best in the world. She smiled to herself as she pushed on through the swirling snow. She was from the city that had produced Melba, the country that had produced Sutherland. She would do her utmost to follow in their footsteps.

In the Maestro's waiting room, Carla von Kahl leaned over Frau Meyer's desk trying to read the form in her hand.

"Who was that? Is the Maestro going to take her? Come on, Frau Meyer, we need to know."

Frau Meyer looked into Carla's laughing face, the red hair tossed back, the brilliant green eyes wheedling. Smiling, she put the form face down on her desk.

"You'll find out soon enough, when the Maestro's ready."

"But I must know. What voice is she?" Carla threw her hands in the air. "Not another mezzo, please Frau Meyer. Tell me she isn't a mezzo. That's all I want to know, just that."

Frau Meyer looked at her watch and tried to look stern. No one could mistake Carla von Kahl for anything but an opera singer. Every expression, every movement was part of a performance. She suppressed the urge to laugh at Carla's extravagant pleading.

"I have to close up now," she said. "But if I were you, I wouldn't worry."

"A soprano!" Carla reached across the desk and flung her arms around Frau Meyer's neck. "Now I'm happy."

Frau Meyer reached up to disentangle herself but Carla had already danced away and was twirling round the room. Behind her a tall, fair-haired young man stood up.

"Come on, Carla, let's go. If we hurry we can still get something to eat at the university. It's too cold to miss lunch."

It took Leonora longer to get home than she expected. Still high on the excitement of her audition she had got on the train in the wrong direction. As she opened the front door and went into the hall, the cold seemed to be soaking into her bones. She could barely feel her toes. She stood in the hall wondering what to do with her jacket, wet and limp from the snow. Would she ever get used to this cold?

"Mädele, you look half-frozen." Frau Felder had come quietly into the hall. "You'd better take that jacket down to the cellar and hang it in the laundry." She looked down at Leonora's feet. "And put on some dry shoes. Then come and have some tea and tell me all about it. You're going to need some warmer clothes now that you're going to stay." She laughed. "Mädele, it's written all over your face. You don't have to tell me it's good news."

No one Leonora knew at home had a cellar but she was beginning to understand why no German house was without one. She went down the steep stone stairs and into the large warm room where the washing machine and water heater were. It was all so practical. A separate room for storage with an old upright bicycle in one corner and shelves where her landlady kept the fruit and vegetables she bottled over summer. She imagined Frau Felder as a young woman speeding along the paths in the Englischer Garten, the skirt of her summer dirndl dress blowing in the breeze. If the bicycle was still ridable Leonora would ask if she could use it when the warmer weather came.

Entering Frau Felder's sitting room was like entering a time warp, as if nothing had changed since she came here as a bride, who knew how many years ago. A couch with a row of plump cushions dented at the top, their corners pointing up like ears; a round table covered with a dark green cloth; the broad window sills above the old-fashioned iron radiators crowded with plants. But most fascinating to Leonora was the tall chest of drawers with its rows of small dolls meticulously hand-sewn by Frau Felder and dressed as her favorite saints. Leonora could pick out Saint Francis and Saint Catherine but Frau Felder knew them all. "One for every day of the year," she told Leonora. "Then I'll be finished." Joining her landlady at the tea table, Leonora thought she looked like a doll herself in her black dirndl with its matching apron, her face as serene as one of her saints; as if in this room from the past she relived a time when she was happy.

Beside the old-fashioned tea-things lay the makings of an angel, the body already finished, scraps of fabric and wire for the wings neatly arranged at its side.

"This will be for you, Mädele. To decorate your room at Christmas." Frau Felder picked up the angel and stood it upright on the stiff gold pleats of its skirt. "Sometimes I give them instruments to play, but yours will be a singer."

She poured the tea, her eyes bright as a bird's. "Drink this to warm you up while I fetch the strudel from the oven. Then I want to hear all about Maestro Roberto Mazzone."

Peering through the window in her room at the student village Carla von Kahl was eyeing the world with very different emotions.

"I hate this weather. It's too soon for snow." She speared a pair of frankfurters from the pan of water simmering on a small portable stove, and dropped them onto a plate. "Sorry Walter, it's the best I can do."

They had given up on finding anything left at the university cafeteria.

Walter dipped a frankfurter into a dollop of mustard. "I thought you liked the snow. Aren't you supposed to be a champion skier?"

"Not any more. It's too risky. How can I go on stage with an arm in plaster?" She broke open a roll and sandwiched a sausage between the two halves. "It happens all the time, even to good skiers." She bit off the end of the roll and went back to the window. "I'd just like to know who that was auditioning for the Maestro. I haven't made all these sacrifices to have someone else taking my place."

"Come on, Carla. Frau Meyer all but told you she's a soprano. And she looks nothing like you. How could she be competition?" Walter reached for another roll. "She's more your romantic heroine, you know, rosy cheeks, blue eyes, dark hair. Like Snow White."

"And what am I, Walter Saville? The witch?" Eyes narrowed, Carla flicked a scarlet finger nail in his direction.

Walter laughed. "Well, yes, actually. Why not? And Princess Eboli and Lady Macbeth. I can't see the new soprano as a problem for you at all. You could work really well together. That's probably what the Maestro has in mind. I think she's interesting." He swallowed the last of his second roll.

Carla eyed him suspiciously. "What do you mean, interesting?"

He smiled to himself, refusing to be drawn. "You should get some tomato sauce. Are there any more frankfurters?"

- 4 -

A month had passed since Leonora's audition. She knew her way around now. No need to ring the bell when you were expected. Push open the door, check that the Maestro was ready, and go down the corridor through the double doors into the studio. There was no point knocking. The studio was soundproofed. Leonora was glad that only she and the Maestro would hear her mistakes.

After a brief greeting and the few seconds it took for her to take off her coat, the exercises began: scales, arpeggios, and the *vocalise,* exercises sung on vowels, sometimes with texts in Italian, French and German. She knew now from the opening chords which exercise would follow. So far, not a single aria.

Today the Maestro didn't interrupt her. One after the other, the exercises flowed. To Leonora they seemed neither better nor worse than usual but concentrating on them left her no time to wonder.

When they were finished, he looked up from the piano with a smile.

"Did they tell you it would be perhaps a whole year before I would let you perform anything but exercises?"

Her expression told him they had but she was unsure how to answer, perhaps fearing to be rude or still in awe of him. Today he would not press her. He admired her courage to come so far alone. But she would need to learn to speak her mind – with good manners, of course – if they were to communicate well.

"Sometimes it is true," he continued, "that singers with raw talent and little training will first have to spend time perfecting their technique. But you came well-trained and have done all I have asked. Now we will work on a scene from Gluck's *Orfeo*. The beginning of Act Three, where Orfeo leads Euridice out of the underworld, up to the famous aria *Che faro senza Euridice*, when he has lost her again. Do you know the opera?"

Leonora nodded. "I know the story."

"Ah, but which one? In Gluck's version Orfeo and Euridice live happily ever after. The original story was quite different." The Maestro leaned forward, his arms on the piano's music rest. "In the ancient Greek version Euridice went back to the underworld and Orfeo was killed by a band of women at the festival of Bacchus." He paused. "They threw Orfeo's head in a river, where it floated away, still calling for Euridice."

"How horrible." Leonora folded her arms against her body, as if she suddenly felt cold. "No wonder Gluck wanted to change it."

"Indeed. But as artists we must consider the whole story. Think about it as you learn the role of Euridice." The Maestro was silent for a moment. "Carla von Kahl will be your Orfeo. Frau Meyer thinks you may have met her. She was at the studio when you came for your audition."

Leonora shook her head. "I was too focused on my music to speak to anyone."

"Then I shall arrange a meeting soon." He stood up from the piano, and handed her a score from a pile on top of the closed lid. "We'll start today with Euridice's recitative, *Ah dovess'io saper*. Just sight read it through."

He was already starting to play when Leonora found the place. She had to react quickly; he hated to waste time. As a student she had rebelled against the boring sight reading practice she had been made to do, but it was thanks to those exercises she could make her way through a new piece without embarrassing herself.

As they finished, the Maestro nodded. "*Bene*. But I didn't hear in your singing that you understood why I started with this. Do you know why?"

Leonora hesitated. "To work on the Italian diction?"

"That of course. But the reason we started here is because this recitative is the key to the tragedy. Tell me what you were singing about."

"Euridice doesn't understand why Orfeo won't speak to her or look at her."

"Yes, but see what she says: 'Has he brought me back only to learn how cruel he is?' When you sing *crudele* I want to feel all Euridice's anguish."

The Maestro tapped the page in front of him, emphasizing his point.

"In this scene we begin to understand that Orfeo cannot win. He can only lead Euridice out of the underworld if he does not speak or turn back to look at her. But if he does not answer her, Euridice will refuse to follow him. It is only a matter of time before Orfeo breaks his promise and turns." The Maestro was silent for a moment as if watching the tragedy playing out before him. "There is such dramatic tension in this scene. You and Carla must make us feel it." He smiled. "Now let us start again."

Her lesson with the Maestro over, Leonora couldn't wait to start learning her part, practicing the phrases in her head or marking them softly under her breath. She didn't need to go to the practice studio for that, and in any case today wasn't one of her days. She couldn't afford to book it for more than two hours twice a week. Her electronic keyboard would have to do. It had a robotic kind of sound but it was useful when she couldn't get to a piano.

As she made her way home, lights were coming on in the shops and houses. Back home the first of the summer heat would be arriving, long sweltering days where people would escape to the beach to cool off. Even in winter in Melbourne it didn't get dark at four o'clock. Leonora longed for the signs that meant Christmas was coming soon, the feeling of warmth in the air in the morning, the magpies warbling in the gum trees. No one had warned her how cold it would be here. Even the birds were quiet.

She quickened her step as she passed the opera house and headed for the U-Bahn station at Marienplatz. She had known she would miss her family and friends and be homesick at times. What surprised her was how soon it had begun. But this was what she had chosen. Euridice was only the beginning.

Running down to the platform, Leonora was deep in the scene, the cold air on her cheeks like the first breeze from the upper world as Euridice began to step towards the light, the people streaming past mere shadows.

- 5 -

It seemed as if Carla wasn't going to turn up. After waiting ten minutes the Maestro stood up from the piano and picked up the phone. Then there she was. In a long black coat over narrow black jeans, her red hair and her scarlet boots the only touch of color, she swept a perfect theatrical bow.

"I'm so sorry, Maestro – the traffic…"

Stepping lightly across the studio to Leonora, Carla held out her hand. The smile she had given the Maestro was gone and her look was challenging.

"Ah, Miss General Motors. We meet at last."

Leonora was taken aback by the hostility in Carla's voice. Where did that come from? But she wasn't about to be put off by a scowl and a sarcastic remark.

Leonora contemplated ignoring Carla's outstretched hand but staying cool would probably annoy her more. She took Carla's hand briefly and turned to the Maestro just as he spoke.

"A less colorful entrance for Orfeo, I think, Frau von Kahl."

Carla smiled, as if butter wouldn't melt in her mouth.

"Sorry, Maestro. Just a little joke."

"Then perhaps you could save such things for times when you are not late. And remember, today you are not playing Cherubino."

But she is, thought Leonora, as Carla took off her coat, tossed it aside and came to where Leonora was standing near the piano. In her black jeans and jumper, her hair tied back in a ponytail, Carla could have come straight from one of those trendy modern productions of *The Marriage of Figaro*. Even offstage some singers were always playing a part; there had been a few at the conservatorium in Melbourne. It must be exhausting to keep up, Leonora thought, and risky. If you were going to draw attention to yourself all the time you'd better have the talent to back it up.

Leonora's score was open on the music stand in front of her. Carla glanced at it ostentatiously, then looked at her own empty hands, as if to say, poor you, still using the music. As if she hadn't noticed, Leonora moved her stand aside. These little tricks weren't going to unsettle her. If the Maestro had chosen them to sing together, that was all that mattered.

Maestro Mazzone allowed himself a moment of amusement: Leonora outwardly poised and as capable of standing her ground as any singer he had known. And Carla, so insecure she was ready to attack anyone she thought could threaten her place, showing her spines like an animal. There was so much fire in her. It just needed to be channeled into her singing, not wasted on petty rivalry. He hadn't brought them together by chance. He knew already they would be a striking partnership on stage.

Smiling, he played the opening bars to Euridice's recitative and aria in Act Three, skipping the preceding duet. Carla opened her mouth to protest, then caught the Maestro's eye and thought better of it. She understood. It was his way of putting her in her place. And making her listen.

She had never thought much of the sopranos she had rehearsed with. They all sounded the same: bright, *wishy washy*. Now, to her amazement, as Leonora sang Euridice's anguish at Orfeo's refusal to speak to her, Carla felt tears at the corner of her eyes. The color of each word, the long grace notes that gave such pathos to the meaning: this voice was something new. She closed her eyes and let the music flow through her, drawing her into the mind of the listening Orfeo, until the aria was over. If she had thought about it, Carla would have expected the Maestro to stop and give notes as he usually did in rehearsal. Swept up in the music, it seemed only natural to her that he should play on. Now it was her turn to sing, Leonora's turn to listen, to take in the richness of Carla's voice in the great aria, *Che faro senza Euridice?*

When it was over, the two singers stood and waited, as if this first experience of hearing each other had left them incapable of speech. The Maestro let them wait. He stood up from the piano. "*Bene*. We'll leave it there for today. And now I have a surprise for you. My dear friend Beata Benedict has asked me to present a small musical entertainment for her New Year's Eve party. I have chosen this scene, and you are to sing. Frau Benedict herself will direct it. I will let you know about rehearsals."

Leonora was astonished. She expected to have to make her way at first by singing at small concerts, weddings, private musical evenings. But performing for *Beata Benedict*, one of the greatest singers of her generation... It was exhilarating and frightening at the same time. Leonora turned to Carla, who was inspecting her with a look that said, you may have passed for now, but don't think the test's over yet. Calmly Leonora met her gaze, taking her own measure. It mightn't be such a bad thing to have Carla's spikiness to goad her along. It didn't seem to affect her performance and that was what counted. Working with Carla would never be boring.

Picking up her coat and music case, Leonora waited to see if Carla would offer to walk with her when they left the studio. But Carla stayed where she was until Leonora had left the room.

In the travel agency window a photo caught Leonora's eye: a long golden beach with surfers riding the waves. It had to be somewhere in Australia. She turned her head to look, lost her balance on the slippery path, and would have fallen if a man coming out of the shop hadn't reached out to steady her.

"It's black ice," he said. "You have to watch out for it because you can't see it. They haven't had time to put sand on the footpaths yet."

There was something familiar about him but she couldn't place where she had seen him before. He could be an athlete, with his tanned face and strong hands.

Leonora was puzzled. "Do I know you?"

"My name's Walter Saville, Wal for short." He gave a rueful grin. "Walter's a family thing. I was there when you came to audition for the Maestro. Carla's told me about you. We're rehearsal partners," he added.

"Ah." Leonora looked up at him.

"Look," he said. "It's too cold to stand here. You look frozen. There's a *glühwein* stand at Marienplatz. That'll warm us up."

Leonora hesitated.

"Come on, I'll shout you."

Only an Australian would say that as an offer to pay; it was a voice from home. She was ready for some company and it would be reassuring to have someone to walk with on the slippery footpath.

Leonora hadn't taken the idea of *glühwein* in the middle of the day seriously but to her surprise there was the stand, dispensing the hot spiced wine in paper cups. Ignoring her protests Walter bought two. "Try it. Most of the alcohol evaporates, it just warms you up."

Leonora took a mouthful, gazing at the ancient buildings around her, the Town Hall and the mediaeval tower the locals called "Old Peter". She couldn't imagine anything more different from the one-story suburban architecture she had grown up with.

She swallowed the rest of her wine. He was right, she did feel better. Was it him or was it the wine? Too soon to tell, she decided, smiling to herself.

Walter caught the smile and thought how attractive she was. He was reluctant to let her go.

"Come on, I'm seeing you to the station. I want to be sure you don't slip again."

When Leonora came up from the U-Bahn it was snowing. She didn't have far to walk but there was more black ice to negotiate and she hadn't brought an umbrella. She wished she had let Walter see her all the way back to Frau Felder's. It felt good to have someone to talk to, who understood what it was like to be so far from home, where everything was so much more colorful and relaxed. And warm.

Other people were walking near the edge of the path where the snow was flattened. Following them, Leonora was relieved to find her boots sinking a little into the snow instead of sliding away under her. She trudged on, thinking about Walter. If he asked her, perhaps she would go out with him.

- 6 -

The entrance hall was a surprise, more like the foyer of a hotel than an apartment building: leather armchairs, fresh flowers on a stand, a man in a dark suit behind a reception desk.

"Miss Ford." It was not a question. "Please go up. You are expected."

With a jolt Leonora realized he had spoken in English. Why did people do that, she wondered? The Maestro would only translate when she was really stuck. She had to learn to take direction in German if she was ever going to get work here.

The lift slid upwards; Leonora barely had time to think before the doors opened onto a hall lined with oriental rugs, where a slim, dark-haired woman in a plain black dress was waiting for her. She was so elegant that Leonora could have mistaken her for Frau Benedict if she hadn't seen photos.

"Please come in, Miss Ford. Frau Benedict is waiting for you in the music room." She gestured to the open door of a walk-in hall closet. "You can hang up your coat here."

Leonora slipped off her coat and changed her boots for the shoes she had brought with her. Her fingers felt clumsy and awkward. Singing for Frau Benedict was like a performance. Nerves were a part of it. *Lampenfieber* was what they called it here. Footlight fever. It sounded friendlier than stage fright, excitement not fear.

She decided to leave her music case in the hall. Carla would not have another chance to imply that she didn't know her work, especially not here.

Following the dark-haired woman, Leonora felt like Euridice

walking behind Orpheus, not knowing what would happen next. And then she was at the doorway of a light-filled room. Tall windows, like those in the Maestro's studio; bookshelves filled with scores; a grand piano with a harpsichord nearby; a long, pale sofa and armchairs, sleek and functional. And Carla, brilliant in orange, arranged dramatically in one of the chairs.

It seemed an age before anyone moved. Then an elderly dachshund shuffled over to sniff at her ankles. Grateful for the distraction, Leonora bent down to pat him.

"Come in and join us, Frau Ford – Leonora. What a perfect name for a singer!"

Leonora felt her nerves dissolve as Frau Benedict came over to greet her. "Come in and sit down. You know Carla, of course."

With a glance at Carla, cool and impassive in her armchair, Leonora took a seat on the sofa. At once the little dachshund, who had led the way across the room like a miniature major domo, cocked his head on one side as if to ask permission, jumped onto her lap and went to sleep.

Carla's eyes narrowed, as if Leonora had arranged this deliberately to draw attention to herself. Glaring across at her, she sized up Leonora's simple pullover and jeans and – surely not – *house shoes?* With a tiny smirk, Carla relaxed into her chair. She uncrossed her legs and stretched them in front of her, displaying her shining ankle boots, a perfect match for her soft mohair tunic.

Leonora was unperturbed. She smiled to herself. Carla would do well not to mistake good manners for meekness.

Beata Benedict observed them shrewdly.

"Poor Dacki, we're going to have to disturb you. It's time for us to start our rehearsal." The little dog pricked up his ears at the familiar word and jumped down from Leonora's lap. Following his mistress to the grand piano he curled up against one of the gleaming black legs and went back to sleep.

Frau Benedict opened the piano lid and sat down. "Come and

stand where I can see you. We are going to present this scene in the original eighteenth century style. But first, let's sing it through."

Leonora followed Carla to the piano. From the corner of her eye she saw Carla watching her and felt nerves clutch at her diaphragm. What if no voice came when she opened her mouth?

A memory of her acting classes slipped into her mind. *Be in the moment.* She would put on Euridice like a costume, would become her. As the first notes on the piano sounded, Leonora let herself slip into darkness, a shadowy figure following another, towards a glimmer of light in the distance.

Afterwards, Carla faced Leonora. "Where did you learn to act like that?" Was there just a hint of emphasis on *you*? Leonora wasn't sure. But Carla didn't wait for an answer. "Sorry, I can't stop now," she called over her shoulder, as if Leonora expected her to stay and talk.

It was only their second rehearsal together and Carla had been anything but friendly. Leonora ignored her and went to get her coat.

As Leonora walked through the foyer she was surprised to see Walter Saville.

"Walter? What are you doing here?"

"Waiting for you. Frau Meyer told me you were seeing the Maestro after your rehearsal. So I thought I'd come down and walk back with you."

He had taken off his beanie, his fair hair rumpled and falling over his forehead. She hadn't realized his eyes were grey.

He fell into step beside her. "What are you doing for Christmas?"

"I haven't really thought about it. I suppose I'll be using the time to rehearse. My landlady told me people celebrate on Christmas Eve here, mostly just with family." She laughed. "She thought I was joking when I told her about our Christmas Day parties on the beach. I'm still not sure she believes me."

Walter was shocked. "You can't be serious about working on Christmas Day. Look, we're having an orphans' Christmas at the student hostel with whoever's around. Why don't you come and join us? I can pick you up and take you home. It's only an old Beetle and it rattles a bit but it goes, and it's got a heater."

"*A heater.*" Leonora looked up at him and smiled. "How can I resist?" The cold weather suits him, she thought. The greyness of the day brings out the grey of his eyes. "But I can't stay long. It's only a week after that until Frau Benedict's party and I have to be in form."

"No worries. I'll take you home whenever you say. And it's *Wal*, remember?"

A gust of cold air hit their faces as they turned a corner, making them both pull their scarves closer to their throats and muffling his words so that Leonora had to lean in to hear him. He turned to face her. "It's funny, though. Walter's a famous name in Germany. They love it. And anyway they have no idea how to pronounce Wal. Like Australians with Volkswagen." He laughed. "It could have been worse. I was at school with a boy called Paris."

By now they had reached the Maestro's studio. Walter opened the door and followed Leonora into the entrance hall.

"I'll call you then."

She nodded. "Ask Frau Meyer to give you my number. It's nearly time for my lesson and I don't want to be late."

- 7 -

The wardrobe mistress looked Leonora up and down. Leonora had already run the gauntlet of the work room, through rack upon rack of costumes, feeling as if everyone was watching her, though only one or two people glanced up. Now she was standing with her shoes off, in a curtained-off corner that reminded her of a hospital. The disapproving expression on the woman's face didn't help. Lips pursed, she measured Leonora with her eyes.

"So, Frau Benedict has sent you to us." The irritation in her voice was palpable, as if to say, *do you realize what a privilege it is for an unknown like you to be fitted for a costume here?* But at least Leonora could understand the clipped North German accent, familiar from her language tapes. The Bavarian dialect was still beyond her.

Pieces of costumes on hangers were hooked over the curtain rail. With a flick of her wrist the wardrobe mistress detached the nearest hanger and passed it to Leonora. "Frau Benedict wants a baroque style. Put these on and then we'll see."

Leonora took the calico petticoat and the padded hip piece, wondering what the actors called it here. Probably not a bum roll, she thought. She slipped out of her clothes, stepped into the petticoat and wound the strings round her waist before tying them in front. Then she put the hip piece in place and tied that in front too.

The lips un-pursed slightly, or was it just Leonora's imagination? "Good. You've worn this type of costume before. Now the skirt."

Leonora held her arms up as the pale blue brocade skirt was

slipped over her head and hooked into place at the back of her waist, over the padding. It was all so brisk and professional, no names exchanged, even though the wardrobe people knew who she was or they wouldn't have let her into the store, an old factory building near the railway goods depot. This was probably an extra job for them in the middle of a busy season, a favor to Frau Benedict.

The skirt was heavy but there was no train. Her feet and ankles would be free. She could walk comfortably though her back might ache from the weight.

"Bra off, please."

The bodice was open at the back with an eyelet and drawstring closure. Leonora slipped her arms into the sleeves as the bodice was held in front of her, and turned round for the strings to be laced and pulled tight.

"Breathe in, as much as you can." With their stiff fronts and boning, these costumes were tight; if you didn't expand your ribs while the strings were laced, taking a deep breath to sing would be almost impossible.

With the strings tied and knotted in a bow at the back, Leonora turned round again. She could see herself in a frameless mirror propped against the wall. The wardrobe mistress moved behind her and looked over Leonora's shoulder.

"This will do." Was there a hint of approval? "You don't need a wig. Frau Benedict will tell you how she wants your hair. I'll find you some shoes but you'll need to wear your own white stockings. Do you know how to look after a costume?"

Her face was stern again, as if reminding a child to remember its manners.

"Never eat in your costume. Cover it with a wrap when you are in your dressing room between scenes. Always hang it up as soon as you take it off. Shoes in the shoe bag, hats on the rack, wig on the stand, props on the prop table." Leonora reeled it off like a nursery rhyme.

The wardrobe mistress smiled stiffly, as if she did not do it often. "You'll do. Do all that and everyone in here will be happy. Now let's get you unlaced and put these things back on their hangers. There are still shoes to try and I've no time to waste today."

The shoes were disappointingly worn and shabby but they fitted well. Perhaps the audience wouldn't notice.

"Don't worry, Miss Ford. We'll color them to match your dress. No one will see the scuffs. Now please sign the book for the costume and shoes. You will be responsible for returning everything in good condition."

Feeling a mixture of awe and excitement, Leonora signed her name. It was something to be wearing a costume from the National Opera for the first time. If she could make it happen, one day she could be in a production here.

"When do I pick the costume up?" she asked.

"You don't." The expression was stern again, as if to say, *we don't hand out costumes to unknowns.* "It will be sent to Frau Benedict."

"I'll take good care of it." Leonora felt awkward. Those sharp eyes were taking her measure again.

"See that you do." The wardrobe mistress nodded, as if she had come to a decision. "Perhaps we'll see you again one day."

Weaving her way back through the costume racks Leonora felt she had passed another test. Wardrobe people were like tigers with their cubs. Treat their costumes well and they would look after you. Treat them badly and the claws would come out. And why not? No one made clothes any more the way the theatre did. She had seen how the seams and bones on the inside of her costume had been bound with pale blue satin, not a stitch showing. The dress was as perfect on the inside as on the outside. That was skill and dedication. How could anyone disrespect that?

Passing through the work room again she walked more slowly, confident now to look around her. Bolts of cloth were spread out on huge cutting tables. Half-finished costumes were pinned on dressmaker's dummies. It must be the new production of *Die Fledermaus*. There would never be a role for her voice type in that, except perhaps for the tiny part of Ida traditionally given to young sopranos starting their career, but Carla would make a wonderful Prince Orlofsky. I must be feeling good to be thinking about roles for Carla, Leonora thought, emerging into the street. I wonder what she's thinking about me?

Leonora didn't see Carla again before Christmas. The snow had set in and Carla left early to spend Christmas with her parents in Starnberg, before the roads became too icy. In the city, snow heaped up beside the footpaths and in spite of fresh sand scattered every day, walking was no pleasure. Still, people crowded the streets, hurrying to finish their shopping. And on every corner Christmas trees glittered.

She'd already discovered that the snow she'd so looked forward to could be treacherous. And she was struggling with the cold though everyone kept telling her it wasn't really cold yet. But what struck her most was how different Christmas was here. The holiday only lasted a few days and most people spent the time at home with their family. Even Frau Felder, who never seemed to leave the house, always busy in her kitchen or working on her dolls whenever Leonora was at home, was to spend Christmas Eve to New Year with her daughter in the country. Leonora had accepted Walter's invitation to spend Christmas with him without thinking much about it. Now she was glad she wouldn't be alone.

All through December Frau Felder had been baking. Leonora had helped press sticky gingerbread paste into old-fashioned wooden molds with patterns of rocking horses, trumpets, stars and dancing children. On the last Sunday afternoon before

Christmas, Leonora was invited to sample the *Lebkuchen* they had made together. She found Frau Felder lighting the last of the four candles on the Advent wreath, the gingerbread shapes piled into its center. In front of Leonora's plate was the Christmas angel, shining in the candlelight. And in the pale satin hands, the promised song sheet, still blank.

"You should choose the song yourself, Mädele. Then we can fill it in before Christmas Eve." Frau Felder reached across and took Leonora's hand. "I've made this angel smaller than usual because I hope you'll keep it and think of your time here when you bring it out each Christmas."

Leonora ran her finger over the stiff brocade wings, surprised at how soft they felt to touch.

"*In Dulci Jubilo. Nun singet und seid froh.* That's what we should put on the song sheet. *Sing and be happy.*"

She began to hum the tune and Frau Felder joined in with a paper-thin wisp of a voice that was just what Leonora would have expected. And so they sat there and sang it all through, one in English and one in German between the Latin phrases, the clear young soprano and the old papery voice together. And to Leonora it seemed exactly right.

- 8 -

On Christmas morning Leonora saw it had snowed again in the night. It was as if a curtain of snow had been drawn across the window in the sloping roof. She got out of bed and went onto the landing, where a window overlooked the street. To her surprise, the road had already been cleared and there were people sweeping the footpath.

It felt strange to be in an empty house on Christmas Day. Her first white Christmas wasn't going to be the romantic postcard vision she had grown up with. Switching on the jug to make coffee, Leonora was thinking more about how to keep warm and protect her throat from the cold than anything else.

In Australia, eleven hours ahead of European time, Christmas Day was nearly over. She would try to phone home while her mother was still up but she would be lucky to get through before the evening, perhaps not even until tomorrow.

Sitting on the edge of her bed to drink her coffee, Leonora caught the eye of the angel doll on her bookshelf. *You chose this,* it seemed to remind her. A life without singing would be unthinkable now. And her next big test was coming closer. She felt a prickle of sweat on her palms against the warm coffee mug. It's just the adrenaline, she thought. If I can't do this, there's no point.

If she wanted to reach the top, the testing would never stop. And she did want to. Whatever it took, whatever she had to give up on the way.

Swallowing the last of her coffee Leonora put down her mug and went back onto the landing. Downstairs the hall clock chimed, as if the old house had been listening and was urging her on. Whatever *happens, she thought, I'm in the right place.*

Driving through the icy streets to pick up Leonora, Walter thought of the sun shining on the beach at Bondi, the crowds of people cooling off in the dazzling water before going home to lunch or picnicking somewhere around the harbor. He could have been there. What was it about Leonora that had made him give that up? It wasn't his way to be taken with anyone so soon. From the first time he saw her, completely focused on her audition, oblivious to Carla whispering and laughing, he'd known there was something special about her. It was more than physical attraction. He liked being with her. She gave herself no airs and graces. Carla was all drama and gesture but Leonora did nothing and still shone.

He found the house easily, the only one with a Madonna over the door. Why was Leonora living in this old-fashioned villa? Could she really be so serious that she'd deliberately hidden herself in this quiet suburb? He pressed the car horn a few times, even though he knew it would offend the sort of people who lived here.

A few seconds later Leonora appeared in the doorway; she must have been downstairs waiting for him. The blare of the car horn didn't seem to have bothered her. Those thick walls and the thick woolen cap pulled down over her ears would've deadened the sound anyway. He got out of the car and found himself looking straight into her eyes and all the things he had planned to say went out of his head.

But Leonora didn't give him time to say anything. With a shiver she got straight into the car and closed the door. By the time Walter settled into the driver's seat next to her, he'd regained his composure. To a degree. He wanted to reach across and touch her arm but it was too soon for that. He switched on the engine and a blast of warm air that smelt faintly of diesel condensed on the windshield. At least she would be warm. He felt oddly protective.

They didn't speak much on the way back into the city. Leonora noticed the cassettes he kept in the car and to his surprise picked out a song by Cleo Laine. He was about to ask her why, when she turned to him. "I dream of singing like that. She has the best technique of any singer I've ever heard."

Always the voice; with singers, sooner or later everything came back to the voice. They could talk about technique for hours. Carla was the same. But he never saw the need for all that analyzing.

The few car park spaces at the hostel were empty and the building had an abandoned look. "Most people have gone home," Walter explained, switching off the engine.

Inside, the building was bland, all white walls and polished pine doors. A Christmas tree with colored lights blinked on and off in the empty lobby. Leonora thought she could hear a faint clatter of dishes somewhere but the place seemed deserted. Leading the way along a corridor, Walter answered her unspoken question. "It's hardly ever this quiet. There are only two of us here. I hope you don't mind."

Leonora was relieved. She wouldn't have to talk too much and she could speak quietly. Noisy rooms could trap you into shouting to be heard without realizing it and leave you hoarse.

They emerged from the corridor into a large common room. A table in the middle was already set. Someone had found a red table cloth and placed a red candle with a sprig of green spruce at each of the four places. A blue and white bowl with a matching porcelain spoon and a wine glass completed each setting, and in the center of the table was a small spirit stove. Leonora picked up one of the bowls, admiring the dragon curled around the inside. Perhaps they were having a Chinese meal.

"Steam boat is ready. Please sit." Leonora turned to see a slim young man in a long blue coat carrying a steaming soup pot. He was too fine boned to be a singer. A dancer, perhaps.

Placing the pot carefully on the stove he smiled. "I am Kim Ah. Welcome, Leonora. Walter has told me much about you."

What exactly, Leonora wondered, but Walter was busy lighting the stove and she couldn't catch his eye.

Kim Ah pulled out a chair from the table. "Sit, please, Leonora. Now I shall bring the dishes from the kitchen. "Walter, please come and help me bring the wine."

Then they were back, one behind the other, Walter carrying a bottle of wine, Kim Ah with a tray of small dishes. Carefully he placed each dish on the table, naming its contents like an offering: *bok choy*, bean shoots, rice noodles, prawns, three kinds of mushrooms, paper-thin slices of beef. Less familiar, a blue-and-white bowl of miniature boiled eggs.

"Quail eggs, Leonora. Very good. Please try." He passed her a pair of chopsticks and a small bamboo basket on a long handle. Filling her basket from the dishes, Leonora thought she was managing her chopsticks quite well but the slippery eggs defeated her. Her efforts to capture even one broke the ice. Laughing, Kim Ah dropped two into her basket. As they each dipped their basket into the steaming broth and waited for the food to cook, Walter poured the wine.

"But isn't someone else coming?" Leonora asked. "There are four places."

Kim Ah smiled at her across his raised wine glass.

"At home in Saigon we always had an extra place. And always someone came."

She was still wondering if he was a dancer when the conversation turned to the performance at Frau Benedict's.

"Walter has told me about this." Kim Ah put down his chopsticks. "But I want to know more, about the costumes and the wigs. Above all, the wigs."

"We aren't wearing wigs. Frau Benedict said it would be difficult to get the right ones, and she preferred our natural hair to a wig that didn't suit the costumes."

"Of course." Kim Ah took up his chopsticks again and selected a mushroom from his bowl. "Beata Benedict is a great artist who understands these things. Not like some who don't even bother to put their wigs back on a stand. After all those hours of work." Swallowing the mushroom he replaced his chopsticks elegantly across his bowl and smiled at Leonora.

"I'm a wig maker and make-up artist," he explained. "If you like I could help you with your hair."

"What's that about hair? Can you do mine too?"

They all looked up at once to see Carla framed in the doorway, wrapped in a dazzling red coat and wearing the red boots Leonora had seen at their first rehearsal. Pulling off her hat so that her hair fell dramatically around her shoulders, Carla came laughing into the room. "Don't look so shocked. Am I too late for coffee?"

"Your timing as always is perfect, Carla." With exquisite politeness Kim Ah rose to his feet and went to help her off with her coat. "We have tea, we have coffee and Leonora has brought dessert."

Taking her coat from Kim Ah, Carla tossed it aside and glided across the room. Her eyes glittered, reflecting the green of her dress.

"Dessert! Don't keep us in suspense, Leonora. And afterwards I want to talk about rehearsals. There's so little time."

The last person Leonora had expected to see here was Carla. She had to admit, Carla knew how to make an entrance. The combination of red coat and bright green dress was stunning. But what was she doing here at all? Leonora couldn't help feeling she was missing something.

Sweeping past Leonora, Carla sat down next to Walter at the empty place and propped on her elbows, her chin on her hands. It's as if she's on a stage, Leonora thought, and we're her audience.

"I suppose I'm gate crashing," Carla admitted, with a smile that seemed to Leonora more gleeful than apologetic. "But all three of my father's aunts were coming to lunch today." She rolled her eyes dramatically. "As soon as they arrived they wanted to know when I was going to get married, as a young woman from a good family should. So I made up an excuse about having to practice for Frau Benedict." Carla tossed her head sending her hair flying again, a triumphant smile on her lips. "And here I am."

"Indeed you are." Kim Ah inclined his head graciously. "And you are welcome to seek refuge here with us…" He paused, a mischievous twinkle in his eye. "…Even from aunts."

"You've no idea what they're like." Carla was warming to her theme. "They never let us forget that their mother was related to Bismarck. They even dress like characters in a Thomas Mann novel, you know, high collars and pearl chokers. It's ridiculous. What?"

Leonora had managed to keep a straight face at the thought of Carla accusing someone of playing a role but Walter's lips began to twitch. Carla threw him an indignant look.

"It's not funny. They're terrifying. And they all smell of those horrible white mothballs." She wrinkled her nose as if to dispel any lingering trace of the pungent aroma.

Walter couldn't hold back any longer and burst out laughing. "Come on, Carla, look at yourself. Who are you dressed as today, the Christmas Elf ?"

The color rose in her face and for a moment Carla looked vulnerable, like a little girl about to cry. The expression passed as quickly as it had come and the familiar gleam was back in Carla's eyes.

"At least I smell of something better than mothballs," she shot back. "It's called *Opium* if you want to know. It hasn't got any in it but some old fuddy duddies still tried to ban it. I wouldn't be surprised if the aunts had a hand in it." She flicked a strand of hair out of her eyes and looped it over her ear. She was smiling again but Leonora had seen that softer moment.

Kim Ah had seen it too. He leaned across and touched Carla's sleeve.

"You're not gate crashing. In my family we always laid a place for an extra guest, and here you are. You've made me very happy. And you make a beautiful Christmas Elf." He smiled and turned to Leonora.

"Come, Leonora. I have some special plates for your dessert."

As Leonora followed Kim Ah into the kitchen she heard Carla's voice behind her.

"I meant it about rehearsing. I can't afford to have anything go wrong in front of Frau Benedict."

It was clear Carla wasn't referring to herself and the words stung. Then she heard Walter's reply.

"Don't worry, Carla." Walter paused, barely suppressed laughter in his voice. "I haven't seen you make a mistake yet."

Smiling to herself, Leonora turned her attention to the pavlova, lifting it carefully out of its tin and sliding it onto the blue and white plate Kim Ah had ready. At home she would have been able to buy the meringue base but here she'd had to make it herself. She'd been to Dallmayr, Munich's most exclusive food store, to track down the passionfruit to pour over the whipped cream topping.

Carla leaned forward ostentatiously to inspect the plate Leonora was carrying.

"Did you make this, Leonora?" she asked, in a voice that implied she expected Leonora to admit she didn't.

Another trap Leonora wasn't going to fall into. Of course

Carla had seen that it was home-made. She cut into the pavlova and slid a wedge onto a plate, handing it to Carla with a smile, as if she hadn't heard the question.

The rest of Christmas Day passed quietly. Carla wanted to rehearse as soon as they'd finished eating but Leonora stood by her promise to herself to go home in the afternoon. She wouldn't have sung straight after a meal anyway. Carla had only eaten the slice of pavlova and had little in her stomach to restrict her diaphragm. Was this another attempt at one-upmanship? Leonora didn't know whether to be amused or irritated. In the end Carla turning up made sticking to her plan to leave early easier.

The next day she made her way into the city to rehearse with Carla. The sun was shining in a clear blue sky. It was still very cold but the frosty air was exhilarating. Heading for the station Leonora tried to put everything out of her mind except getting ready for the New Year's Eve performance, the first night of the Fasching carnival. They had their costumes. They knew their music. What they needed now was to practice the movements Frau Benedict had set for them, gestures taken from those used by singers in the Baroque period. She wanted her guests to be transported to an eighteenth century court and the performance had to be authentic. Everyone was to come in a costume befitting the period.

Carla had given Leonora the address of a studio she rented in Schwabing, near the University. Leonora found the house easily and pressed the bell. The door clicked open, revealing a row of doors along a corridor. At the end, Carla was waiting in front of an open door. Following her inside, Leonora was astonished. She had expected a "cell" with a piano like those at the conservatorium. The room, although not as big as the

Maestro's studio, was spacious. In the center a grand piano stood on a large oriental rug. There were chairs, music stands, a bookshelf with scores. Leonora put down her music case and looked around her.

"Carla, this is amazing. It's more like an apartment than a studio."

Carla gave her a sharp look. "It *is* an apartment. It belongs to a violinist who rents out this room to musicians when she's travelling. There's space for us to move here and no one will disturb us."

Stuffing her gloves into her coat pockets, Leonora took off her hat and scarf and turned to face Carla. She looked workmanlike today in jeans and pullover, with her hair in a simple pony tail. Leonora doubted that Carla ever needed to think about money. But it was the music that mattered and behind all the game-playing she knew they would both have to make their way on merit. Carla would face the same competition as everyone else. When it came down to it, there wasn't so much difference between them. And those aunts sounded awful.

Determined to take charge this time, Leonora took off her coat.

"Come on, then" she said. "Let's walk it through."

In Frau Benedict's music room the comfortable sofa and chairs had been moved out into the hall. In their place rows of small gilt chairs were arranged in a half-circle.

When Carla and Leonora arrived an hour later, a young man was playing the accompaniment to Carla's aria, the Maestro at his side beating time with a pencil. With a final flourish, he called them over. "Leonora, Carla, come and meet your orchestra. This is Tilman Konrad. It's a good sound, isn't it?"

The young man stood up and bowed slightly, making Leonora think of a character from an old-fashioned movie. "Tilo. Please

call me Tilo. I think Maestro means the piano, not my name."
In his black jeans and shirt, granny glasses hiding his eyes, he
was an unassuming figure. He would be easy to work with, she
thought. But there was character in his face, and even the few
bars they had heard told her that here was what the Maestro
called a real musician.

The Maestro smiled. "Tilman is a very promising young
conductor. I hope for great things from him. But for our *Orfeo*
he will play the piano and I shall follow the tradition of playing
the recitatives on the harpsichord, and conduct from there." He
gave Leonora and Carla a searching look. "Though, if you have
done your work as you should, I think not too much direction
will be required."

The rehearsal was over quickly with only a few notes at the
end. Leonora was feeling confident when in an aside over her
shoulder, as if she had only just thought of it, Carla said, "You
know Frau Benedict has invited us to stay for the rest of the
evening after the performance? I hope you've got something to
wear when we change out of our costumes. Eighteenth century,
of course."

Leonora didn't know. Why hadn't anyone told her? How was
she going to organize a costume in time? She only had three days
to put something together.

How long had Carla known about the invitation? Had she
deliberately waited until the last minute to pass it on to spoil
Leonora's chances of finding anything in time? To make it look
as if Leonora hadn't bothered to get a costume ready and then
dazzle everyone with her own perfect outfit?

All the way home Leonora agonized over the problem of what
to wear, so preoccupied she nearly missed her train. Then an
idea came to her. She would ask Kim Ah to help her. He would
know what to do.

She hurried out of the station into the snowy street.

- 9 -

It was quiet in the small bedroom Frau Benedict had turned into a dressing room. Leonora closed her eyes and tried to relax as Kim Ah twisted her hair into a loose bun high on her head. He had already braided Carla's hair and pinned the gold laurel wreath into place. Make-up was simple for both of them, pale powder on their skin, a little red on their lips and cheeks. Frau Benedict wanted them to look elegant and graceful. In an eighteenth century court scenes from opera were often played by members of the nobility. Some were accomplished musicians, like the sister of Frederick the Great, Princess Wilhelmine, Markgräfin of Bayreuth, who composed operas and concert pieces, wrote plays and delighted in dressing up and taking part in performances.

Leonora opened her eyes. Her mind had wandered. Going through her moves wasn't going to work now. She had to trust her memory.

Looking into the mirror Leonora saw her reflection; Kim Ah in his black working clothes was tying a pale blue ribbon across her forehead; beyond him Carla, silently mouthing her words.

Picking up the veil that was the only touch of ancient Greece on Leonora's costume, Kim Ah deftly placed the comb sewn into a corner of the filmy material, into her hair, leaving the end of the veil to hang loose until she was ready to drape it around her shoulders.

Glancing across at Carla and back again at Leonora, Kim Ah nodded. "I think Frau Benedict will be very pleased with you both. I'll be close by if you need me again."

Quickly replacing his brushes and combs into his work bag, he left the room as softly as he had come.

Carla was already wearing her costume of mulberry satin knee breeches, ivory-colored stockings and cotton undershirt with deep frills of lace at the wrists and neck. Slipping on her shoes, she put on the long embroidered waistcoat that matched her breeches. She would put on the brocade coat with its silver and gold thread just before they went on stage.

For Leonora it was more complicated. She needed Carla's help to lace her into her dress. In the eighteenth century only poor women had clothes laced at the front so that they could dress themselves. It was a status symbol to have clothes laced at the back, needing the help of a maid.

Leonora was already partly dressed under her wrap. Now she stepped quickly into the ivory satin underskirt and into her shoes. She took the blue brocade bodice and its attached skirt from its hanger and slipped it over her head, sliding her arms into the sleeves and pulling the stiffened bodice into place. It was as far as she could go without help. Carla had been focused and professional during their rehearsals but not exactly friendly. And then there was the matter of the invitation. Leonora didn't feel like asking for a favor now but she had no choice. If only she had thought to ask Frau Benedict for a dresser.

"Shall I lace you up?"

Leonora looked up, surprised at the softness in Carla's voice, as if she had dropped all her play acting now that the real performance was about to begin. She nodded, grateful to get ready without breaking her concentration.

Carla hooked the overskirt closed at the waist, and began the lacing, pulling the bodice closed as she worked from top to bottom.

"Say if it's too tight, Leonora."

"It's fine. Tell me when you get to the last three or four eyelets so I can make sure there's room to breathe properly."

"Okay, now." Leonora breathed in, pushing against the stiff brocade and holding her breath until she felt Carla tie off the ends of the laces and tuck them under the bodice.

"Look in the mirror, Leonora. You're perfect."

It was as if she was looking at someone else. She turned to look at Carla, now wearing her brocade coat and carrying a golden lyre.

"You look amazing too. I feel as if we've stepped back in time, just as Frau Benedict wants."

Carla put a hand on her heart in a graceful gesture, smiling at Leonora with a warmth she hadn't seen before.

"You know, that blue brings out the color of your eyes." Carla laughed, smoothing the mulberry silk of her waistcoat. "Luckily, I can't say the same for myself."

Leonora turned back to the mirror and pulled the loose end of her veil over her shoulder. "I'm just not sure about the veil."

Carla leaned forward, appraising Leonora's reflection.

"Try draping it across your neck and over your other shoulder. Then it won't hide those little bows on your bodice."

"Like this?" Leonora looked up at Carla in the mirror.

Carla nodded. "It's just a symbol to suggest ancient Greece. Think of it as a prop and it won't worry you." Restless for the performance to begin, she began to walk slowly up and down.

Leonora stayed where she was, concentrating on her breathing, steadying her nerves.

A few minutes later the Maestro knocked. In silver-grey brocade and satin, he was a picture of elegance.

"Maestro, you look magnificent." Carla skipped like an excited child, all thought of nervousness forgotten.

He held out a coat-tail and pretended to sigh. "Indeed, I was tempted to come as Machiavelli, bejeweled and splendid, but the orchestra must not outshine the stars! I have no further notes for you. Trust that everything you have worked on is there and give yourselves to the performance. Then you will do very well."

At the door he turned and smiled. "I'll see you on stage. *In bocca al lupo.*"

"*Into the mouth of the wolf.* What superstitious creatures we are." Carla took a deep breath. "*Hals und Beinbruch,* Leonora. *Break a leg.*"

The sound of the audience reached Carla and Leonora as soon as they left the dressing room and stepped into the corridor.

There's no other sound like it, Leonora thought, as they took their places behind a screen just inside the door of Frau Benedict's music room. Beside her she sensed Carla drawing herself up, gathering energy like an animal preparing to spring.

Frau Benedict, glittering in lapis and silver as Astrafiammante, Mozart's Queen of the Night, had come herself to call them. Now they listened to her introducing them, to murmurs of acknowledgement from her guests.

Leonora felt small beads of sweat dampen the palms of her hands. Nerves were a familiar part of performance but she had never before felt like running away. With an effort she pulled herself together. She owed it to herself, the Maestro, Frau Benedict, everyone who had come to hear them sing. Even Carla, who needed Leonora to give her best performance, in order to shine in her own. And would never let Leonora forget it if she did not. Taking slow, even breaths, Leonora balanced her weight, one foot a little forward, ready to step off. With each breath she withdrew deeper into her role as Euridice, fearful, insecure, one moment full of joy, the next believing the worst. As Leonora, all her steps were mapped out; as Euridice she must sustain the illusion of not knowing what lay ahead.

When the harpsichord plucked its first notes, she was ready.

On cue they moved forward into the light and Carla began to sing:

Ah vieni, o diletta, vien con me
Ah come with me beloved...

From the corner of her eye Leonora caught sight of the audience and almost missed her entry. Candlelight flickered on silk and satin, casting bizarre silhouettes on walls and ceiling: the curved beak of a Venetian mask exaggerated in shadow, a minuscule galleon sailing on an opulent wig; as if Gluck himself might be there.

Startled, she caught herself just in time.

Sei tu? tu or qui? Ah, è sogno, è vero!
Is it you? Ah! Is it a dream, or true...

As she sang, all Leonora's nervousness left her and her voice rang steady and clear. Euridice pleading, Orfeo resisting, tension building. She felt the audience breathing with her as she begged him to look at her. She knew she had never sung this better.

Then Orfeo turned and the audience held its breath, exhaling in a great sigh as Leonora stepped slowly backwards to the screen, and Carla took center stage for Orfeo's lament.

Che farò senza Euridice, che farò senza il mio ben
What shall I do without Euridice, without my beloved...

Behind the screen again Leonora stood in the darkness, listening, the audience still as painted figures on a frieze, the flicker of candlelight the only movement. Carla is one of those lucky ones, she thought, who sing even better in performance. She was singing gloriously, receiving at the end the few seconds of silence before the applause that pays tribute to a great performance.

Surprising Leonora, Carla turned upstage almost immediately to call her to take their bow together as they had rehearsed. The applause continued as the Maestro and Frau Benedict joined them, acknowledging Tilo and Walter at the piano. In the excitement Leonora had forgotten that Walter would be there as page turner. She returned his smile, but she couldn't think beyond this moment. Still half Euridice in her mind, her performance was already a blur, as if all the hours of learning and practicing had been poured out with the music, as if memory itself had been suspended. It would come back to her soon enough. Until then, standing there with Carla receiving compliments and shaking hands, Leonora felt only relief that she had done her best; for now, nothing else mattered.

Kim Ah had come up with the idea of dressing Leonora as a shepherdess: "You only have to look at the china figurines from the time. We can dress up a dirndl, they've hardly changed since the eighteenth century." Frau Felder came home in time to lend a dress and with some extra drapery around the hips, and a little straw hat, no one would suspect how hastily Leonora's costume had been put together.

Carla's was far from home-made. From a professional-looking garment bag that had concealed her outfit until now, she took a dazzling Harlequin suit. Leonora caught a mocking glint in Carla's eye as she started to get dressed in her modest dirndl but Carla didn't comment, busying herself instead with taking off her make-up and replacing it with a white pancake base. She was still smoothing it on when Kim Ah returned to help them get ready. He had changed his black clothes for the traditional full length Vietnamese blue coat, with a matching headdress of stiffened brocade. *Like a halo*, Leonora thought, as he bowed gracefully to each of them in turn.

"Your scene was very beautiful. So sad, but beautiful." He held out a small shepherd's crook with colored ribbons twined around it. "Leonora, I made this for you. It will be the finishing touch. What do you think, Carla?"

Carla looked up. Home-made or not, Leonora's costume

worked. But Carla would not give her the satisfaction of admitting it. Turning back to her make-up she picked up a brush.

"Kim Ah, will you check my face when I've finished? I'll be wearing a mask but if I take it off later I want my eyes to look perfect."

She caught his knowing glance in the mirror; those smiling eyes missed nothing. He saw her register his look and nodded.

"Of course. But first, let me help Leonora."

Carla grinned. *One up to Kim Ah.* No one could say she wasn't a good sport. Carefully she began her eye make-up, finishing with a theatrical scarlet dot in the inner corner of her eyes – did that really make them look larger and more sparkling? Carla had to admit it had turned out well, *and* without Kim Ah's help. She smiled at herself in the mirror as she pulled on a close-fitting black cap and, the last touch, tied on a black satin mask.

Satisfied with her own appearance, Carla turned a critical gaze on Leonora. With her hair done and the tiny straw hat pinned on at an angle, she looked annoyingly perfect.

"You know, Leonora, a shepherdess might make a good substitute for Columbine." Carla gave her most feline smile. "I wouldn't even mind if people thought we planned our outfits together."

An apparition in a torn smock and battered Lederhosen brought her satisfaction to an end.

"Walter! What on earth are you wearing?" Carla leapt to her feet and looked him up and down. "You look like a ..." – she struggled for words, aware that Kim Ah and Leonora were laughing their heads off behind her – "like a ...*scarecrow*."

Walter grinned. "I'm a shepherd, what else? Leonora's the Marie Antoinette play version and I'm the real thing. Come on, Carla, where's your sense of humor?"

Carla snorted. "Well, I think you look terrible. And carrying that silly little white lamb doesn't fit with the rest of your outfit.

It's too clean, and you look so *grubby*."

Walter just laughed. "It's only stage dirt, Carla, painted on. It won't come off on your shiny diamond suit. And anyway the lamb is for Leonora. Come on Carla, smile, just a *little* one."

Carla gave a last huff and shrugged.

"All right, but *don't* come too close and don't touch me. I'm not going to test-run whether your stage dirt comes off or not." She stood up and twirled on the spot, her eyes glittering behind the mask, her white face and scarlet lips accentuating her impish expression. "Well?"

"*Very* well, Carla. The *Commedia* would be proud of you." The Maestro and Frau Benedict appeared in the doorway, left open by Walter. "May we come in?"

Carla as usual was the first to respond, dropping into the graceful bow Leonora had seen the day they met at the Maestro's studio. *"Maestro, Frau Benedict, please."*

Leonora had begun to enjoy Carla's chameleon-like play-acting. Harlequin was perfect for her, as if no single color could reflect such a mercurial personality.

"Carla, Leonora, your performance was all that I hoped for. Thank you, my dears." Holding out her hands to them, Frau Benedict kissed each of them in turn. "And how enchanting you both look, don't you agree, Roberto?"

The bright light of the dressing room caught the crystal drops on Frau Benedict's crown, scattering tiny baubles of light across the walls and ceiling as she turned to the Maestro.

"Indeed, but no more enchanting than you, dear Beata. And I too was pleased with their performance. But we must not give them too much praise. An artist's work is never done." He turned to Walter with a chuckle. "If these ladies are enchanting, here is a delightful contrast. But perhaps you will turn out to be the poor prince in disguise. However," he looked at Walter, serious now, "they must not stay late; half an hour, an hour at most after midnight, to enjoy their success. It is easy to strain the voice trying to be heard when so many people are talking. I shall expect all of you to be fresh and ready to work when I see you next week."

"Come, Roberto." Frau Benedict slipped her arm through the Maestro's. "We shall not lecture these young people any more tonight. They know what they have to do. Let us leave them to enjoy themselves. They must be hungry for their supper."

Walter was the first to speak. "What is it with those two? Is there something I'm missing?"

"Ah, that's the great mystery." Carla twirled again, ending her pirouette with a neatly pointed toe. "At the least, they are old, old friends. But are they, were they ever lovers? Like Goethe and Charlotte von Stein, no one knows for sure."

Walter grinned. "At least there's someone who tells the Maestro what to do. Trust him to want you to go home early. We don't always have to do what he says, you know."

"*I* do." Leonora picked up her crook and tucked the toy lamb under her arm. She tapped Walter gently on the shoulder with her crook. "Come on, shepherd boy, let's go and eat."

"You mean, let's go and enjoy our applause." Carla danced ahead of them to the door. "Then we can eat. Come on, Kim Ah. You can pack up later."

Linking arms, with Carla ostentatiously placing herself next to Walter at one end and relegating Leonora to the other, they went out into the candle light.

- 10 -

Leonora slept late on New Year's Day though she had respected the Maestro's wishes and hadn't stayed long at the party. Not because she wasn't enjoying herself. It was thrilling to have people come up to her and thank her for her performance as if she were already someone to take notice of. With so many people wanting to speak to her she'd only managed one dance with Walter. After the midnight unmasking she'd decided it was time to go and Frau Benedict's driver had taken her home.

Carla had been planning to go out for coffee afterwards with Kim Ah and Walter. Leonora half wished she could have gone with them, but then there would have been the temptation to stay up talking, to arrange another date with Walter.

The day ahead seemed grey and dull like the weather. It happened sometimes after a performance. But knowing that didn't help. Perhaps she'd call past the hostel later today.

Leonora washed and dressed quickly, amused to see traces of the ringlets Kim Ah's curling wand had made in her hair. She combed the curls into loose waves and the pile of music she had planned to go through caught her eye. If she didn't look at it today she wouldn't be ready to work on it with the Maestro.

For now the hostel and Walter would have to wait.

Leonora was surprised at how quickly life returned to normal. People were back at work as soon as the New Year's Day holiday was over. For her too life returned to its usual routine, as if the glittering evening at Frau Benedict's had happened weeks not days before.

In her lessons with the Maestro, Leonora was back to singing nothing but exercises; he seemed in no hurry to give her new repertoire. When she asked if there was anything she could work on with Carla, he only smiled and said she was in Italy for a few weeks, doing a round of master classes.

The exercises were to extend her range at top and bottom, strengthen her breath control and vary the tone of her voice to express meaning and emotion. Leonora understood that. Yet the exercises seemed endless. She was reminded of her piano teacher at the conservatorium who made her play scale after scale and one Czerny study after another, before he would hear a single piece. Once she had dared to ask if she had to play them all. *Let me remind you, Miss Ford, it was Czerny who taught Liszt. If those studies were good enough for Liszt, they are certainly good enough for you. You will never master the technique to play well if you do not do this work.*

It was just as well she didn't want to be a pianist. She would never have been able to keep up the hours of technical practice. Now it seemed that singing was no different, except that there was a limit to how long the voice should be used at a stretch. But she had to extend that too. There were exercises to improve her vocal stamina so that in time she would be able to sing the most demanding operatic role without damaging her voice, as fresh at the end as at the beginning. It was a struggle to be patient.

If at least she could have rehearsed with Carla and Walter or gone out sometimes, it would have been easier. But Carla was away and Walter's parents had persuaded him to go home to Australia for a few weeks. Leonora thought wistfully of long summer days with family and friends; the mid-winter days here were so short. Her first pleasure at the snow had been tarnished like the snow itself, heaped up in muddy piles beside the footpath. Repeating her daily practice routine over and over was like trudging through the icy sludge, every step an effort.

She was lucky sometimes with last minute student tickets to concerts and the theatre, and there were galleries and museums to visit. But these were occasional distractions. She decided to go into the newspaper office and put an advertisement for piano pupils in the classified section. Carla had said she could use the studio any time it was free. One or two hours a day would be a start to saving some money to live on when her scholarship ran out.

Leonora put the volumes of exercises she was working on into her music case. She knew all of them by heart now: Concone, Marchese, Abt, Vaccai. She enjoyed singing them all, she just longed to be performing again as well. She was beginning to feel as dreary as the weather.

"You seem distracted this morning, Leonora. Two missed entries already."

"I'm sorry, Maestro. I just lost concentration for a moment."

Facing the Maestro across the piano, Leonora braced herself for a rebuke. The Maestro was punctilious about preparation and never continued a lesson with anyone who was not fully engaged.

But instead of sending her to the practice room he got up from the piano stool and came to stand beside her.

"I know you have prepared your work, Leonora." He picked up the pencil she kept on the shelf of the music stand in front of her and circled the missed entries. "But you must learn to put your personal life aside when you are in the studio."

Mortified that she had wasted even a few minutes of her precious lesson, Leonora hung her head.

The Maestro looked at her gravely.

"You have been blessed with a voice that will allow you one day to sing the great lyric soprano roles of Puccini's operas. Mimi, Manon, Butterfly, Tosca. Glorious roles. Is that what you want?"

"Yes, Maestro."

"Don't waste your talent, Leonora. You have made a promising start. You are fortunate to have impressed some influential people. They may speak well of you somewhere. But that is all. You will have to prove yourself in audition and performance again and again. You must learn to get used to that."

Leonora waited for him to continue, still expecting him to send her away to practice.

To her surprise he nodded, as if satisfied to have made his point, and returned to his seat at the piano.

"The exercises we have been working on are your daily medicine. They will keep your voice well, tell you where you need to take care, to work more or perhaps less. Now let us begin again as if this lapse in concentration had not happened."

He played the opening chord for the first exercise and Leonora began to sing, grateful to have escaped with such a mild rebuke.

The exercises soothed her as she ran through them one after the other. It was as if the Maestro's lecture had brought the dreariness into focus and dissolved it. Today she felt she was at last singing on pure technique, in that magic place where emotion and control came together and even a simple scale could be glorious.

At the end of the last vocalise Leonora looked across at the Maestro, waiting for him to speak. She was relieved to see him smile with his usual warmth.

"*Bene*, Leonora, I think we can agree you have made up for today's shaky start. I spoke earlier of auditions. You have after all convinced me that you are ready. The sooner you have sufficient repertoire prepared, the sooner you can begin."

Willing herself to stay calm Leonora waited for him to go on.

"There is a summer festival production of *Aida* coming up. You should try for the role of the High Priestess. It's a cameo, no more, but the music is ravishing." He paused, assessing the effect of his words. "You know of course that the role of Aida herself will never be for you. It requires a different type of voice to do it justice, and great experience and stamina. It can destroy a voice that is not right for it." He stood up and took a score from the table near the piano. "You must always take care, Leonora. The vocal cords are unforgiving. Once damaged, the bloom is gone from the voice forever. People may push you to sing roles that are not right for you, for their own purposes. But you must be strong. In the end, you are the one responsible for looking after your voice. Learn the part of the High Priestess, Leonora, but leave the music of Aida to others. Your time will come."

He handed Leonora the score.

"To be a great singer can demand great sacrifice. I think you know that." He smiled. "Next time let me see that your concentration has improved."

Unsettled after her session with the Maestro, Leonora called past the student hostel to ask about using the piano there and perhaps find out when Carla and Walter were coming back.

The hostel no longer looked deserted. The area in front of the building was still covered with snow but here and there a few blades of grass were showing through. Someone had swept the path.

Pushing through the main door it was as if she had walked into a different climate. How did people manage with this change of temperature all the time – layers of clothing to withstand the cold outdoors, then tropical warmth inside? Even a few minutes in a shop were enough to have to take off your coat. The frequent change from cold to hot could play havoc with the voice. Leonora was glad she was staying in an old house. It was heated well enough to keep her warm but wasn't too drying for her voice.

There was no one in the office. She turned to leave, only to see Kim Ah coming towards her.

"Leonora! Perfect timing! Now that you are here I shall take a break and make some tea. We shall speak of Hildeberg."

"Hildeberg?"

"The festival in June. *Aida*. Aren't you going to audition?"

"How do you know that?"

"Carla told me, of course. Perhaps I will be there too. But first we will drink tea."

Her head full of questions, Leonora followed Kim Ah to the small communal kitchen, where he set the electric kettle to boil, before leading the way to his room.

Tiny though it was, it was as neat and elegant as Kim Ah himself. There was the usual pine furniture provided by the hostel: desk, bookshelves, a small table and chair, a bed covered with a woven throw to make a couch for daytime. But the centerpiece of the room was a small cupboard of dark wood, inlaid with mother of pearl. On it were old family photos, a bowl of perfect apples, a container with incense sticks and a small lamp in the shape of a lotus flower.

"My family, Leonora. Let me introduce them."

Reverently Kim Ah pointed to each photo in turn. "My mother and father, my grandparents, my great-grandfather and -grandmother on my mother's side. Sadly, the pictures of my other great-grandparents were lost." He smiled at Leonora. "It is our custom in Vietnam to revere our ancestors, to keep the memory of three generations on our family altar. It is my duty to remember them, and for me, a link with home."

Leonora studied the serene faces, belying the turbulent times through which they had all lived. She knew so little, but enough to know that none of them had experienced a true peacetime in their country. There was strength in the eyes that looked back into hers. She was moved and calmed, as if they were speaking to her, telling her to live her life courageously.

"Thank you, Kim Ah," she whispered. "I am honored to meet

them."

"And they you. Now take off your coat. There's a hanger behind the door."

In the kitchen a piercing whistle announced the boiling of the kettle.

"Come, Leonora. Did you know it will soon be Tết, our New Year? I have some special tea with lotus seeds in it. We shall drink tea and dream." He laughed. "Don't worry. The lotus is for flavor, it has no other effect. It is very delicate, you will enjoy it."

There is nothing he does that is not elegant, Leonora thought, as she watched Kim Ah take a spoonful of tea from a gleaming red packet with a picture of two dancing children on the front. "Red is the lucky color for us at New Year," he added as he put the tea into a small blue and white teapot with a bamboo handle, and placed it with two matching cups on a lacquer tray. "The children are a symbol of renewal."

He led the way back into his room and placed the tray on the table. Pouring the tea into the cups, he handed one to Leonora.

"Tết is a spring festival. We go to the temple to make offerings, and decorate our homes with peach blossom. And we drink tea. Whenever we go to a friend's house to visit, they will offer us tea. It is a gesture of respect that we always accept."

Leonora took the cup, feeling the warmth between her fingers. The clear green tea gave off a faint scent that reminded her of aniseed, only more subtle. She took a sip.

"It's delicious, Kim Ah. I've never had tea like this before."

She could see he was pleased at the compliment.

"It is special for us too. I have it sent to me by a Vietnamese friend in Paris. He still has family in Saigon." He picked up his cup and gazed into it. "I was only a child when my parents sent me to France for safety after the fall of Saigon but one day I will go home again. Until then, whenever I am homesick I drink tea and play music. Have you heard the Vietnamese flute?"

He reached across to a cassette player on the table and pressed a button. The rich notes of a melody in a minor key filled the room.

Leonora listened intently, trying to see the flute in her mind. "It's woodwind, isn't it?"

Kim Ah nodded. "Bamboo. When I hear it I can see the rice fields – so green – and the children taking the ducks to fossick in the water channels. It gives me hope."

He refilled their cups and for a few minutes they sat drinking their tea without speaking, listening to the sound of the flute.

Leonora put her cup back on the tray. "Tell me about *Aida*, Kim Ah. The Maestro wants me to audition for the High Priestess. It's a tiny part really but he thinks it would be good for me. Where is Hildeberg? What do you know about the production?"

"It will be *huge*, Leonora." Kim Ah's eyes danced. "*Aida* is always huge, sometimes even with elephants. This production will be very traditional. I know that because I have seen the designs. I have been engaged to work on wigs and make-up."

When Kim Ah smiles, his whole face gleams, Leonora thought, like light shining through polished amber, like the smiling Buddha statue she had seen in a museum.

"Have you seen the costume for the Priestess?" Remembering her manners, she stopped herself. "What am I thinking, I haven't even congratulated you and I'm already trying to pick your brains."

"All the costumes are beautiful but I shouldn't say too much. It is for the designer to introduce her work to the cast when the time comes. But I can tell you about Hildeberg."

Leonora leaned forward.

"Hildeberg was once a monastery, a beautiful gothic building in the countryside not far from Dresden. Now all that is left is a ruin, the remains of a tower and a row of arches that once were part of a wall. Every year in the summer festival, an opera is performed in the open air, in the park that still surrounds the ruins. The date is always chosen to coincide with the full moon. If the weather is clear, it is an amazing sight. Can you imagine the final scene with the moonlight shining down on Radames and Aida in the tomb?"

Leonora nodded, her excitement rising. She had to get this part.

"Everything has to be brought in for the performance," Kim Ah continued. "Every single thing. But the directors love it. They have an open space where they can do anything they want in a spectacular setting. The festival itself has been going for over a hundred years. Subscriptions are often passed on through families from one generation to the next. It was already next to impossible to get tickets even before the Berlin Wall came down and people from all over the world could travel to the festival. It's a unique thing to be part of." He paused. "You must try for the High Priestess, Leonora. I know you can sing it, and when the director sees you I'm sure he will cast you."

Leonora caught her breath. "It's strange how things can suddenly turn around. This morning I was feeling stuck in a rut, nothing to sing but scales and exercises, and now I have this audition to prepare for."

Kim Ah observed the excitement on Leonora's face. "Carla and Walter are auditioning too."

"How do you know? Are they back already?"

"Carla is coming back today and Walter will be back next week. I heard it from the office staff yesterday."

Leonora jumped to her feet. "Oh! I nearly forgot. That's why I'm here. I came to ask whether I could use the piano sometimes. I'd better go down and see." She took her coat and turned back into the room. "Thank you, Kim Ah. I always feel better for seeing you."

He nodded gently. "I too. I think that means we have become

good friends. Now you'd better hurry. The office closes round about now."

Leonora ran down the stairs, her head full of Hildeberg and *Aida* in the moonlight. By the time she got to the bottom she had completely forgotten why she had come. Waving to the young woman in the office, Leonora went out into the street. Clasping her music case with both arms, as if to impress the score inside it into her body, she gave herself up to the excitement surging within her. Somewhere in those pages the High Priestess was waiting for her. She would look at the part on the train. By the time she got home she would already have some of the notes by heart. Next stop Hildeberg.

- 11 -

Munich, February 1991

Leonora sat in the glass-enclosed booth in the corner of the empty factory building, waiting to be called for her audition. She had been there for half an hour already. They were obviously running behind. Luckily the glass panes muffled the sound of the audition taking place on the main floor. From what she could hear, it was a male voice. At least she wasn't going to have to follow another soprano.

Auditions were difficult to enjoy. However positively you tried to look at it, you were up for judgement, examined from every angle, an ant under a microscope. Being able to sing the role was a given. After that it came down to personality, appearance, the director's vision of the character. Luck.

Leonora sighed. So much of what would get her the part would be outside her control. She was lucky to be here, she knew that. But the longer she had to wait, the more difficult it became to stay calm. She ran through the music again in her head and felt a sudden panic. Which came first, *Possente Fthà* or *Immenso Fthà*? She opened the score and checked. *Possente Fthà*. She had been right.

The door opened, and a head poked round it, followed briefly by its owner, a cheerful young man in black wearing wire-rimmed granny glasses.

Tilo. Seeing him here felt like a good omen.

Now he was leading the way into the huge empty space of the factory. The ceiling with its slatted skylights loomed high above, a vast echo chamber. Glancing up, Leonora's heart sank. There would be no time to judge the acoustic. She could only do her best to adjust to it as she began to sing.

At the far end of the floor three figures waited behind a trestle table, two men and a woman. As Leonora got closer she recognized the director, Kurt Stahl, from photos she'd seen. He nodded pleasantly as she introduced herself and handed over her audition form. One on each side of him, the other members of the panel sat impassively, as if barely registering her presence.

Leonora's mouth felt dry. Waiting for the next move, she swallowed surreptitiously.

"Frau Ford, good morning." Kurt Stahl voice was deep and clear, an actor's voice. "We are going to ask you to do something you may find unusual in an audition." He gestured towards a structure in the middle of the room, a set of steps leading to a high platform. "In this production the High Priestess will appear high above the stage. She will be pre-set at the beginning of the act, waiting for some time, high up in the dark. How do you feel about heights?"

"It wouldn't be a problem for me."

"Good. Then please go and stand on the platform and sing from there. Tilo will start to play as soon as you are in position."

Leonora began to climb the steps leading to the platform, counting them so that she would only need to glance down briefly if she was asked to walk down again as part of the audition. From the top, the figures behind the table looked small and far away. If she stretched up, she would touch the ceiling. She wondered briefly if this was the actual height of the platform or if it would be even higher in the theatre. Although she didn't suffer from vertigo, she'd been reassured to see the safety rails on either side of the steps and surrounding the platform. From the corner of her eye she could just see the piano. It was far enough away to make it difficult for her to hear it when she was singing.

Below, Tilo began to strum the two bars of rhythmic chords leading into the invocation to the god Phtah. The acoustic was surprisingly resonant, with only a slight echo. Leonora sensed she would need to sing a fraction ahead of the beat to stay exactly in time with the piano. As she sang, she imagined the awe-inspiring effect the temple scene would have at night among the ruins at Hildeberg. The Maestro was right; the melody was haunting. It gave her goose bumps every time she sang it.

The scene finished and Leonora waited. Below her, the audition panel compared notes and she thought she saw Kurt Stahl write something on her audition form. At last he looked up.

"Thank you, Frau Ford. Tilo, we'll take a short break now. Back in fifteen minutes, please."

Leonora came down the steps in a smooth progression without hesitating, in case the audition panel was still watching her. But they had already left the table and turned their attention elsewhere.

Tilo caught up with her as she left the room. "You did really well in there. So far you're the only one that has managed to stay completely in time with the piano." The granny glasses had slipped down his nose and he pushed them back in a gesture Leonora guessed was habitual. She smiled. It was kind of him to take the trouble to tell her that she had judged the acoustic accurately.

They reached the booth where Leonora had left her coat. She turned to Tilo and asked impulsively, "Why did you disappear so quickly after *Orfeo*? We didn't really get to meet."

"I'm not much of a one for parties." Behind the granny glasses Tilo's eyes twinkled. "I'm a musician, I haven't learned to wear a costume. And anyway, I was playing at a recital the next day. I didn't want a late night." He looked at his watch. "I'd better go back." His glasses had slipped down again and he pushed them back. "I think you've got a good chance, Leonora. I'll keep my fingers crossed for you."

On the way home Leonora was oblivious to everything around her: the clatter of wheels on the rails; snatches of conversation; the woolen smell of damp overcoats. She went over and over what she knew about Hildeberg, picturing the set, the costumes. She *had* to get the part. If the stations hadn't been announced over the intercom she would have missed her stop.

A gust of freezing wind blew into the stairwell as she followed the stream of people getting off the train. Sheltering behind them, she braced herself for the walk home.

On the street a few people were putting up umbrellas. Leonora was wondering whether it was worth struggling with an umbrella in this wind, when she thought she heard her name. Walter?

She turned round, and there he was. She stared at him, in shock. Despite all her intentions not to get involved with anyone she had missed him while he was away more than she liked to admit.

"Wal! What are you doing here?"

He laughed. "What kind of reception is that? You knew I was back, Kim Ah said he'd told you. I came to meet you, of course. Frau Felder said you'd probably be on this train or the next one."

Leonora was touched. Standing there he seemed to exude the sun and warmth of home. When he put his arm round her it felt like the most natural thing in the world. Steps matched, they walked on, perfectly together.

The force of the wind blowing into their faces kept them silent until they turned the corner into Lindenstrasse. Away from the main road the wind dropped but they walked on without speaking until they were almost at Frau Felder's front door.

Though it was still afternoon, the sky was dark again and the porch light was on. Its rays touched the faces of the stone Madonna and child over the door, so that they seemed to float in the air.

Walter's arm still round her shoulders, Leonora fished in her bag for her key. But before she could put the key in the door Frau Felder appeared, as if carried on the waft of apple and cinnamon that came with her.

"Come in quickly, Mädele." Beaming, she bustled ahead of them into the hall. "Show Herr Saville where to hang his coat, and go in and sit down. *Kaffee* will soon be ready and you must eat the strudel while it's hot."

Leonora could see Walter taking in the atmosphere of the old house and its antiquated furnishings. When she showed him into Frau Felder's sitting room he was charmed.

"What a great room." But whatever else he was going to say went when he saw the steaming bowl of strudel Frau Felder placed in front of him.

Not until two helpings had been consumed and the last drop of coffee drunk, would Frau Felder allow any talk of the audition, though Leonora knew she was dying to hear. She gasped in amazement at the ladder and makeshift platform and made Leonora describe Kurt Stahl several times over. Walter was quiet as Leonora told her story, smiling now and then, as if about to say something, then holding himself back.

"It's not just Kurt Stahl." Leonora couldn't keep the longing out of her voice. "It's Hildeberg, the cast, everything. I'll be on tenterhooks now until I hear." She turned to Walter. "*You* know what it's like."

He nodded. "I do. A bit like you and the platform, when I auditioned as the messenger they seemed to care more about whether I could ride than the singing." He grinned. "Of course I told them I was practically born on horseback."

Leonora felt as if her chest would burst. "Have you heard anything yet?" She held her breath as a thought struck her: if only one of them was successful, they wouldn't see each other for weeks.

"They offered me the part this morning."

Leonora froze; fear that she had missed out clutched at her stomach. She tried to smile as if it didn't matter – she didn't trust herself to speak.

Walter could have kicked himself. He hadn't meant to say anything yet but Leonora's question had caught him off guard and he'd blurted out his answer without thinking.

He tried to lighten the mood. "Carla's convinced you'll get the High Priestess, and she always knows what's going on." He turned to Frau Felder. "If Carla thinks Leonora will get the part, it's a good sign."

Frau Felder reached across and patted Leonora's hand. "There are others who also know what is going on." She gestured to the row of saints on her cupboard. "I shall find the one we need to help us." Her eyes twinkled under the tiara of neat grey plaits. "Now we shall drink a little of my home-made schnapps to cheer ourselves up. We must wish Leonora luck and toast Walter's success."

Opening the cupboard below the saint dolls, Frau Felder brought out a small bottle and poured the clear liquid into tiny glasses. "Juniper, an old family recipe. A spoonful in a cup of black tea or hot water is the best remedy for a cold that I know. But be careful, it is very strong."

Smiling, she handed Leonora and Walter a glass, and raised her own. "May there be good news very soon."

The schnapps smelt enticingly of fruit. Cautiously Leonora took a sip. At first taste it was smooth on her tongue, then it exploded on her soft palate with a burst of fire. Strong was an understatement. She pretended to take another sip before putting her glass down. She looked at Walter, willing him to help.

Frau Felder stood up and went to her cupboard, as if to commune with the small figures.

Quick as a flash Walter took Leonora's glass and poured its contents into his, then into the nearest pot plant. When Frau

Felder turned back to them, they were sitting there as naturally as if they had never moved.

"Let me think," she said. Then she beamed. "Perhaps I should just ask them all."

She picked up the schnapps bottle, looked at it thoughtfully, then put it back in the cupboard. "I think one glass must be enough. I would offer you more but until the juniper berries are ripe again we may need this for medicine."

Walter kept a straight face. "I'm sure not even the worst cold could resist your schnapps, Frau Felder."

Later in the hall, he whispered to Leonora, "Your landlady's fantastic. That schnapps was just about pure alcohol. It may not cure a cold but you'd be past caring."

That's what I want to be now, Leonora thought as she closed the door behind him, past caring. She didn't know what was harder to bear, the tension of waiting or getting the answer she didn't want. In the end, she thought, waiting was preferable, uncomfortable though it was. Until she heard, there would still be hope.

All the next day Leonora waited, writing letters home and trying to study. She left her door ajar so that she would be sure to hear the phone. It was a house where the phone seldom rang. Frau Felder entertained her friends with *Kaffee und Kuchen* every Thursday, a weekly ritual that took place without the need for invitation. Every Sunday afternoon her daughter called her and they chatted for a few minutes but apart from that, the phone was for making appointments, for emergencies. Frau Felder's generation didn't use the telephone frivolously.

Leonora was careful to observe the same restraint – she didn't want to lose the privilege of being able to make and receive calls. But no matter how many times she went out onto the landing and listened, the phone remained stubbornly silent. After two days of waiting, she gave up. Surely they would have called her by now if they were going to. She needed to get out into the fresh air and clear her mind.

Picking up the letters she had written, Leonora went downstairs and put on her coat and boots. She would go to the post office and afterwards for a walk in the Englischer Garten, the park that stretched all the way from the *Aumeister* beer garden to the inner city. She was just fastening the gate behind her when Frau Felder called her back.

"Leonora! Telephone!"

She ran back into the hall and picked up the phone, in her haste nearly dropping it back onto the handset and cutting off the call. Frantically she pulled off one of her thick woolen gloves, and transferred the phone to the safety of her bare fingers.

"Leonora? Are you there? It's Carla."

Disappointment hit Leonora like cold water; she stood holding the phone but finding no words.

"Leonora?" Carla sounded impatient.

"Yes, sorry." Leonora broke off, hoping her voice didn't betray her feelings. "I was confused for a moment. I was expecting another call."

In the background she could hear Carla's earring tapping against the receiver like a faint rattle of castanets. Vaguely she wondered which opera character Carla was channeling today.

"Leonora, listen. Are you saying the people from *Aida* haven't contacted you yet?"

"No, not yet." Leonora tried to sound casual, as if it didn't really matter.

"Well, they will. Do you want to know how I know?" Leonora heard the earring rattle again, then Carla's voice, triumphant. "I've seen a cast list."

Leonora was bewildered. How was it other people knew what was happening when she knew nothing? Should she really believe Carla?

"Come on, Leonora, I've seen your name on the list, say something."

"But why would they let you see a cast list? I don't understand."

"I'm understudy for Amneris. It's a wonderful role, Leonora. In the production in Verona she had a real panther on a leash."

Leonora smiled in spite of herself. Amneris, Aida's jealous rival. Carla would know how to play the drama to the full but it was early in her career to be taking on such a big role.

"I know people will say I'm too young for it but I'm not expecting to do a performance. The public wants to see a big name not a beginner. If I'm lucky, I'll get to sing once or twice at rehearsal. That's the only reason the Maestro is letting me do it, for experience. They won't double-cast your role, though. You'll be doing all the performances."

"You're forgetting, it won't be my role unless they offer it to me."

"They will, I told you. But that's not why I rang. I'm going home to Starnberg this weekend to start working on the score and I want you to come with me. There's plenty of room and there's a music room with a grand piano. We can work as much as we like and relax afterwards. I could pick you up on Friday afternoon and bring you home on Sunday. Will you come?"

Carla sounded so confident that Leonora would be offered the role of High Priestess that she was beginning to believe it. Surely she would know by Friday. If it turned out Carla was wrong, she'd just have to swallow her pride and work on something else.

Leonora made up her mind. "Yes, I'd like to come. Do you know my address?"

"I do, the Maestro told me." Carla laughed. "It was partly his idea for us to work together. I'll see you on Friday then." She paused, as if thinking something over. "I might ask Walter too."

No sooner were the words out of her mouth than she hung up. Even at a distance Carla's exits were dramatic.

Leonora put down the phone. She'd make an excuse not to go if she didn't get the part. She couldn't bear to be the odd one out, even to spend time with Walter.

On Friday morning Leonora woke up tired after a night tossing and turning. Bracing herself for a rejection, Leonora didn't hurry when Frau Felder called her to the phone.

"Leonora? This is Tilo Konrad. We are offering you the role of the High Priestess."

She could hardly take it in.

"Tilo? Did I really get it?"

"You did." She could tell from his voice he was smiling. "I promised to keep my fingers crossed for you and it seems it worked."

She let out a sigh of relief. "I can't wait to start."

"Don't get too excited. Most of the rehearsals will be in the old factory where you auditioned. Cold and draughty, in other words. But we need the space to fit everyone in."

Then he was gone, leaving Leonora smiling into a silent phone. She wouldn't need to cancel the weekend with Carla after all.

- 12 -

Carla pulled up outside Frau Felder's at four o'clock, punctual to the second. She was curious to see what Leonora would be like away from the studio. Could anyone really be as earnest as Leonora seemed to be? Since *Orfeo* she had begun to think of Leonora as a colleague, someone with a talent as great as her own. Then she was surprised to find herself wanting to be friends.

Carla had wheedled her father's BMW convertible for the weekend. A pity it was too cold to have the top open – it wasn't so dashing with the hood closed – but they'd make good time on the autobahn. Turning down the sunshade on the driver's side, she looked at herself in the mirror, smiling at the thought of how her father disapproved of this feminine touch in what he regarded as an entirely masculine car. As soon as she could afford it, she was going to have a car just like this.

Pleased with her reflection she pulled up the collar of her emerald green coat, and picked up her fur hat from the passenger seat beside her. How disapproving Leonora had looked until she heard it was *faux* not fox. One last check in the mirror, eyes sparkling with amusement at the memory, and Carla got out of the car.

Leonora opened the door quickly, as if she had been waiting behind it. She was dressed warmly, a pale blue scarf tucked into the neck of her black coat.

"You look very serious today, Leonora. Why all in black? We're not going to a funeral."

As soon as the words were out, Carla wanted to take them

back. What had possessed her? She'd only meant to poke fun a little.

For a moment Carla thought Leonora would turn around and go back into the house. But she'd seen the car waiting at the kerb and her lips twitched.

"Black, Carla?"

Carla relaxed. "All right. It's my father's. He wouldn't buy the color I wanted."

They were both laughing as they got into the car. Carla turned to Leonora.

"Sorry, Leonora. I didn't intend to be mean. You look good in black, just a bit serious." She waited for Leonora's reaction, not wanting to start the car until the air was clear. "I didn't mean to offend you."

Leonora fastened her seat belt and settled back in her seat. "You didn't. And you weren't far wrong about the funeral. If I'm only going to have one coat it needs to be one I can wear anywhere."

Carla bit her lip. It would never have occurred to her to think of that. She turned the key in the ignition and headed for the autobahn. Once they were on it there would be no speed limit and she was looking forward to putting the car through its paces. She was a good driver, her father had seen to that. He wouldn't have trusted her with it otherwise.

"I'll stay in the slower lanes, Leonora, don't worry, but everyone will be going at least 130. We'll have a smooth ride, I promise you. Put on some music if you like."

There was little conversation on the journey to Starnberg. With no speed limit on the autobahn, Carla needed to focus on the road ahead. Cars flashed by in the faster lanes, once two Porsches, one behind the other, at a speed even Carla thought ridiculous.

Dusk was setting in as they turned onto a winding narrow road. Rows of majestic fir trees rose on either side, branches flattened like outspread hands, still bearing layers of snow, striped with bands of light from the car's headlights.

"We're nearly there, Leonora. Look, you can see the gate now. We always leave it open."

She turned through tall wrought iron gates into a curving drive and stopped, leaving the engine idling. "When I come home, I always stop here to look at the house. When I was little I thought it was a castle, because of the tower. You can see it from here."

In the twilight the house seemed to float against the surrounding trees.

Leonora caught her breath. "*A dim tower in a forest green.*"

Carla looked at her, intrigued.

"It's a song by Elgar. *My love dwelt in a Northern land: A dim tower in a forest green was his.*"

"A *dim* tower." Carla was smiling as she drove towards the house. "Honestly, Leonora, don't you ever think about anything but singing?"

But she was pleased. She loved the house her great-grandfather had built. Though she spent less time there these days, it was still her base, the place she always wanted to return to. It was where she grew up. She could never be close to anyone who had no feeling for it. Leonora had passed that test.

As they pulled up in front of the house a light came on over the door, and a stout middle-aged woman came out to meet them. Carla jumped out of the car and ran to hug her.

"Bärchen, it's so good to be home." She turned to Leonora. "Leonora, meet Frau Bär, who takes care of the house and us."

Then, as if she couldn't wait another moment to be back home, Carla dashed ahead of them into the house.

Frau Bär's face softened.

"Please excuse her, Leonora. It's always the same. She loves this old house so much she can't wait to run inside and check that everything is as she thinks it should be. Now come in quickly, out of the cold."

Frau Bär led the way into the hall. "Now, Carlinchen, you can make up for leaving your guest at the door by bringing in her luggage. I will introduce her to the portraits while we are waiting." From the way Carla went meekly to do as she was told, Leonora guessed that Frau Bär had been with the family a long time.

The inside of the house was more homely than Leonora had expected, in spite of the grand staircase and the two full-length portraits facing them from the first landing. This was her first experience of a country house; the antlers decorating one of the walls were confronting, but oddly gave the hall a more domestic feel.

"They liked to hunt, years ago." Frau Bär had followed Leonora's gaze. "Poor beasts. At least this family hunted for the table." She stopped, as if she would have said more, but thought better of it. "But those days are long gone. Now let me tell you about the portraits."

Turning towards the staircase she pointed first to the handsome man with a monocle and upturned moustache, then to the painting of a smiling red-haired woman with knowing eyes.

"Graf August von Kahl, who built this house. And his wife, Gräfin Elisabeth-Lore." Frau Bär pronounced the second name with reverence, her lips pursed as if only a perfectly rounded vowel could do it justice. Leonora was intrigued by the mixture of deference and intimacy in her voice.

While Frau Bär was speaking, Carla had come back into the hall. She caught Leonora's eye.

"Yes, Leonora. Bärchen's favorites, my great-great grandfather the Count, that noble man. And my scandalous great-great grandmother who left him to be on the stage. He put her portrait in the attic. Vati – my father – often played up there when he was a little boy, and vowed to put her back on the wall one day." Carla's eyes gleamed with the same knowing look as the portrait. "Some people say they have even seen her walking on the landing upstairs."

"Now stop that nonsense, Carlinchen, and take your guest to her room." Frau Bär tried to suppress a smile. "Supper will be ready in half-an-hour."

Carrying Leonora's bag as well as her own, Carla led the way up the stairs past paintings of mountain scenes and more portraits. On the first landing the bronze head of a small child smiled from the shadows as they passed. Leonora felt as if she had left all sense of time behind.

At the end of a long passage on the second floor, Carla opened a door.

"You'll be sleeping here in the tower room, Leonora. In the morning you'll be able to see the lake, if the weather's clear."

Tossing the two bags onto the bed, Carla turned to Leonora, still standing at the door.

"What do you think? Do you like it?"

Leonora stepped further into the room, which ended in a semicircular window seat beneath large bay windows. The furnishings were simple, as if the bed, chair and old bamboo bookcase had always stood in the same place, carefully preserved and cared-for. Someone had loved this room.

"It's beautiful, Carla, thank you."

"I used to curl up in here and read all day." She picked out a book from the bookcase and handed it to Leonora. "This was my favorite. You might enjoy it."

Leonora took the book, wondering if she would really be able to read it in German. It didn't seem likely but she could try. She was seeing another side to Carla: the gracious hostess.

In her childhood home, she seemed gentler, as if deferring to the personality of the house. Because it did have a personality; Leonora had felt it as soon as she came through the front door. Carla picked up her bag and smiled her Cheshire-cat smile. "Let's go and see what Bärchen has for supper. We can drop this off in my room on the way."

Next morning, Leonora woke early. She watched lazily as the light slid through the slats of the wooden shutters on the windows. In a moment she would get up and open them, to see if the lake would reveal itself.

After supper they had stayed up until midnight, playing piano duets and singing through old cabaret songs. Leonora had expected to sleep late. Instead she had woken at first light, as if her mind was refusing to let her waste a moment.

She opened the windows and reached for the s-shaped catch that held the covering shutters closed, pushing them out and back. Between the fir trees a path sloped down to a jetty, and there was the lake, glimmering beneath long strands of mist, the sun above it, a dull red disc on the grey sky.

She stood and looked until the frosty air made her pull back and close the windows. Six months ago, she couldn't have begun to imagine a weekend in a house like this, with someone like Carla. Somehow she had landed on her feet.

Had the streak of adventure that brought her parents to Australia driven her to face the unknown in Europe? Or was it something deeper?

Below her, patches of light rippled through the mist on the water. Leonora gave up trying to find an answer. She would get dressed and go for a walk. If she stayed on the path she wouldn't get lost.

Tiptoeing downstairs a few minutes later she was surprised to find Carla already up. Half the fun of knowing Carla was seeing what she was wearing. This morning it was grey corduroy knee breeches, a felt jacket with silver buttons, dark green stockings, and neat walking boots: Cherubino in a village *Marriage of Figaro*. Or a figure from a catalogue: what the well-dressed Bavarian youth is wearing. Leonora smiled. On the youth it would probably look traditional. On Carla it was exotic.

"Carla, I thought you'd still be asleep, so I was going for a walk before breakfast. You look fantastic."

Carla spread her arms, as if presenting herself for inspection.

"Country clothes. Wait till you see the hat." She spun round, ending in her favorite theatrical bow, leg stretched in front, toe elegantly pointed. "But now you're here we'll have breakfast. We can go for a walk later." Slipping off her jacket, Carla slung it carelessly over the banister. Leonora was amused to see she was wearing traditional woven braces with a pattern of edelweiss straight from *The Sound of Music*, no detail of her costume overlooked.

Walking through the house in daylight, Leonora realized it was larger than it seemed by night. Yet everything was surprisingly unpretentious. Even the music room with its walls of books and grand piano felt homely. Following Carla through the house, it occurred to Leonora that for all her flamboyance and sharpness, there was nothing pretentious about Carla either. Take her or leave her, she was always true to herself.

Last night they had eaten supper in the kitchen but this morning Carla led the way further along the main corridor into a small dining room.

Here the furnishing was more formal, a palette of green, from the grey-green silk on chairs and walls to the velvet curtains, a green so dark the folds seemed painted on in black.

Carla's eyes sparkled. She was clearly enjoying the effect the room was having on her guest.

"Yes, Leonora. This is the *green* dining room. After the tower, it's my favorite."

"I can see why. It's like a scene from *La Traviata*." Moving to the table, Leonora touched the curve of a chair back. "Violetta could come in at any moment."

Carla shook her head, laughing.

"Ah, the soprano's one-track mind. Actually, you may be right. Elisabeth-Lore designed this room. It's been refurbished a few times but nothing's been changed. She was always playing a part. Or so the family tradition goes."

So that's where she gets it from. Leonora was struck again by Carla's resemblance to the portrait on the stairs: the glint in her eyes, the hair, the forthright stare.

"Now Carla, don't be teasing Leonora with your superstitions." Frau Bär came bustling in with a laden tray and began to set out its contents: rolls, a platter of cold meats and the most beautiful coffee pot Leonora had ever seen, delicate tulips curving over its pale green surface.

Following Leonora's gaze, Carla smiled, her eyes more catlike than ever. "That was Elisabeth-Lore's too. I thought we should get her on side before we start to work."

"Never mind Carla's stories, Leonora, come and sit down before the coffee gets cold."

"Okay, Bärchen." Carla planted a kiss on Frau Bär's cheek. "I'll be good." She leaned forward, the glint still in her eyes. "Why don't you pour, Leonora. Good practice for *Traviata*."

Whatever Carla intended – from teasing Leonora with a role she would never sing, to rubbing in that she would be handling a precious heirloom – Leonora was not about to rise to the bait. Taking her place at the table, she picked up the coffee pot. It felt perfectly balanced in her hands, its elegant spout delivering a fine stream into the porcelain cups, not a single drop falling where it should not.

So far Carla hadn't mentioned Walter. All through breakfast Leonora had wondered whether to ask, then held back, not wanting Carla to read too much into the question. Now, as they prepared to go for a walk round the lake, she saw an opportunity to find out without seeming too obvious.

"What do you want to work on when we get back?"

Gazing at herself in the hall mirror, preoccupied with placing her hat just so, Carla was vague.

"I don't know. Maybe run through your part first, then you can play for me and help me memorize Amneris." She tilted the hat first to one side, then the other. "Isn't this a fantastic feather? It's from a pheasant's tail. Vati found it."

Leonora could only agree – the feather was magnificent. Luckily it was pointing upwards or it could have been a danger to anyone who got too close. "So it's just us, then?" she persisted.

"Ah." Carla turned round with a cheeky grin. "Yes, I did say *I might* ask Walter. I wanted to be sure you'd come. But then I thought it could be fun with just the two of us. Bärchen is going to stay with a friend for the weekend and we'll have the house to ourselves."

She turned back to the mirror and gave her hat a last tweak. "Sometimes it's no fun being an only child. Do you have brothers and sisters, Leonora?"

"No." Leonora hesitated, unsure how much to say.

Carla spun round to face her.

"Then you've got room for an honorary sister."

Caught off guard, Leonora could only nod but it didn't matter. Carla had taken her acquiescence for granted and was already steering her to the door.

"Once round the lake, and then it's *Aida* all day. Come on."

When they reached the lake, the mist had cleared. Looking up, Carla quickened her pace and Leonora hurried to keep up with her.

"Is it going to snow?"

Carla shrugged. "Usually there's a kind of scent in the air when it's going to snow. And the sky would be darker." She stopped and took a long breath through her nose. "Nothing yet."

They walked on in silence, stepping over the tree roots that broke through the narrow path around the lake. Trees rose beside them, receding into a deep forest. Leonora imagined the snow falling across the landscape, drifting over the water.

As they came full circle to where the path wound back to the house, Leonora turned to look before the lake was lost to sight behind its screen of trees. "This could be the landscape the wanderer saw in *Winterreise*. It's beautiful."

Carla smiled. "What an incurable romantic you are." But Leonora could see she was pleased.

Predictably perhaps, Carla had changed her mind and was keen to work on Amneris first, with Leonora playing the piano. Leonora didn't mind. She enjoyed being able to stretch her fingers again. She was usually only able to play for an hour or so here and there, mostly the accompaniment to whatever she was learning. She warmed up with a Chopin waltz, happy to find she had not forgotten it.

Carla seemed impressed. "You play really well, Leonora. Did you start off wanting to be a pianist?"

Leonora placed the score of *Aida* on the piano's music rest. "No. I always wanted to be a singer but I loved playing the piano. My mother's the pianist. She taught me. When I was about three years old she used to hear me playing as soon as it was light enough to see, strange tunes I made up myself."

Carla settled herself in the curve of the piano and leaned forward. "Tell me about where you live. We've never really spoken about it."

Leonora suppressed a smile. What was that old expression?

Chance would be a fine thing?

"There's not a lot to tell. Home is an old house with a big garden not far from the beach. It was a good place to grow up. People say Melbourne is the most European of the Australian cities but it's still very different from here. Wherever you are in Australia you're never far from the world beyond the city." Images flooded her mind, the majestic red gums along the river near where they camped with friends every summer; looking up at the stars at night, astonished by their brilliance; the sounds and sharp scents of the bush. "It's so vast and ancient it has a life of its own, a kind of music, beyond words." She sighed. "It's a pity it's so far away. I think you'd like it." She paused, a small smile on her lips. "It's dangerous."

"Dangerous?" Carla's eyes lit up. Leonora could see she was intrigued by the idea, attracted even. The tales of spiders, snakes and sharks, dangerous water and burning, dehydrating heat were unlikely to daunt her; she would see them as warnings to be heeded. It would take something deeper, out in the bush, beyond her control, to shake her.

Still leaning against the piano, Carla propped her elbows on the lid and cupped her chin in her hands, as if curious to know more. But all she said was:

"Do you miss your family?"

Leonora looked down at her hands resting lightly on the edge of the piano keyboard as she had so often done at home, playing duets with her mother. "My father died when I was little and my mother brought me up on her own. It's been just the two of us for most of my life. I miss her a lot. I worry about her being alone when I'm so far away. But I always knew I'd have to go away to study."

Carla looked thoughtful. "So did I. I don't mind being away from home, especially when the Prussian aunts come to stay. But Vati and Mutti are always there to come back to." Her face softened. "It must be hard, not being able to go home whenever you want."

A new thought struck her. "What sort of school did you go to? Did they make you wear a uniform?"

Leonora was getting used to Carla's sudden changes of topic. "A girls' school. Yes, we wore a uniform. Navy blue everything with a white shirt, and a checked dress in summer. Why?"

Carla thought for a moment. "It must have been awful wearing the same thing every day. I'd probably have run away just to be able to put on something different."

Leonora laughed. "I can believe that." Carla's outfit today was more reminiscent of a scene from *Hansel and Gretel* than *Aida*. She'd probably go off to change at some stage into something more suitable for Amneris. Leonora was amused to find herself looking forward to that. She opened the score. "Where shall we start?"

As it turned out, Carla stayed in the same clothes all day, reflecting the setting of her home rather than the opera. Breaking only to eat the soup Bärchen had left for them, they worked on through the score, sometimes singing, sometimes memorizing in silence, pacing themselves through the rehearsal to keep their voices fresh.

At last Carla closed her score with a snap. "I'm starting to think I can really sing this part. But we've done enough for one day. There's pizza to make for dinner and we can open some wine." Her eyes sparkled. "And perhaps play some loud rock and roll on the stereo."

She turned towards the window. "It will be getting dark in a few hours and we can watch the moon rise. I always hope for moonlight when I come home."

Carla was serious about seeing the moon. As dusk fell she led the way up to the tower room. Leaning against the frame of the bay window, she looked out into the night. The snow had held off and the sky was clear.

"Come and stand here, Leonora. This is the best place to see the moon rise."

Slowly a glow outlined the treetops. Within moments the moon floated free above them, revealing row after row of black spears, like a child's folded paper cut-out.

Oblongs of moonlight patterned the floor as light slipped through the windows.

Then Carla spoke, her voice a whisper. "I used to lie in bed watching the moon. I'd say a poem or sing a song to it and feel so secure and happy."

Leonora waited for Carla to go on.

But as if she had revealed too much, Carla turned away from the window and switched on the light.

"All that *Romantik* has made me hungry. The moon will still be there later. Now it's time to eat."

Leonora shook her head and followed Carla down the stairs.

Next morning Leonora again woke early. She pulled the quilt up under her chin and listened; the house was quiet. Half asleep, she let her thoughts drift.

Something tugged at her mind and she remembered. In the early hours of the morning someone had come into the room. At first she thought it was Carla but as her eyes adjusted to the darkness she saw it was someone else. A tall woman with Carla's red hair, but not her face, standing by the bed.

Then, as suddenly as she had appeared, she was gone.

Leonora remembered struggling to work out if she was awake or only dreaming that she was. Then nothing.

This morning the memory was as clear as if it had really

happened. Idly Leonora wondered what it meant. She decided not to tell Carla. She would only make too much of it. After all, it was just a dream, hardly surprising in these surroundings.

Feeling the quilt soft against her face, she traced the ridge of tiny herringbone stitches separating the squares and wondered how many hands had made them. She would miss waking up here. Tomorrow she would be back at Frau Felder's, back in the routine of study and getting ready to start rehearsal.

And then there was Walter. She had meant to concentrate only on her singing until she could see her way ahead. But now she found herself wavering. Perhaps being with him wouldn't distract her from her plans.

A knock on the door interrupted her thoughts, and Carla's tousled head appeared.

"Ah, Leonora, you're awake. I hope you slept well." She gave Leonora a mischievous look. "Hurry up, there's work to do."

Without waiting for an answer, she disappeared behind the door.

Leonora threw back the quilt and got out of bed. Today would belong to music. Time enough to think about Walter when she got back to Munich.

In the kitchen Carla was making batter, attacking the mixture with a wooden spoon.

In black pullover and jeans, a red scarf draped round her shoulders, hair now brushed back and shining, she radiated energy. Her eyes gleamed as she put down the spoon and poured the batter into a jug.

"Sunday breakfast, Leonora. Pancakes." She gave Leonora a keen look. "Did you sleep well?"

Leonora nodded. She was getting used to being asked if she had slept well. Frau Felder asked her often enough. It seemed to be the custom, a form of politeness, like being asked how you were. But Carla seemed more than usually interested.

She laughed. "Maybe I should have asked if you've woken up yet. But how was it in the tower?"

"Perfect. I slept like a log."

"Truly?"

At the stove, Carla began to pour batter into the pan. She didn't need to say any more for Leonora to know that she wasn't finished with her questions yet.

The morning passed quickly as they worked through sections of *Aida* from memory. Leonora had just sung the last note of her part, and was thinking how well they worked together, when Carla swiveled round on the piano stool to face her.

"Leonora Ford." Carla looked Leonora up and down, as if taking her measure. "Your name. You should change it."

Leonora was beginning to get used to Carla's bluntness. Taken at face value it could even be useful. But this piece of advice she could resist. She gazed down at Carla, perched on the piano stool.

"Why?"

"It's the name of a car; an opera singer can't have a name like that."

"Well, I can. And actually, like Mercedes Benz, the Ford car was named after a person. In fact, my family has a remote connection with Ford." The connection was limited to buying the family car but she wasn't going to tell Carla that. "Would you be telling me to change my name if it was Daimler or Benz?"

"Maybe, I don't know."

"Come on, Carla, times have changed since Nellie Mitchell became Nellie Melba. I like my name. I'd need a better reason to go to the trouble of having a stage name as well."

Carla sighed. "You are very direct. I like that."

Leonora burst out laughing.

"Well, so are you, if it comes to that."

Carla got up from the piano. "Tell me, did you really not see Elisabeth-Lore? I put you in the tower room specially."

"What do you mean?"

"There's a family tradition that she always comes to look at singers, but only the very good ones. I thought she would be sure to come for you."

Still determined to say nothing about her dream, Leonora tried to look as if she didn't take Carla seriously.

"She did, didn't she, I can tell by your face." Carla was triumphant. "I knew she would." She reached across and gave Leonora a hug. "Now you'll *have to* come again." She turned back to the piano and closed the lid. "Help me put the cover on. Then we'd better get going. I promised to get the car to Munich before it gets dark."

Back in her room in *Lindenstrasse* Leonora poured herself a cup of tea and sat down to write a letter home. She'd thought about recording a cassette but she'd have to go into the post office to mail it. A pre-paid air letter form could be sealed and posted as soon as she'd finished writing. Even so, it would be five days or more before it reached her mother.

She unfolded the thin blue sheet and smoothed it out. In her first week in Munich, to the amusement of everyone in earshot, she had asked at the local post office for *ein Luftbrief* – a letter made of air. It was called "an airmail-light-letter" – *ein Luftpostleichtbrief* – they explained. It had become one of her favorite words, with all those consonants a perfect diction exercise: *Luft-post-leicht-brief*. It made her smile every time she thought of it.

She began to write. There was so much to tell.

- 13 -

Leonora arrived early at the factory building where she had auditioned. She'd been called before the start of the main rehearsal for a technical walk-through with the members of the Chorus who would be her attendants.

The *Aida* set was marked out in tape, a different color for each Act, covering half the factory floor. The platform where she would stand in Act One was already in place. With its single railing at the back it looked horribly narrow and its height took her breath away. From the top there was a drop of two or three meters to rows of steps fanning downwards into a semicircle. Her palms were clammy. What had she let herself in for?

At the foot of the front steps a woman in a purple coat was arguing with the technical manager, Herr Schmidt, a short man with a shaved head and fierce expression. Leonora was about to introduce herself when the woman turned round and scowled at her, before pointedly turning her back and continuing the argument.

"I'm not going up there and that's my last word. You'll have to change it."

Herr Schmidt took a step back and shook his head.

"We're not going to change it Birgit. If you don't want to do it we'll have to find someone else."

"We'll see what the union says about that." Birgit spat out the words; turning on her heel she pushed past Leonora and flounced off as if she did not exist, leaving Herr Schmidt to greet her on his own.

"Frau Ford, welcome. I am Josef Schmidt. Everyone calls me

Sepp." He gestured at the structure behind them. "It's not as bad as it looks."

Leonora felt much the same as Birgit, but she followed Sepp to the back of the set where narrow ladder-like steps led up to the platform and watched as he leaned on the handrail.

"Firm as a rock." Now that Birgit was gone he looked more cheerful. "The steps are only for rehearsal. In Hildeberg you'll have a lift. We'll take you up and down just like an elevator. One of the assistant stage managers will go up with you and make sure you are safe."

Leonora looked up at the platform.

"I can see why they asked how I felt about heights. Can I try it on my own now?"

"Of course. I'll take you up myself. Just put this on." *This* was a narrow webbing belt with a mountaineer's clip attached to another length of webbing at the back. "You should ask wardrobe to give you a rehearsal skirt so that you can practice with it."

Leonora wondered at how calm he was: a man who would take everything in his stride and deal with it. Sepp close behind her, she began to walk up the stairs. At the top he showed her where to stand, clipping the webbing belt to a strong safety rail at the back. The platform was wider than it looked from below and she felt more secure than she had expected. Once she was clipped in she could focus on looking straight ahead and try to forget how high up she was.

Sepp seemed completely untroubled by the height, concerned only to make sure that Leonora knew exactly what she had to do.

"Let the clip slide along the rail as you come back to the stairs. One of the ASMs – the assistant stage managers – will be there to unclip you and take you back down. You will get used to it and think nothing of it."

Leonora hoped he was right. Going up and down in the rehearsal room was one thing, but doing it in the dark in full costume would be another matter altogether.

They reached the foot of the stairs without a hitch.

"Well done, Frau Ford."

"Leonora, please."

Around them people were starting to arrive for the main rehearsal. Sepp looked at his watch. "Now I'd better go and sort out that problem with the other priestesses."

The number of people in the room was building up. The full company was called today, Chorus and non-singing extras as well as principals and understudies. No one took any notice of Leonora as they came in, trailing snatches of conversation.

"It's a bit much being asked to shave my beard just for rehearsals."

"Is it full body make-up, does anyone know?"

"You wouldn't get me up there for any money."

Unsure where she was expected to sit, Leonora decided to play safe and stand near the door until she could see how things worked. After the experience with Birgit she preferred not to risk encroaching on anyone's place.

It was a relief to see Tilo Konrad come through the door.

"*Hallo* Leonora! Come with me. I'll show you where the principals are sitting. Herr Stahl is going to talk everyone through the production first."

Tilo led the way to where the Chorus members were seated in a semi-circular block of chairs with the first two rows left free, and showed her to a seat in the second row.

"Aida, Radames and Amneris will have the chairs in the front row, but they are not called for this rehearsal. You'll be able to see well from here."

He took his score and a pencil case out of his bag, and checked his watch. "I'd better get going. I'm conducting this morning. Maestro Domenico is working on the music separately. He'll only come to the production rehearsals once all the movement is blocked in."

Tilo's glasses had slipped down his smallish nose. In the gesture Leonora remembered, he pushed them into place again. Smiling he tucked his score under his arm and picked up his bag. "I'll see you in the break."

Leonora watched him go, grateful for the way he had put her at ease. Her small role was going to have its challenges. Tilo would be at every rehearsal. Knowing he was out there watching was a good feeling.

The rehearsal room was full now, the buzz of conversation a constant drone. From her position in the second row, Leonora scanned the room for Carla and Walter but there was no sign of them. Perhaps the understudies weren't called yet but Walter should have arrived by now. Everyone was expected to be present 15 minutes before the start of rehearsal.

A wiry young woman in overalls strode to the front of the Chorus section and raised her hand. Immediately the sound dropped and everyone turned towards her.

"Good morning ladies and gentlemen. I am your stage manager, Barbara Fischer." She grinned and pointed to a bright red fish brooch pinned to the bib of her overalls. "Fisch for short. Please be ready to start in ten minutes."

Walter was cutting it fine. With the hood of his old green anorak thrown back and his blond hair shining under the lights, he was attracting admiring glances as he came across the room. In the first row of the Chorus seats Birgit waved him towards the chair in front of her, a proprietary hand on its back. Outwardly calm Leonora waited for Walter to take his place. Who did that woman think she was, making such an obvious pass at him? The strength of her reaction shocked her.

He took the seat next to Leonora, apparently unaware of the ripple of admiration that followed him. "Car trouble. I got here just in time. Kurt Stahl is right behind me."

As he spoke, the director entered the room, followed by the set designer, a tall woman in a long black dress carrying the set model. After shaking hands with Fisch, he moved across to the table where the production team would sit. Leonora looked at him intently. At her audition she'd been too nervous to observe him closely. She was intrigued now to see how ordinary he looked. You could pass him in the street and not notice him, one of many middle-aged men with an intelligent face and a thinning hairline. Yet this was one of the greatest opera directors alive.

Often the stage manager had to call for silence at the start of a rehearsal, but today everyone was already quiet, waiting to hear the director speak.

"Ladies and Gentlemen, welcome." He looked around the room, taking in every face, as if making contact with each person there. "We have a lot of work to do. I know I can rely on your discipline and professionalism to make it as easy for us all as possible."

Disziplin, Professionalismus. Leonora relaxed. His German was clear and precise. If he always spoke like this she would be able to follow; perhaps not everything but enough to take direction.

He paused, his gaze sweeping their upturned faces.

"The singers will know this opera is set in the city of Memphis in ancient Egypt, but some extra performers in our cast may not. Bear with me and refresh your memory as I tell them the story."

He turned to the actors, assembled at one side of the room; they would fill out the stage as soldiers, slaves and priests. His voice was calm and controlled, a voice that would carry however softly he spoke.

"Aida, the daughter of the King of Ethiopia has been captured by the Egyptians and made a slave to the King of Egypt's daughter, Amneris, who is in love with the Egyptian General Radames. But *he* secretly loves Aida and she him."

He smiled, acknowledging the ripple of interest from those

hearing the story for the first time.

"When the Ethiopians invade Egypt to rescue her, Aida is torn between her love for Radames, who will lead the Egyptian army against them, and her love for her father and her country."

He paused again, holding their attention. "And what of Amneris...watching... jealous and suspicious?"

His eyes narrowed as if seeing her before him, willing them to share his vision.

"When Radames returns victorious the King of Egypt offers Radames marriage with Amneris as a reward. Hearing this, Radames confesses his love to Aida and they plan to escape together. But unbeknown to him, among the prisoners he has taken captive is Aida's father, Amonasro, who persuades Aida it is her duty to find out from Radames where the Egyptian army plans to invade Ethiopia."

The actors were leaning forward in their seats.

"Amonasro hides and overhears Radames tell Aida the secret route. When Amonasro reveals himself, Radames realizes he has betrayed his country. He surrenders to the High Priest and Amneris, who have followed him, allowing Aida and her father to escape."

Turning back to the full cast, Kurt Stahl was speaking to everyone now.

"And so we come to the end: Radames is tried for treason and condemned to death; he refuses Amneris' offer to save him if he will marry her and is sealed alive in a tomb. Longing for Aida, Radames prays that she will be happy, wherever she is. And then he hears her voice: she has hidden in the tomb, determined to die with him."

He waited, letting his words sink in.

"There is much to reflect on. Verdi was a supporter of the Risorgimento, the movement to unite Italy; he was a member of the first Italian parliament. The struggle for freedom, love of country, conflicting loyalties – we find all these in *Aida*. But I do not believe we should focus too much on politics. We are here to tell the story and above all, to serve the glorious music."

A rustle of acknowledgement ran through the room. Kurt Stahl raised his hand, smiling.

"And now let me introduce you to our set designer, Anna Gardini."

The set model had been placed onto a small table and brought to the front where everyone could see it. Leonora marveled at its detail, perfectly to scale. As they watched, Anna Gardini gently placed two figurines, a man and a woman, center stage.

"Ladies and gentlemen, you already know that this set will be erected in front of the ruins at Hildeberg. I have designed it to create a sense of the smallness of human beings against the massive architecture of ancient Egypt. And to symbolize the powerlessness of Aida and Radames against the might of Egypt."

She paused, as if waiting for her words to take effect.

"Most of you will be performing on the stage floor; at times some of you may be standing on the steps, nothing unusual for an opera company."

A murmur went through the Chorus and there was relief on more than a few faces. Anna held up her hand for quiet.

"I can assure you that full engineering stress tests have been carried out on the structure and a safety certificate has been issued. But I ask all of you to be aware of safety on the set and speak to Fisch immediately if you have any worries."

Turning back to the model she placed the figure of the high priestess on the top platform. "Only a few people will be on this level."

Walter turned to Leonora, dropping his voice so that no one else could hear.

"It's too high. You shouldn't have to do this." He looked worried. "It's an opera, not a circus."

Leonora's heart skipped a beat at the warmth in his eyes. "Don't worry, I've tried it. It's fine. And anyway, some parts of *Aida* have a lot in common with a good circus. Like the messenger galloping in on a real horse."

Walter laughed. He leaned across to whisper in her ear, but it was too late; Kurt Stahl was speaking.

"I'll set the priestesses first. Ladies and gentlemen of the Chorus, stay if you wish, but if you go out, please do not come back into the rehearsal room until you are called."

Fisch was on her feet immediately, marshalling people towards the exit. A few stayed in their chairs and took out a book or began to study their scores. Leonora got up and went across to join the woman in purple and the other priestess at the edge of the set. Neither of them bothered to acknowledge her.

When the room was completely quiet, Kurt Stahl left his seat and came over to them. He wasted no time with small talk but got straight down to business.

"Sepp tells me you have already been up on the platform. So now we will talk through what I want you to do. Do not believe because you will just be standing there that you do not need to act. I want you to remember what has gone before."

He paused, making eye contact with each of them before continuing to speak.

"Can there be another opera that opens with such power? In the first few minutes Verdi gives us the incomparable *Celeste Aida*, and the dramatic trio where Amneris sees that Radames loves Aida, and determines to get revenge. And then the war chorus."

Pacing the floor in front of them, he raised his arm, waving an imaginary spear.

"Guerra!" He stopped and spread his arms as if to encompass ranks of soldiers all around them. "Verdi gives us fourteen lines of harmony for this chorus, a massive wall of sound.

"And then – as if all this were not enough – the magnificent aria where Aida pours out all her anguish, the sublime *Ritorna Vincitor!*"

He stopped his pacing and stood facing them.

"She knows that victory to her lover means slavery or death for her father, who has invaded Egypt. Torn between them, she asks the gods to take pity on her suffering."

His voice dropped to a whisper.

"*Numi pietà... May the gods have pity...* This tumultuous aria ends so softly. *Perdendosi*, fading away: that is what Verdi has written above the vocal line."

Leonora was mesmerized.

Kurt Stahl turned to her and smiled.

"And now it is your turn, Leonora. As Aida's voice fades away we are transported into the temple. We go from the passion and drama that has gone before to a scene of magic and mystery that is no less intense. Such a small solo, but so very beautiful. You must hold the powerful emotion these opening scenes have created." He lifted his hands, palms upward. "And remember, there will be applause at the end of Aida's aria, perhaps for several minutes."

Leonora tensed; she would have to hold the pitch in her mind. As long as she could hear the harps clearly, the key change wouldn't be a problem.

"Right, let's get you up there. Sepp, we're ready." His tone was brisk now. The director had replaced the performer.

Sepp was already at the foot of the steps.

"Leonora, this is Renata. Birgit you met at rehearsal this morning."

If you could call being ignored an introduction, Leonora thought. But they had to work together. She smiled politely and held out her hand.

Renata nodded and shook hands but Birgit scowled and turned away.

Sepp watched them put on their safety belts and clip them onto the rail, checking that they were secure. When he was satisfied, he gave the cue for them to climb the stairs, Renata first, Leonora in the center and then Birgit. At the top Leonora moved forward to her place in front of them. The platform felt crowded now, Renata and Birgit uncomfortably close behind her. Leonora looked down at the tape marking where the incense burner would stand. There was no room to move. She would just have to get used to it.

Down below, Tilo had taken his place at the piano.

"Can you hear me, Leonora?" Kurt Stahl's voice sounded far away.

"Yes."

"Good. Sepp will have speakers up there for you on the Hildeberg set. You will be able to hear the orchestra and all your cues. Now let's just sing it through. *Lights coming up...*"

Tilo began to play. To Leonora's relief the sound carried and she managed to come in on time.

Then in the middle of her first long note, she felt a sharp poke in the back, making her voice jump on the quavers at the end of the bar. She managed to steady herself and sing on. They were so close together on the platform, she'd have to learn to deal with the occasional bump. Then she felt another push and heard Birgit behind her, hissing under her breath. *Why should you take our jobs.*

Leonora froze. On this high platform in the dark she would be vulnerable. Whatever tricks Birgit used to put her off, no one would see them. Perhaps she didn't mean Leonora to get as far as the performances if she could make her miss an entry or sing badly in rehearsal.

Leonora took a deep breath and pulled herself together. She leaned into the muscles in her back, bracing herself. She imagined the great columns of the temple, the shadows and flickering lights, the blue-grey incense spiraling around her. Instinctively she lifted her hands in the gesture of invocation seen in painted scenes from Egyptian tombs. If Birgit pushed her now, it would be impossible to keep her balance.

But there were no more jabs, as if to ensure she could never predict when the next one would come.

Going down in reverse order, Leonora was thankful Birgit was ahead of her. From now on she would be on her guard.

At the foot of the stairs Fisch was waiting for them.

"You're done for the morning, Leonora. Be ready to start again at two. Birgit and Renata, you stay to rehearse with the rest of the Chorus. Places quickly please."

Suddenly everyone was on the move and any chance to speak was gone. Glad to get away, Leonora went back to her seat, where Walter was waiting with her bag and coat.

As soon as the door of the rehearsal room closed behind them, Walter put his arms round Leonora and held her close.

"What happened? You never miss a note." His face was pale. "I won't be able to look when you're up there."

Leonora leaned against his shoulder, feeling the warmth of his breath in her hair. She drew back so that she could look into his face, and smiled up at him.

"No, you won't. You'll be in the wings with the horse and you'll never make it out front into the audience in time, even if they let us, which isn't likely."

She slipped her arms into her coat and Walter wound her scarf round her neck, pulling her gently towards him. As if they had always known it would happen, their lips met.

Walking out arm in arm, Leonora was at ease again.

- 14 -

Walter's car was double parked, blocking the car in front. Cheeky as a small boy caught raiding the pantry, he opened the passenger door. "Don't worry, it's Kurt Stahl's. The director's always the last to leave."

Walter's carefree attitude to life was part of his charm. Leonora wondered how far he would push the boundaries; she didn't know him well enough to judge.

"Come on, Lou. It's only a car space." Walter was looking at her with amusement. "Haven't you ever done anything like this?"

Leonora got into the car. She wasn't going to be drawn. "Maybe." She let the shortening of her name pass. Australians shortened everything. She quite liked *Lou*. It had a good sound to it.

Settling himself into the driver's seat, Walter leaned across and switched on the cassette player. The way he was smiling at her set butterflies dancing in the pit of her stomach.

"It's Billie Holiday," he said.

"Of course." She stole a sidelong glance at him as they drove off. Had he known that or had he checked the label to impress her? She turned her face towards him, his profile clear cut against the window behind him. The butterflies danced again. She wanted to reach out and touch him.

She'd promised herself no distractions. It unsettled her.

Outside the inn where they stopped to eat, the trees were putting on new leaves, a faint haze of green along their branches. After the long cold winter, spring was beginning to show itself.

Preparations for the first full run of Act One were complete and people were moving to their places. Carla was already in her seat. Leonora and Walter hurried to join her. As if a switch had been turned, the buzz of conversation died and the room fell silent. Everyone craned forward to catch their first sight of the three principal singers but it was Lily Benjamin they wanted to see most, the great African-American soprano who would sing Aida.

There was a subdued round of applause as Lily Benjamin took her seat. The Chorus sounded less than enthusiastic. Leonora was surprised. "What's that about?" she mouthed at Carla. "Difficult to work with," Carla murmured under her breath. "But who cares, if she's as good as everyone says?"

The applause for Gianluca Alba, the tenor in the role of Radames, was rapturous by comparison, polite but strong for Ilse Berg, the Amneris. Tall and thin, Leonora could hardly imagine her as the thwarted and vengeful Amneris.

Now Fisch was on her feet making the formal introductions in English.

"Lily Benjamin insists on being directed in English," Carla whispered, under cover of another round of polite applause. "But not for you, Leonora," she added with a glint in her eye. "It's back to German for you."

Carla straightened in her seat and looked innocent as Fisch sent a reproving look in her direction before continuing her instructions in strongly-accented English.

"We're running Act One straight through so that we can time it. Please be ready when you are called."

Hooking her thumbs into the buckles on the bib of her overall, she looked across to where Birgit was sitting.

"And please observe all safety regulations. Come straight to me or Sepp if there are any problems. We will not tolerate any slackness."

Her instructions over, she beamed at everyone.

"That's all I have to say, except *enjoy yourselves*. Act One beginners, places please." The Chorus hurried to line up on either side of the set and Fisch clicked her stop watch on. Maestro Domenico raised his baton and Tilo began to play the Prelude. The music rippled under his fingers, bringing to life on the piano the strings, woodwind, all the lush texture of the orchestra, until the last rising chord died away. Then Maestro Domenico held up his hand and paused so that Fisch could allow for applause in her timing before giving the cue to start the opera. In Hildeberg there would be no house curtain to raise, only lights illuminating the dark stage.

Gianluca Alba, a small man with dark good looks, was dwarfed by the massive set behind him. Could he be believable as the great warrior Radames? Thoughtfully the director had cast a singer of similar height as the high priest Ramphis, but the two figures seemed insignificant in front of the high platform.

Suspense crackled in the room.

In the brief opening scene with the high priest, Radames only sings seven words: *La sacra Iside consultasti?... Oh lui felice... Have you consulted holy Isis?... Oh happy man...* Holding nothing back, Gianluca sent the words echoing round the studio in full voice, these few notes already enough to convince everyone that this was a Radames who would fill the stage. Leonora felt the gooseflesh prickle on her arms. And then there it was, the famous aria, building to the final high note that risks everything, like leaping off a high diving board. Everyone in the room burst into applause, some people even stamped their feet, calling out *bravo*, until Maestro Domenico held up his hand for Fisch to cue the next entrance.

The Chorus had edged downstage during the aria and now had to shuffle back into place. With a reproving frown, Fisch gestured them to hurry up. Ilse Berg was already on stage and ready to sing.

Dressed comfortably in a modest tracksuit, Lily Benjamin still managed to glow like a figure from a papyrus painting. She looked remarkably gentle for someone who had upset one company so much that the Chorus left a rehearsal in protest.

Now she waited meek as a dove to make her entrance in the trio. But Ilse Berg was watching Lily in a way Leonora sensed was due to more than the rivalry between their characters. There was an undercurrent of tension on the stage, as if something had been pulled too tight and was about to snap.

Lily's first notes reached Leonora like a physical shock. She felt a tightness in her chest as if a weight of grief was about to give way. The room blurred in front of her; the first few notes had moved her to tears.

Carla scribbled a few words on the palm of her hand and slid it discreetly along the side of her chair so that only Leonora could see: *that's why they put up with her.*

Leonora could only nod and hope the lump in her throat would subside before she had to sing. One of the assistant stage managers was beckoning her to stand by for her entrance.

With Renata and Birgit, Leonora climbed the stairs behind the set. She wouldn't be able to see Walter when he made his entrance but she could hear him. She was relieved to hear his voice ring out confidently before disappearing into the roar of sound as the priests and captains of the army joined the ensemble.

Then it was as if the entire cast held its breath. But instead of Lily singing one of the most dramatic of Verdi's arias, it was Kurt Stahl they heard, announcing that he would rehearse the aria separately. They would pick up from the temple scene.

High up on the platform, Leonora braced herself; without Lily her entry would be easier and with the whole company watching them it was unlikely Birgit would make trouble today. Maestro Domenico conducted the opening chords with a wide beat she had no trouble in following and as the voices of the priests and priestesses joined in, she felt her voice floating on the beauty of the sound rising towards her.

Spirito animator, spirito fecondator...noi t'invochiamo...

Spirit of life, spirit of fruitfulness...we invoke you

A moment of silence and Fisch clicked her stop watch. Act One was over.

It took a few minutes to get down from the platform and have their safety lines formally checked and released by Sepp. By the time Leonora went to get her things, Walter had disappeared. Instead Carla was waiting for her. She had let her hair loose and the studious-looking glasses were gone.

"*Mein Gott*, Leonora. Did you ever hear such fabulous voices? I can't wait to hear Lily Benjamin sing the aria." Carla did a little skip on the spot. "I knew the Maestro wouldn't send us to just any production, but this..." She left the sentence dangling, as if she had run out of words.

Leonora nodded, only half-listening, wondering where Walter was.

Carla tossed her head impatiently. "They've finished with Act One for the day so they've sent Walter to work with the horse wrangler. He asked me to tell you."

Leonora was deflated. Carla didn't even try to mask her disapproval.

"Come on, Leonora, what's the matter with you? You've had a fabulous rehearsal. I heard Kurt Stahl say you were brilliant."

Leonora knew how hard it was for Carla to praise her peers, even one who had a completely different voice. She wouldn't make this up. The shadow lifted from her face and her eyes lit up.

"Did he really say that?"

In spite of herself, Carla softened.

"I'll have to stay for Act Two but I could drive you to the station."

Leonora shook her head. "Best not. They might need you here." She picked up her music case. "Anyway, I think I'll walk home through the Englischer Garten. But thank you. You're a good friend, Carla."

No one had ever said that to Carla before. Bemused, she followed Leonora with her eyes as she left the rehearsal room. She was beginning to understand what the Maestro saw in her. Leonora was someone you could trust.

Frau Felder was in the hall, watering her plants. "Back so soon, Mädele?" Looking more than ever like one of her dolls, her eyes shone like glass beads.

Leonora hung up her coat and put her music case on the hall table. "The rehearsal went so well, they decided they didn't need me this afternoon. So I walked home. It's amazing to walk through fields in the middle of a city."

Frau Felder dribbled a few more drops of water onto her favorite wax flower plant. Leonora's glowing face told its own story. No doubt she was living on *Luft und Liebe*, air and love, and had forgotten to eat. She smiled. She wasn't so old that she couldn't remember what it was to be young. She put down her watering can.

"I made goulash and dumplings this morning. I kept some for you. And then I have a surprise."

The thought of the spicy caraway-scented goulash made Leonora realize how hungry she was. Gratefully she followed Frau Felder into her kitchen. They had become close in the few months she had been living here. Frau Felder treated her more like a granddaughter than a tenant, but never intruded.

When she had finished eating, Frau Felder looked approvingly at the empty plate.

"You must keep up your strength, Mädele. Plenty more walks in the fresh air, too. Now come and see your surprise."

In the sitting room, Frau Felder's sewing things were laid out as usual on the round table. Frau Felder picked up a cloth bundle lying beside the open work basket, and began to unroll the cloth, revealing the body of a doll fashioned from light brown silk, the head and tiny hands made of fine porcelain. She picked it up and held it upright, balancing the little head above the torso.

"This will be for you, Mädele, to remind you of your first opera in Germany." She took a piece of linen from the bundle and pleated it into narrow folds round the body of the doll. "I'll start the costume as soon as you know what you are going to wear."

Leonora took one of the tiny hands and cupped it in her palm. "Thank you, Frau Felder. I'm sure she'll bring me luck."

Impulsively she leaned across and gave the old lady a kiss.

Frau Felder beamed and patted her shoulder. "Run along then. I'll call you if that young man of yours telephones."

Later that afternoon, Frau Felder called Leonora down to the phone. Leonora picked up the receiver, so convinced it was Walter she didn't wait to hear him speak.

"Wal? Where are you? Have you finished your riding rehearsal?"

But the voice at the other end wasn't Walter's.

"Leonora? It's Fisch. We've got a problem."

"What's happened?"

"It's Lily Benjamin. She wants you to go shopping with her."

"*What? Me?*"

"I know it sounds mad, but she doesn't want to go on her own. And when she heard you were Australian she asked for you, said she felt comfortable with Australians." Fisch sniffed. "Apparently she finds everyone else's accent difficult."

"But I'm working with Maestro Mazzone tomorrow morning. No one cancels a session with the Maestro unless it's a matter of life and death."

"She knows about your lesson. She's already spoken to the Maestro. She wants to pick you up from his studio afterwards, at eleven."

The phone felt heavy in Leonora's hand. She stared at it. In her small debut role Leonora was as far apart from Lily in the theatre hierarchy as it was possible to be. She'd hardly expected even to meet Lily Benjamin. It was part of her contract to be available for work. But *shopping*? She couldn't begin to imagine it.

"Leonora? Will you do it?" Fisch sounded rattled.

Leonora sighed. "All right. But what if she's not happy afterwards?"

"I'll pick up the pieces. I definitely owe you for this."

Leonora felt a flutter of excitement. Lily Benjamin might turn out to be a different person when she was off duty. And there could still be time to meet Walter later in the day.

Humming a scale under her breath to begin her warm up, she headed back up the stairs to prepare for her lesson with the Maestro.

- 15 -

The Maestro was warming up with a Schubert impromptu.

"*Buon giorno,* Leonora. How was your rehearsal yesterday?"

"Incredible, Maestro. Those voices…" Leonora broke off, trying to find words for what she felt. "I can hardly believe I'm in the same cast."

The Maestro continued to play softly while she placed her music on a stand and adjusted its height. When she was ready he brought his warm-up to an end with a perfect cadence, like an *Amen* after a hymn.

"*Ecco.* Are you ready to sing?"

Though the Maestro expected his singers to complete their daily vocal exercises before they arrived, he always asked the question.

"Yes, Maestro." Her voice was confident as she answered.

"*Bene.* Then we shall work on Mimi." He leaned forward, his forearm along the piano's music rest. "I want you to audition for the Sankt Hubert Opera. They have *La Bohème* in their winter season and an excellent development program for young artists at their opera studio. We could launch you very successfully from there."

Leonora took a step back, as if she had been pushed. She was only just beginning to feel at home in Munich and now the Maestro was talking about moving on. Nothing could have shocked her more. Her throat felt dry as she forced herself to speak.

"Would I still be able to work with you?"

"Of course. But we must think about the future. You must

show what you can do in the smaller opera houses before the big opera houses will consider you. When your opportunity comes you must be ready."

His expression was kindly but his voice was firm. Even though they might not perform the great roles until they were more mature, singers were expected to have their careers well-established by the end of their twenties. This was a critical time for Leonora.

He rapped his knuckles lightly on the music stand to signal Mimi's knock on Rodolfo's door in Act One of *La Bohème*, struck a D major chord and sang: *Chi è là?*, Mimi's cue to enter.

With an effort, Leonora gathered herself together and began to sing.

The Maestro seemed stricter than ever today, honing every musical phrase and spending most of the lesson on the recitatives. Only in the last few minutes was Leonora allowed to sing Mimi's aria *Mi chiamano Mimi*, once.

At the end of the aria he closed the piano lid, his usual signal that the lesson was over. He smiled as he waved her towards the door. "Enjoy your shopping."

Leonora looked up from repacking her music case and caught the twinkle in his eye.

"Maestro? Was it *your* idea?"

He laughed. "Do I concern myself with such things? But I think it will do you good. There is much you can learn from Lily Benjamin. Away from the stage she is just a person like any other."

Leonora looked unconvinced. "I've heard she can be difficult."

"Ah." The Maestro got up from the piano and came to stand beside her. "It can be lonely at the top of the mountain, Leonora. There are so many critics, so few people to trust, too many people eager for gossip. Take my advice and make up your own mind."

Leonora's mind was spinning as she made her way along the corridor to the office. There was no sign of Lily Benjamin and Frau Meyer was not at her desk. There was nothing to do but wait. She gazed round the familiar room. Studying with the Maestro had been her goal for so long that she hadn't planned beyond it, not in any detail. Now he had reminded her that she couldn't just let things take their course: if she was serious about her career she needed to make it happen. And that meant being prepared to move on at any time. But so soon? The shock had left her struggling for answers. What was she to do about Walter?

"Frau Ford?" A young man in a dark suit had come quietly into the room. "I'm Max, Frau Benjamin's driver. Frau Benjamin is waiting for you downstairs in the car." He gave Leonora a rueful look. "She doesn't like to wait. Can we be quick?"

He turned as if there wasn't a second to lose and sped back through the door and down the stairs, Leonora at his heels, running to keep up with him. In the street, a few hundred meters away, a dark blue Mercedes was parked with both passenger side doors open. Max clicked his tongue in annoyance then covered the sound quickly with a cough.

"Perhaps you could explain to her?" he whispered to Leonora. "I asked if she could just open the windows if she wants more air. She only has to press a button." He sounded worried. "It's dangerous having the doors open like that."

"Well there you are, honey. Get in." Lily Benjamin's elegant head appeared behind the window of the rear door.

Up close she was dazzling, a face sculpted in dark clay glowing against the bright apricot color of her jacket and matching jeans. A scarf wound tightly round her head was expertly draped to show off the silken tiger curling elegantly round her skull.

"Some name, Leonora. I guess your parents were into opera in a big way, huh?"

She smiled, her lifted cheeks emphasizing the symmetry of her bone structure. Whatever people said about her, Lily Benjamin could charm the birds from the trees if she wanted to.

Leonora returned the smile. "It was my grandmother's name, nothing to do with *Fidelio*."

"Well there's a thing. I was named after my grandmother too. Tiger Lily Benjamin. That's my full name. I don't use it on the stage, out of respect. She was the original. But the tiger's still there." She raised a hand to the crown of her head, her pale pink nails gleaming like rose quartz. "But don't worry honey, I never scratch *real* deep."

All this time they had been sitting in the car, the doors still open, Max waiting in the driver's seat.

At last, with a final tweak of her scarf Lily was ready.

"Max, we're getting out now. The door please."

Max leaped out of the driver's seat and ran round to stand smartly to attention beside the open door. Leonora got out first, and waited on the footpath for Lily to follow. Holding out her hand for Max to help her, Lily slid her legs elegantly out of the car and stood up in one sinuous motion.

"Now, Miss Leonora, I'm ready to shop, and I mean *shop*."

Leonora had done enough window-shopping to know where to go. It wasn't far to *Odeonsplatz* with its luxury boutiques. They could start there.

Passing a huge photo of Lily as Aida and a display of the CD from La Scala in a shop window, Leonora wondered how far they would get before she was recognized. Lily had camouflaged herself with a pair of large sunglasses but she was still a head-turning figure.

How lonely it must be to travel so much. To be on the road with no one to share simple everyday things. It no longer seemed so strange that Lily had looked to her for company. Leonora was beginning to understand that the Maestro had wanted her to know if she reached the top there was a price to pay.

The shopping trip didn't last long. Lily was soon recognized in a city known for its love of theatre and music. The interruptions and requests for autographs made it impossible to stop and look at the shop windows, and Lily wasn't keen to go inside if she wasn't interested in buying anything. It was no different at the aristocratic Tea Rooms, where Leonora had thought they might be undisturbed. The service was impeccable and the manners of the people who approached their table exquisite. As they sipped their coffee, Lily acquired the cards of a Prince and two Counts. "It's no good, honey," she said as another admirer approached. "We'll have to go back. I really only wanted to stretch my legs anyway. Take a break from the pressure."

Leonora was surprised at how graciously Lily greeted the autograph hunters and the people who just wanted to shake her hand and tell her how she inspired them.

"Always be nice to your audience, honey," Lily explained as they walked back to the car. "Without them you can't succeed. When you're on stage and you feel them breathing with you, there's nothing like it. It can really lift your performance. And," she added, laughing, "I want every single one of them to go to that music shop we saw and buy, buy, buy that CD! Our audience is our bread and butter. Never forget that."

Where was the temperamental diva in all this? The demanding star that could show her claws if her standards weren't met. So many singers competing for the same opportunity meant emotions were high and disappointment keen. Perhaps it was easier to disparage someone than admit to being out-performed. There was a name for it back home, the tall poppy syndrome: if someone stands out from the crowd cut them down to size. She'd had a taste of it already with Birgit. Was it only going to get worse?

All day since her lesson, the Sankt Hubert audition had been nagging at the back of Leonora's mind. By the time Max dropped her off at the wardrobe store, she could think of nothing else. Her head ached with questions and she had no answers. The costume fitting was a welcome distraction.

In the work room a space had been closed off with fabric-covered screens to form a dressing area. Since *Orfeo* it had become familiar territory: the white sheet covering the floor to protect the costumes; the mirror propped against the wall; the photocopies of Anna Gardini's costume designs taped to the inside of one of the screens; the clothes rail crowded with costumes.

The *Aida* wardrobe mistress, Frau Ruprecht, was already there, neat and efficient with an old-fashioned floral smock protecting her clothes. She took a body stocking from a calico bag and handed it to Leonora. "Please get undressed and put this on, Frau Ford. There's an empty hanger on the rail you can use for your clothes. While you are changing, I'll see if your wig is ready."

Leonora undressed quickly, her eyes darting along the rows of costume designs until she found the High Priestess. She was surprised to see the bodice of the dress left one breast bare. No one had mentioned that. Slipping into the body stocking she hoped it would be an illusion, painted onto the fabric of the dress.

It was cool in the work room. These old factories were a godsend to opera companies but they were difficult to heat. If the temperature could be controlled at all, it would be set to what was best for the costumes. It didn't seem to worry the wardrobe staff who added or removed layers of clothing as the room warmed or cooled. Some of them even wore hats. Taking her cue from them, Leonora slipped on her coat while she waited. Before she had time to button it up, Frau Ruprecht was back.

Putting an ornately dressed wig onto the work table, Frau Ruprecht shook out the costume draped over her arm and held it out for Leonora to slip over her head. The simple dress fell in narrow pleats to her ankles; the linen of the bodice was artfully draped and sewn to fine netting, the bare breast painted on the net as she had guessed. Assessing the fit with a keen eye, Frau Ruprecht lifted the shoulder seams and marked the adjustment with a pin.

"That's better." Next she turned her attention to the dress, arranging the folds before standing back to check the hem. "The length is good. Now walk a few steps. The skirt must be narrow, but you need to be comfortable."

Leonora took a few steps across the sheet. Though she wouldn't have to move on her platform, the restricting skirt would alter her walk as she made her way there and got into character.

"It's fine. We won't have stairs at Hildeberg and I don't have to move on stage."

"Good. Now for the jewelry." Frau Ruprecht took down a flat cardboard box from the shelf on top of the clothes rack. "The wig will be heavy, so Frau Gardini has painted your necklace and bracelets on fine leather to keep the weight down." Lifting the lid she took out a magnificent golden collar decorated with lozenge shapes in lapis, coral and turquoise, and placed it around Leonora's neck, covering her to the top of her breastbone, and across the shoulders.

Silently Frau Ruprecht handed her the matching wrist cuffs, and turned her to face the mirror.

Peering over Leonora's shoulder, Frau Ruprecht looked her up and down thoughtfully.

"The lights will drain the color from your skin. You'll need body make-up on your arms and feet." Her face in the mirror was stern. "And you'll wait till it's dry before you get dressed. I don't want to see any finger marks on your costume."

Leonora studied her reflection, wondering how much she'd need to cover with the flesh-toned body wash. It was notoriously messy stuff.

With the costume checked to her satisfaction, Frau Ruprecht moved quickly to put things away. Gently she lifted off the collar and replaced it in its box, almost as if it were a living thing.

"You'll have a dresser, but I want you check that the collar is back in its box after every performance. Frau Gardini painted it herself. And the cuffs. They'll have their own box when they're finished. There's a headpiece too. The wig staff will look after that. Now, please get dressed quickly, while I fetch our assistant wig master."

As she hung up her costume and put her jeans and jumper back on, Leonora wondered what she would wear on her feet. Nothing had been said. If she was to have bare feet she hoped the floor would be well swept. You could cut your feet if you trod on a loose nail or screw that had been missed.

While she waited Leonora had time to examine her wig. Someone had painted long Egyptian eyes and a mouth on the polystyrene head it was resting on. The painted eyes gave Leonora an eerie sense of someone looking back at her.

The wig was longer and thicker than she expected, rows of thin plaits finished with beads in the gold, blue and coral of the collar. The plaited fringe was beaded too.

"Do you like it?"

Leonora turned sharply at the familiar voice as Kim Ah appeared between the screens, reminding her of the first time she'd seen him, coming out of the kitchen on Christmas Day.

"Kim Ah! I should have guessed from the wig. It's spectacular."

Kim Ah slipped off his shoes and stepped neatly across the sheet. He was in black as usual, in a collarless silk shirt and narrow black jeans.

"So good to see you again, Leonora." He kissed her lightly on each cheek, exuding the faint scent of cinnamon she would always associate with him.

"I enjoyed making this wig even more when I heard it was for you."

He pulled out a small stool from under the work bench, and placed it in front of the mirror.

"Please sit, Leonora. Anna Gardini will be here soon to check the wig design, so we shall be quick." Deftly he pinned Leonora's hair into pin curls and pulled a piece of stocking over her head, before placing the wig, gently pulling the fringe to sit just above her eyebrows. "The headpiece must sit just on top of the beads on the fringe," he explained, placing a broad gold band painted with stripes of lapis and turquoise, low on her forehead. At the center of the band a golden snake curled, its head rearing up, the tail pointing down. "The tail of the snake should sit between your eyebrows, just above your nose. How does it feel?"

"It's quite heavy but it's comfortable." Even without makeup, in her jeans and jumper, Leonora saw herself transformed. She turned her head slowly from side to side a few times, the plaits swinging with the movement. "I'm just a bit worried about being able to hear. I'm so far above the stage, it's hard to hear even without a wig."

Kim Ah lifted the plaits that covered Leonora's ears.

"I'll wire these so that they stand out a little bit and clear your ears. It won't show from the audience."

Leonora leaned forward to get a closer view in the mirror. "It's funny, sometimes it's not so much the singing we worry about, it's all these other things."

A quick movement of the screens and Anna Gardini's face appeared in the mirror, a slim figure in jeans and paint-streaked calico working smock, Frau Ruprecht in attendance behind her.

Walking slowly around Leonora, the designer checked the

wig from all angles. Frau Ruprecht and Kim Ah stood silently, waiting for her verdict. At last she turned. "*Sono molto contenta, grazie.*" And as quietly as she came she slipped out through the screens.

No sooner had Anna Gardini left than Frau Ruprecht began to bustle and the calm was broken. "Right then, Frau Ford. Wig off as quickly as possible. I still have another four fittings to do today."

- 16 -

Munich, April 1991

For the next few weeks Leonora's world shrank to the four walls of the rehearsal studio. She hadn't told Walter about Sankt Hubert, as if keeping it to herself made it less real. She was falling in love with him but if they couldn't stay together when she moved on, it wasn't in her to have a casual affair. And she would never give up singing. She could no more imagine living without singing than speech.

The trouble was she wanted him too.

The intensity of the rehearsal process was giving her a breathing space she desperately needed. Meanwhile there were roles to learn. If she was to be ready when the audition came around there could be no let-up.

Snow and ice were gone now and the air was milder. Outside Frau Felder's house new leaves covered the linden trees like lace. Green was everywhere. Leonora began to understand why the poets made so much of it.

On fine days she got up early and walked through the Englischer Garten to her lesson with the Maestro. Flowers began to appear in the meadows beside the path and every day more people came to walk their dogs or take an early morning stroll. If there was time, she met Walter at a café on the city edge of the park and they would make their way to rehearsal together.

One morning as they sat at their usual table in the café, Walter decided he had waited long enough.

"Stay with me in Hildeberg, Lou. Nobody would care." He reached across and took her hand. "It's our chance to be together. Don't you want that?"

The color came into her cheeks and went again.

"Yes." She spoke so quietly he had to lean forward to hear. "But not in Hildeberg." She hesitated. "I need to be on my own, if I want to. There's so much tied up in this role for me."

She shook her head, not finding the words to say more. A strand of hair had fallen across her forehead; gently Walter pushed it into place, his fingers lingering on her cheek, cool from her walk.

"You can be on your own any time, I promise."

"But if we were staying together I wouldn't want to be, that's the point. It would be too difficult."

She could see in his eyes he was disappointed, as if it hadn't occurred to him that she would say no. "It's only for Hildeberg, Wal," she went on quickly. "After that, we can see." It was on the tip of her tongue to tell him about the audition but he spoke first.

"Where will you stay, then?"

She hesitated. He looked so crestfallen and now she was about to add salt to the wound. "Carla has an aunt who lives in Hildeberg. It's a big house. I can stay there too."

"With Carla?" He was shocked. "You'll be lucky to have a minute to yourself."

Leonora reached across and laid her hand on Walter's arm. The last thing she'd wanted was to upset him.

"Carla will be busy with Amneris. There'll still be plenty of time for us."

The look in her eyes was melting his resistance. "If you say so."

"I do. You'll see."

Leonora relaxed. But the opportunity to tell him about the audition had passed.

ACT TWO

- 17 -

Hildeberg, June 1991

Leonora was ready and waiting with Frau Felder beside her when Carla arrived in a small station wagon to pick her up. She jumped out of the car and ran to where they were standing with all her usual élan.

"I tried to get the BMW again but Vati won't let it go for more than a weekend, so I wheedled this out of Mutti."

But that wasn't what Leonora was staring at. Today Carla's hair was jet black, cut shoulder length, with colored beads worked into the fringe and at the sides. Had she really dyed her hair?

After greeting Frau Felder, Carla turned to Leonora and burst out laughing. "Of course it's a wig. Don't you like it?"

Carla was on her way back to the car before Leonora could answer. With a quick goodbye to Frau Felder and a promise to phone when they arrived, Leonora stowed her bags in the back of the van and took her place in the passenger seat.

The countryside sped past them on the autobahn heading north east towards Dresden, where they would turn off towards the ancient town of Hildeberg in the former East Germany. Leonora had asked Carla to tell her when they passed the old border between the divided German republics. "You'll see it," was all she had said.

The wide band of no-man's land, where only a few years before there had been electrified fences, still ran like a scar across the open country. Here and there between villages an abandoned guard post was still standing, as if an authority somewhere had run out of money or interest. The old border post had become a tourist stop selling postcards, facsimiles of travel permits and other mementos of the darker past. In spite of the bustling food and drink section, there had been no attempt to brighten it up. It was still a bleak place.

Carla had warned her that Hildeberg was only beginning to recover from the years of shortage and neglect when building materials were scarce, often unobtainable, even if there was money to pay for them. People patched up their houses as they could.

In the herringbone of streets that made up the historic Old Town, the story told itself. Separated here and there by old coaching entrances, narrow houses leaned towards each other, discolored patches of broken plaster between their timbering, like scabs on a wound, paint peeling from window frames and shutters. A grey film darkened the walls, as if the dust of centuries had never been swept away.

As Carla negotiated the narrow laneways that zigzagged in and out of each other, bringing them back more than once to where they had already been, neither of them spoke.

Then, as if the sun had broken through clouds, they came into a wide square and found themselves in another world. On all sides the old houses had been restored, their plaster work washed in bright colors between the newly darkened timbers. Crumbled molding had been repaired and picked out in contrasting shades. Even the old cobblestones glistened as if they had been polished.

Now they were in another maze of one-way streets. Left, right, right again. The pavement was little more than a kerb against one or two steps leading to the front doors of the houses. Carla pulled up in front of an open door, where a woman was standing, shading her eyes against the sun.

Carla jumped out of the car. "Tante Irmgard, here we are."

"Carla, at last." Folding Carla in her arms, her aunt held her for a moment. "And Leonora, welcome."

Leonora's first impression of Irmgard von Kahl was her dramatic presence. You wouldn't need to see her enter a room to know she was there. Against the light Leonora couldn't make out the color of her eyes but they were bright and full of fun. The way she held herself reminded Leonora of the portrait of Elisabeth-Lore above the stairs in Starnberg. It struck her that this was how Carla might look one day.

Smiling, Irmgard von Kahl looked her niece up and down. "That's a very becoming wig, my dear. Now, do you remember where to park the car?"

Carla skipped on the narrow pavement like an excited child. "Of course I remember: through the old carriage entrance into the courtyard at the back, by the elder bush."

"Exactly. Come up when you are ready." Irmgard von Kahl turned towards the house, then back again, like an actress following a stage direction, eyes twinkling. "I picked the first asparagus from the garden this morning. Do you remember how you loved to help me when you were a little girl? There'll be more ready tomorrow." She smiled across at Leonora. "Before the border opened, the family needed a permit to visit me and they were rarely given."

Inside the narrow house, steep stairs led to the upper floors but only the ground and first floors were in use. Irmgard von Kahl lived on the ground floor. The first floor was a separate apartment with two bedrooms, bathroom, sitting room and small kitchen. "Before the border opened," she explained, unlocking the apartment door, "people had to take their holidays at home. Now they can go to Italy, the South of France. But we still get plenty of visitors for the festival. I enjoy it." Leading the way into the small sitting room, she placed the key on the sideboard. "Now I'll leave you to unpack. Come down when you are ready."

As if a delightful idea had just occurred to her she turned back again.

"Please know how very welcome you are, Leonora. As Carla's friend, why don't you call me Tante Irmgard too?"

She shines, Leonora thought. When she speaks to you, it's as if you are the most important person in the world.

She sat down in one of the armchairs, running her fingers across the fawn and black plush. The furnishings here were a far cry from the elegance of the house at Starnberg. Yet there was an air of comfort in the way the room was arranged, flowers and books on the table. She felt at ease.

"Wow." Carla dropped her bags and sank into the other chair. "This furniture looks like something left over from the nineteen-fifties, but it's almost new."

Leonora leaned back in her chair. "Brilliant. We're living in the fifties in a house that's hundreds of years old. I've never been anywhere so ancient before." A gentle creaking sound interrupted her.

Carla smiled at Leonora's puzzled expression. "It's the floorboards settling. All very old houses make noises. It's as if they're breathing." Frowning, she turned her attention back to the chair, tracing the design printed on the fabric. "Tante Irmgard was probably lucky to get this. People had to take what was available."

Leonora wondered if Carla had ever needed to give much thought to where things came from. Unlike the von Kahls, Leonora and her mother had no inheritance to call on. They had to live on what her mother earned. But they'd always had what they needed and when they bought something, they had a choice.

Yet here in the former German Democratic Republic, the von Kahl name and inheritance hadn't helped Tante Irmgard. She too had lived on what she could earn. In the state-run theatres she would have received a set salary, nothing like as much as she could have received in the West. Why had she stayed?

"Tell me about your aunt, Carla. She has an amazing presence."

Carla smiled, pleased at the compliment.

"I just wish I could have seen her act. She made her début in Berlin when Brecht was there. She saw Helene Weigl play *Mutter Courage*. They say that Tante Irmgard was just as great in the role when she played it later, and unforgettable as Lady Macbeth. When I came here as a little girl I was too young to go to the theatre but Vati and Mutti went. They still talk about it."

Carla shifted her position, and crossed her legs.

"When the Wall was built, the family wanted Tante Irmgard to leave but she refused. She said that people needed theatre more than ever. And she loved this house. If you left, you had to leave everything behind. She had her place here. Theatre was her life. And there were great directors, like Harry Kupfer. For Tante Irmgard nothing else mattered."

Carla stopped, head bent, as if a new thought had struck her. She looked up and met Leonora's gaze. "We're like her. We have to sing, whatever happens and wherever it takes us. I knew it the first time I saw you." She took a breath. "Not all singers are like us." She stopped, as if there was something more she wanted to say but thought better of it.

She means Walter, Leonora thought. She felt a stab of guilt that she still hadn't told him about the audition.

Carla swung herself up out of the deep chair.

"Come on. Let's have that asparagus."

The next morning Leonora woke with a flutter of excitement in her stomach. The second cast would be standing in for today's tedious technical rehearsal, when lights would be set, scenery changes rehearsed and the sound system checked, but there was no second cast for the priestesses; they had to be there in person to practice with the lift.

Leonora was nervous. She washed and dressed quickly, choosing jeans and a cotton shirt with sleeves she could roll up if it was hot. She wouldn't need make-up today.

In the kitchen she found Carla unpacking slices of ham, coffee standing ready in the plunger. Today was important for Carla too. The singers covering roles as understudies never knew when they might be called on.

Perhaps silence is a kind of ritual, Leonora thought, like a tennis player bouncing the ball the same number of times before serving. She nodded at Carla and pushed the plunger down through the coffee, as if she could sink with it back to the land of the Pharaohs.

Carla and Leonora arrived at the Hildeberg Festival site, eager for their first view of the wild landscape. Granite rocks towered like fortresses over the ruins of the abbey where crumbling arches repeated the pattern of the massive crags above.

The set was already in place, dwarfed by the cliffs behind it. Technicians were swarming everywhere, marking out positions for scenery, adjusting and testing lamps on the lighting rig. In front of the stage a temporary production desk had been set up, sheltered by a tarpaulin. The lighting designer, the set designer, the director, the music staff, the stage manager – everyone had a place with an individual monitor that would give them a close up view of what was happening on the set. The lighting board was massive.

Carla and Leonora looked at each other. The magic of the opera owed as much to these people as to the singers and the orchestra. If one part failed, it would damage the whole.

Fisch spotted them and came over, workmanlike in khaki overalls, her signature fish a tiny silver nose stud. "The dressing rooms are up on the hill but you're not in costume today. I'll send someone to show you up later." She paused to check three mechanics trundling a scenery truck across the stage. "There's a temporary green room with tea and coffee in that portable cabin over there. Someone will call you when we're ready for you."

Carla turned towards the green room. Leonora lingered, hoping to catch sight of Walter but there was no sign of him. She was about to follow Carla when she heard her name, and saw Tilo Konrad waving to catch her attention. His eyes were wide behind the granny glasses, nervous and exhilarated at the same time. Under his arm was a thick folio-size orchestral score.

He smiled and shifted the heavy score to his other arm. "I'm standing in as conductor today. There's no orchestra, only piano – there'll be too many stops and starts. We'll be lucky to get to the priestesses before the first break. Are you nervous?"

Looking up into his kind face Leonora felt her nerves subside.

"Not really. But the set is so open I feel as if my voice will get lost in all that space. And there's no chance to redeem myself if I make a mistake. My part's over in a blink."

Tilo ran his fingers thoughtfully along the edge of the score.

"I'm not sure it's much different with a big role. Miss one entry and people remember. But that's not going to happen to you. I'll be there to give you your cue."

He shifted the score again and looked at his watch. "I'd better go."

It was over an hour before an assistant stage manager came to tell Leonora that Sepp and Fisch were ready to rehearse the lift and set up the sound check.

The first run-through was without Birgit and Renata. There was more space than she expected and the lift went up smoothly.

She was still on her guard about Birgit. It might not be anything as obvious as pushing her in the back again but an accidental bump or treading on her foot – Leonora wouldn't put it past her.

Kurt Stahl wanted the audience to see the priestesses shimmering behind spirals of incense, posed like painted figures on the walls of the tombs in Thebes. As she sang, Leonora would waft the dry ice "smoke" away from the brazier as if throwing on more incense; between each verse of the prayer they would move their hands and arms slowly into new positions.

The incense brazier was already in place. Standing behind it, well away from the edge, it didn't feel as high up as it had in the rehearsal room but the test would come when they rehearsed in the dark.

The first run was purely for the technicians and there was no need for Leonora to sing. When Sepp had checked everything carefully, the ASM gave the cue and the lift came down as smoothly as it went up. Leonora felt deflated: so much emotional energy wasted on nerves and then not to sing.

The dressing rooms at Hildeberg were in low houses built into the side of the hills surrounding the ruins of the abbey. A narrow path curved round the hill to the back of the stage. If it rained, there would be portable cabins behind the stage to shelter in, though the performance was likely to be postponed if there was more than a brief shower because the audience would be sitting in the open.

Because Leonora was only in two scenes, with plenty of time to come down for her entry, she was given one of the upper rooms in a house overlooking the tree tops. It was small but everything she needed was there: a dressing table, with plenty of lights around the mirror, a chair with wheels, a clothing rack for her costume and a small armchair. In one corner of the room was a washbasin. She tried the taps – there was hot water. She would need it. As a minor principal she hadn't expected her own bathroom but there was a separate shower block close by.

Seating herself in front of the dressing table, Leonora switched the mirror lights on and off, luxuriating. It was the first time she'd had a dressing room to herself. Tomorrow she would bring her things and make herself at home. There was nothing more to do now but wait for her call.

To everyone's surprise the technical set-up went without a hitch and the afternoon began with a shortened run of Act One to rehearse the Chorus scenes. Leonora and the priestesses were pre-set on the high platform at the beginning of the opera, waiting for the lighting cue that would reveal them later in the scene. It was still daylight and they could be seen but the lights would be rehearsed just the same. Radames' aria *Celeste Aida* was cut and the piano went straight into the staccato chords announcing the King of Egypt's entrance.

In a few bars Walter, as the messenger, would gallop onto the stage and make his dramatic announcement. Horses were nervous animals. Leonora crossed her fingers at her side until she heard Walter's voice and knew he was safe.

She couldn't put off telling him about Sankt Hubert any longer.

The next morning the cast assembled in the town hall for the *Sitzprobe*, the final orchestral music call before the dress rehearsals on stage.

The singers were arranged behind the orchestra, the principals in the front row in the order chosen by the conductor, Leonora at one end, Walter at the other. Carla was behind them in the row reserved for the understudies.

The room was buzzing with the news that Lily Benjamin had gone to New York for a few days. Her understudy had just been told she would be singing.

Leonora turned and whispered to Carla. "I hope she's ready. Why does Lily do this?"

Carla's eyes glistened with excitement. "Because she can. She's like Callas. People will put up with anything to hear her sing." She tossed her head. "It's the understudy's job to be ready. I just wish Ilse Berg would give *me* an opportunity. "

- 18 -

At the first dress rehearsal, held with piano accompaniment not orchestra, there was still no sign of Lily. The understudy sang from the side of the stage while an assistant stage manager walked through Lily's moves. Gianluca Alba sang his part at half voice and dropped the top note at the end of his first aria an octave with a shake of his head, as if in protest at Lily's absence. The atmosphere buzzed with suppressed gossip as the rehearsal rolled on. Seated behind the production desk, Kurt Stahl kept his thoughts to himself.

Leonora marveled at how calm he was. Like a captain steering his ship through a storm, he knew what to do. He must have seen all this before. Perhaps he'd even expected it. The pressure on Lily was enormous – the critics could be merciless if her performance was less than sublime. Her prima donna behavior might be a safety valve the director was prepared to tolerate. What must it be like to live in the spotlight like Lily where everything you sang or did was open for comment? Leonora had already seen how even going shopping was difficult.

The next morning Lily turned up for the first orchestral dress rehearsal, gliding onto the stage where Kurt Stahl was giving notes to the assembled cast before curtain up, as if she had never been away. The Chorus ignored her completely. In a vivid lime-green wrap that offset her coloring to perfection, Lily smiled serenely, ignoring them in her turn.

Kurt Stahl just nodded and went on with his notes.

The orchestral rehearsals were supposed to belong to the conductor but if there was a problem on stage, there was no choice; the rehearsal had to stop. Today it seemed as if everything that could go wrong did and it began to feel like the technical rehearsal all over again. Gianluca refused to sing anything more than once while Lily sang everything full-voice, irritatingly fresh and rested. Tempers were fraying.

High up on the platform, the lights bored into Leonora's eyes, making them water. The body make-up was taut and itchy on her skin and the wig was uncomfortably hot. It was the first time she was working with the microphone fastened into it – when she moved her head, would it distort the sound? She would have to rely on the technician to give her notes afterwards.

Behind her, Birgit kept up a drone of complaint under her breath. With Birgit's muttering and the thick wings of hair over her ears, Leonora strained to hear the solo harps that were her cue.

She got through the first part of the prayer. Birgit was still muttering. Leonora breathed a sigh of relief when the sound of the war chorus below drowned her out and she heard Renata whisper, *Birgit, just shut up!* Suddenly everything stopped and the conductor's voice crackled over the loudspeaker.

"Fisch, the singers can't hear the orchestra. There's no point going on until the fold-back system is working." He coughed, as if to cover his frustration. "I can't waste time like this. I'll work with the orchestra on its own until you tell me the problem is fixed. Ladies and gentlemen, letter A please."

The orchestra began to play the dance of the priestesses as the cast waited to be told what to do. Poor Fisch. But her voice over the intercom sounded cheerful as ever.

"Ladies and gentlemen, please clear the stage and return to your dressing rooms. Sepp, stand by to bring down the priestesses."

Tradition held that a hitch or two at the dress rehearsal wasn't a bad thing – it put everyone on their toes for the performance.

But too much was going wrong today. Even Birgit was subdued as the lift took them back to stage level where an ASM was waiting to collect their microphone packs. Kim Ah would unfasten the mouthpiece from the wigs later.

Picking up her wrap from the wings, Leonora trudged back up the hill. It was chilly and there were storm clouds in the distance. She shivered. They didn't need that problem as well.

She made it to her dressing room as the first drops of rain began to fall. Collapsing into the chair in front of her dressing table, she rested her chin on her hands. Her wig felt heavy and itchy and she was longing to take it off. Pulling her wrap more tightly around her, she reached for the book she'd brought with her, a tissue in each hand to keep the make-up off the pages, but she couldn't concentrate. Outside it was raining hard now. Even the weather was against them.

At last Fisch's voice came over the intercom. Rehearsal was suspended for the day; they could go.

One by one Leonora pulled the hairpins out of her wig and eased it from her head, the headdress still attached. Her hands were so cold she'd probably mess up the wig completely if she tried to unpin the headdress herself. She put her collar and wristbands back in their box and hung her dress on its hanger. She was still rubbing at her makeup when Carla arrived, scattering drops of water as she threw back the hood of her anorak and upended a large umbrella on the floor. Instead of the black wig, she had plaited gold beads into her own hair, sending them clicking whenever she tossed her head.

She observed Leonora with a critical eye, and handed her a towel. "You've missed a bit under your chin."

"Is that all?" Leonora caught Carla's eye in the mirror. "I think I'll be finding patches I've missed long after *Aida's* over."

The wind drove the rain into their faces in stinging gusts as they ran down the pathway to where Kim Ah was standing under a large colored umbrella, a comical contrast to his black coat and neat beret. Beside him Walter's umbrella was a business-like black.

"No, Carla, we're not going to swap," Walter got in first. "You don't want people to think he's going to a funeral, do you?"

Carla looked up into his face, her eyes full of laughter. "Have it your own way, then. But I think it spoils his style. You, on the other hand, Herr Saville, I'm not sure you have any to spoil."

When the four of them arrived damp and bedraggled, Irmgard von Kahl sat them down in the kitchen to dry off.

Soon there was tea on the table and *kugelhupf* still warm from the oven.

Watching and listening, her gaze was drawn to Kim Ah. As the others laughed and chatted, he sat quietly, cradling his tea cup in his hands. Catching her eye, he set the cup gently back in its saucer, revealing the pattern on its bowl: a painted dragonfly hovering over a water lily.

"I was thinking of home. Dragonflies are a symbol of freedom in my country." He sighed. "Not so free just now."

Irmgard von Kahl looked at him kindly. She knew a little of his story from Carla, how his family had escaped at the end of the Vietnam War. He would tell them what he wanted to in his own time; she would not probe.

She picked up her own cup and studied it thoughtfully. "There's always hope. I've learned that." She waited for a moment, then spoke his name, *Kim Ah*, phrasing the syllables like a singer, her voice rising on the first and falling on the second. "It has a good balance. Does it have a meaning?"

Kim Ah looked startled. "In all the time since I left Vietnam I've been waiting for someone to find me out." He put down his fork, the amusement draining from his face as he told his story.

"My birth name is *Lom*, the dragon. Written *L-o-n-g*." He paused, letting the point sink in. "When I came to the refugee camp there were many jokes. It was not ill-natured but I grew tired of it. So I decided to change my name."

He traced the outline of the dragonfly on his cup with the tips of his fingers, his expression somber. "I met an American at the camp whose name was Kim. In Vietnamese *kim* means golden. It seemed like a good omen. The Golden Dragon is very auspicious." A glint of amusement was back in his eyes.

"The next time I was asked my name, I said *Kim*. Whenever I did this I got the same reply: *Kim? Ah...*" Smiling, he picked up his fork. "So *Nguyễn Long Vân* became *Kim Ah*, a new name for a new life."

The room was hushed, as if no one knew what to say. Carla was the first to speak.

"How sad to give up your name."

Kim Ah shook his head. "It wasn't the worst thing. And I am still *Anh Long*, Elder Brother Dragon, when I speak Vietnamese."

Outside it was growing dark. Carla reached up to the green glass lamp hanging low over the table and switched it on. The light touched the cups, a flicker of movement on the dragonfly wings. A deep sense of friendship pervaded the room. Walter and Kim Ah got up to leave, as if Kim Ah's story had left them all with nothing more to say.

"Get some sleep, Lou." Walter's breath was warm on Leonora's cheek. "I'll call for you in the morning."

Leonora hesitated. It wasn't too late to go out and she needed to tell him about Sankt Hubert.

Behind her Carla's beads clicked gently. Leonora turned to catch her expression but she was already dancing away.

"You can have the first bath, Leonora, and then you'll want an early night. Such virtue." She spread her arms like wings and twirled, setting the beads flying. "Such *Disziplin*."

"Wake up, Leonora. Come *on*." Carla was shaking her, pulling the quilt out of Leonora's hands as she tried to keep hold of it.

"What's the matter?" Leonora squinted at the clock on her bedside table. "It's too early."

Carla tugged at the doona again and it slid off the bed. "It's about tonight. *Ilse Berg has decided not to sing.*"

"What?" Reluctantly Leonora got out of bed and put on her dressing gown. "How do you know?"

"Fisch rang me. They want me to stand in."

Carla was white with excitement. Even her lips were pale. With her hair still tousled from the night and her green eyes alight, she could be playing the young Elizabeth I called from her bed to be told she is Queen.

"It's exactly what I want, to sing the whole role with the orchestra." Her eyes were round as marbles. "Do you think they'll let me do a performance?"

Carla's confidence was breathtaking. Leonora could almost feel sorry for Ilse Berg.

"No, but if anyone can wangle it, you can. Get yourself through this rehearsal first. Does the Maestro know? If you ring him now, maybe he can get here in time."

"I will." She crossed the room in a bound, then turned back at the door, smiling wickedly. "Clever me not to have to put on all that messy make-up."

She slipped away, leaving Leonora musing over how Carla would present herself in the role of understudy to the star. *That* would be interesting.

Leonora had given up any hope of a restful day. All morning Carla had been running in and out of rooms, leaving a trail of restless energy. Keeping out of her way was like dodging firecrackers at Chinese New Year.

Tonight's rehearsal was to start at sunset. For the first time the temple scene would take place in darkness. The thought of it was daunting. As the afternoon drew to a close, Leonora busied herself packing her bag for the theatre. As well as the electric jug, Tante Irmgard had found her an old track suit: she could take the worst of the make-up off in her dressing room then wear the track suit home and scrub the rest off in the bath. A cup, some tea bags and a few magazines she could read without worrying about brown finger marks, and she was ready. Everything else she needed was already in her dressing room.

"Leonora, you've got to help me." Carla burst into the room, her hair standing on end. She had unpicked the braids.

"The more I brush it, the more it frizzes. I can't go to rehearsal looking like this."

She grabbed a chunk of hair and pulled it round where she could see it. "Scissors, quick. I'll have to cut it all off."

Leonora was surprised to see Carla so nervous, but this was a big opportunity. If she sang well, she would impress a lot of important people. Leonora put down her bag and put her arm round Carla's shoulders.

"No, you won't. If anyone cuts it, it will be Kim Ah. But try washing it first."

"Of course, why didn't I think of that?" She ran her hands over her hair, squashing it down, and was gone again in a flash. A short time later she emerged from the bathroom, her hair sleek and shining. "Lou, you're a genius. I'll only be at the side of the stage but I'll be singing with *Lily*. Today of all days, I didn't need a bad hair day to put me off." She frowned at the thought, her eyes green as glass in her pale face. "After your scene, you'll go out front to listen, won't you? I need a friend out there."

Leonora was touched. This was Carla stripped of her usual drama. "Of course I will. So will Walter, and Tilo will be there, taking notes."

"I left the Maestro a message this morning. Do you think he'll come?"

Leonora wasn't sure how to answer. "It's a long way to drive. If he can, he'd only just make it for the start of the rehearsal. If he can't, you know he'll be thinking of you."

Carla nodded. "He always says to imagine we're singing to him, whether he's there or not." She picked up her score from the table. "One thing I *can* show them. I don't need this. I know every note."

The theatrical grapevine was living up to its reputation. When Walter arrived to pick them up, he had already heard the news from Kim Ah. At the festival site there was a feeling of expectation in the air.

The backstage crew had been busy since the early hours. The car park was ready for the invited audience and signs were everywhere. The set was in place, the stage was empty and all was tidy. Only the production desk among the rows of seating showed that it was still a rehearsal.

Huge screens on either side of the stage concealed the backstage working area. After wishing Carla good luck, Walter walked up with Leonora to her dressing room, carrying her bag.

Kim Ah was already there, smoothing the sides of Leonora's wig with a long-handled comb.

He smiled, his small teeth neat as a child's. "I'm glad you've come in early." He gestured at a small table set up near the main dressing table. "They want to put Carla in here with you, Leonora. It's only for today. Do you mind?"

"Of course not. I've shared with Carla before, remember. And anyway, she won't be in costume. But isn't it a bit much to expect her to come up and down all the time? It's all right for me, once I go on stage I'm there for the whole scene."

Kim Ah shook his head. "She'll have a chair backstage where she can wait if there's not enough time between scenes." His lips twitched. "Ilse Berg is going to walk through her part while

Carla sings at the side. She doesn't want the understudy to go on stage."

Walter was bemused. "Then what's the point of having one? And we thought Lily was the difficult one. I don't understand why Kurt Stahl puts up with it." He handed Leonora her bag. "Now I'd better go and check on the horse." He laughed and gave her a hug. "Much easier to manage than some opera stars!"

Kim Ah put the last pin into Leonora's wig and made ready to go. "You can put this on yourself, if you like. I'll be back before the half hour to put in the mike and fix your headdress."

He reached into his bag and brought out a jar. "I've made you some cold cream to take off your make-up. Try it and see."

Leonora unscrewed the lid and dipped a finger into the soft cream. It smelled clean and cool. Turning the lid over to put it back on, she saw a tiny dragon etched into the plastic. Kim Ah smiled, satisfied, his head slightly to one side. Some artists took everything for granted. Not Leonora. She noticed.

She put the jar onto her dressing table and looked up to thank him. But like a shadow he had slipped away and she was alone.

As it turned out, Carla didn't appear before the start of the rehearsal and Leonora had her dressing room to herself. Her only visitor was Kim Ah, coming back to put the final touches to her wig and check her make-up, before she went down to the stage area for the company costume call on set. Anna Gardini was waiting to check every cast member personally. Lily was there too, chatting to her handmaidens, who seemed to have forgotten they were ignoring her. Even in the simple shift of a slave girl, she was head-turning. Seeing Leonora, she beckoned her over.

"Now you just make the most of this, honey." She laid a slim hand on Leonora's arm. I'll be listening out for you." The handmaidens gazed, wide-eyed. With Lily's greeting, Leonora's stock had obviously risen.

When Anna Gardini came over to speak to Lily, she included Leonora in her inspection, sparing her the need to wait around on the chilly stage. That's what Lily intended when she called me over, Leonora thought. Could all those stories of how difficult she was really be true?

And yet Lily herself had told Leonora she had claws. It was a puzzle.

Equally puzzling was Ilse Berg's absence from the wardrobe check. If she was going to walk through her role, she'd need to be in costume. And where was Carla?

There was no time to find out before the call came through for the priestesses to be pre-set on their platform above the stage. An ASM arrived to shepherd them onto the lift, and then Leonora was standing in darkness with Renata and Birgit, with only a tiny circle of light from the ASM's torch to see by. Until the light came up on them, they would be unseen. Leonora was glad she had the incense burner in front of her. She couldn't lean on it but it meant she wasn't standing right at the edge. Behind her, Birgit was quiet for once. Even she was enthralled by the drama of an understudy singing.

The orchestra began to play the Prelude. Soon they would hear the glorious voice of Gianluca Alba in *Celeste Aida*. At every rehearsal Leonora had looked forward to the aria. Today she could hardly wait for him to finish because after the aria Carla would sing her first notes as Amneris in the trio with Lily and Gianluca. Leonora wanted to hear Carla safely launched before she started her own performance.

At last Carla's voice came through the speaker, amber-gold between the brilliant high tones of the tenor. If only they had let her perform on stage.

Then Leonora's hands were clammy again for Walter's entrance. She had never seen him ride the horse and images of him thrown and lying still on the ground flashed through her mind every time until she heard his voice. His moment over, the war chorus began.

The priestesses would be next. After waiting so long in darkness, the brilliance of the light was blinding. Without the television monitor set up to one side, and the sound over the speaker, Leonora would have been lost. The ripple of the harp chords reached her clearly and she began to sing.

How technical it is in the end, she thought afterwards as the lights faded: the emotion contained in the breath and the color of the voice. After so much practice, so many repetitions, Act One was over. It had gone well.

Carla was already there when Leonora got back to the dressing room. Her energy filled the small space like vibrating air.

"Ask me how it feels." Her eyes flashed with excitement. "How am I going to live when it's over?"

"You will." Leonora slipped her dressing gown over her costume and switched on the electric jug. "Because there will be plenty of other things."

Carla took a mouthful of water from the bottle she'd brought with her.

"I just wish they'd let me act the part as well. Did you hear me?"

"Only over the speaker. You sounded brilliant."

"Better than Ilse Berg?" Carla's eyes sparkled. "I bet that's why she didn't want me on stage."

Leonora dropped a tea bag into her cup. "You don't think she just wanted to make sure of her moves?"

"Well, maybe that too. But you'll know I'm right when you hear me in the duet with Lily." Carla glowed with confidence. "Remember, you promised to go out front to listen. Hadn't you better hurry up?"

"I'll come down as soon as I've made my tea. But shouldn't you go now? You don't want to be out of breath when you get there."

"*Cara Leonora, always so practical.*" Carla had the Maestro to a tee. "But you haven't asked me what I thought of you. *Magnifica, bellissima…come una angela.*"

Swinging the water bottle in her hand, Carla danced out of the door, leaving a tremor on the air like the overtone of a note that has all but ceased to sound.

Several rows of chairs had been left empty behind the production desk. This would be the last chance for any members of the company to watch when they were off stage. The final dress rehearsal would be treated as a performance. Walter was already there.

Leonora slipped into the seat beside him just as the lights came up to reveal Amneris reclining on a couch, surrounded by her handmaidens. It was strange to be watching Ilse Berg, now in full costume, but hearing Carla's voice.

Ah vieni amor mio m'inebbria, fammi beato il cor…
Ah come beloved, enrapture me and fill my heart with joy…

Carla was singing of love so ravishingly that tears came to Leonora's eyes. She knew that this was a voice that one day would take the world by storm.

Leonora was already washed and dressed by the time Carla came back to the dressing room, glowing with triumph.

"I gave it everything I could. Afterwards Maestro Domenico came specially to congratulate me." Her face was radiant. "But I want to know what you think." Leonora was touched.

"It was magic, Carla. You made me cry."

"The Maestro didn't come, though. He left a message with Fisch; he had an engagement he couldn't change." She sighed.

"I really wanted him to hear me."

Leonora turned to face her. "He will. One day you're going to be famous for this role. I mean it."

Standing beside Leonora, Carla stared solemnly into the mirror.

"*Arrivederci, Amneris*. I promise we'll meet again." She turned to Leonora, eyes dancing. "And Lily will be singing Aida."

The final "General" dress rehearsal always ran like a performance. Leonora couldn't see Ilse Berg missing it. Not after having rested her voice. Leonora suspected that was the real reason she hadn't sung. But it had given Carla a chance to show what she could do. Now she was buzzing around the sitting room like a bee in a bottle, trying to convince herself it could happen again.

"Do you think she's going to sing at the General? If she doesn't, they'd *have* to let me go on, surely."

"*If* she doesn't sing, yes." It was another two days until the General. Plenty of time for Ilse Berg to recover, but it was no use saying so to Carla. It would only upset her.

"Lily congratulated me afterwards too. Did I tell you that?" Carla plumped into one of the armchairs and threw her hands in the air. "She told me the Maestro's coming to the General as well as the opening night. If only I could get the chance to sing."

"Then maybe you should be resting your voice." It was meant as a light-hearted comment.

But Carla's eyes widened. "You're right. In fact, I should be resting altogether." She gave Leonora a reproving look and got up from the chair. "I think I'll have a quiet day. You should too."

As if that wasn't exactly what she had been trying to do. Leonora gave Carla the last word and held her peace.

- 19 -

To give the cast a longer break before the first performance two days later, the final dress rehearsal, the General, was held in the late afternoon. This was the last step in the build-up to opening night, like a wave drawing back before reaching its greatest height.

To Leonora's relief, Carla didn't have to wait long for Ilse Berg to confirm that she would sing. Carla's restlessness had been making concentration impossible.

Leonora was looking forward to the quiet time before the performance. Thinking she might be nervous and forget something, she had already set out her make-up before she went home after the last rehearsal. Her costume would be hanging on the rack and her wig waiting on its stand. All she had to do was get ready.

Except that when she arrived, everything she had arranged so carefully on her dressing table was gone. Only her makeup box was left, in the center of the towel where her makeup should have been.

Cleaners never touched anything. Would Kim Ah have tidied up for her? Her fingers trembling, Leonora opened the box. It was empty.

There would be an audience of invited guests, some well-known, friends of Kurt Stahl. How could she go on without makeup? Panicked, she searched her room. There was nothing in the waste bin, nothing behind the costume rack.

She checked her watch: there was still time to find Kim Ah and borrow what she needed. Her breath came out in a gasp as a weight lifted and she dashed out of the room. Too late she saw the wooden block on the path outside her door. Her ankle rolled as she tripped and fell.

By the time Leonora had limped down the hill, her foot was beginning to swell. But all she had to do onstage was stand and sing; if she strapped her foot she could manage. The crepe bandage she used to flatten her hair under her wig had disappeared with the rest of her things but Kim Ah would have a spare one in his kit.

He was in the prompt corner speaking to Fisch when Leonora found him. She gritted her teeth and walked over as steadily as she could.

Fisch gave her a sharp look.

"Are you okay, Leonora?"

Leonora forced herself to smile. "I just want to borrow a wig bandage from Kim Ah."

Fisch was unconvinced. "You were limping." "What's wrong?"

Leonora shrugged. There was no point trying to conceal it. "I twisted my ankle. It's all right, I can still sing."

Fisch shook her head. "You'll have to be cleared by the nurse before I can let you go on and there's not enough time for that before we start." Her face clouded. "Birgit will have to take your part and one of the ladies of the Chorus will stand in for her."

Birgit. Leonora bit her lip, suspicion a bitter taste in her mouth. No doubt by now her makeup would be back in its place and the wooden block cleared away.

"I'm really sorry, Leonora." Fisch was upset. "I'll call one of the ASMs to take you to first aid."

Leonora was in shock; she hadn't expected this. Stunned, she could only stand and wait, her eyes brimming with tears. A gentle touch on her arm broke into her misery.

"No one else will wear your wig, Leonora. Or your collar and cuffs." Kim Ah's eyes gleamed. "Birgit will have to make do with her own costume. I will see to that."

The two days until the opening night had seemed a long time until it was all Leonora had to recover. Propped against the arm of the couch, her legs stretched out in front of her, she gazed at her bandaged foot in frustration. There was nothing she could do but rest. At least she hadn't broken any bones.

Pacing up and down the room, Carla buzzed with indignation. "You can't let Birgit get away with this, Leonora, you have to tell Fisch."

"What can I say?" Leonora adjusted the ice pack on her foot. "I can't prove anything." Her voice shook. "All I care about is singing on opening night tomorrow." She hung her head. "If they let me."

- 20 -

On the morning of the General, Tante Irmgard drove Leonora to the clinic. If the decision went against her and she wasn't allowed to sing, it would be as much as she could bear without adding Carla and Walter's distress to her own. Irmgard von Kahl's years in the theatre had taught her to take disappointments in her stride. If need be, she would help Leonora to do the same.

It was a different doctor on duty, a small woman in a white coat that reached to the top of her white lace-up shoes. Motioning to Leonora to a chair, she sat down at her desk and shuffled through the previous doctor's notes. The hands on the wall clock above her hardly seemed to move. At last she stood up.

"Now, Frau Ford, let me see your foot."

Leonora held her breath as the bandage was unwrapped. The swelling had gone down but the bruise now reached to her toes. Her heart sank. Was there any point telling the doctor it looked worse than it felt? She sat rigid, her eyes focused on the badge pinned to the white coat: *Frau Doktor Grimm*. Leonora was too miserable to see the dark humor in it.

Doktor Grimm was silent as she applied a bruise cream to Leonora's foot and rebandaged it. Leonora watched anxiously. She could manage better if the dressing was not too bulky.

"Let me see you walk to the door and back again, Frau Ford."

The ointment on Leonora's foot was soothing. It was more comfortable to walk and she felt steadier. Surely now Doktor Grimm would give her verdict.

But she went back to her desk and leafed through the notes again. Leonora felt as if her chest would burst.

At last the doctor spoke.

"I think you are well enough now, Frau Ford, for everyday activities. However, my colleague has written that you need to stand for some time during the opera. So I must place some conditions. There is to be a chair for you somewhere in the wings. And I would like the company nurse to check on you during the performance. I will write this on your certificate." She looked up. "The Festival management must decide if they accept and allow you to perform."

It was only half a victory. Leonora had her certificate but she still had to convince Fisch and Sepp she wouldn't be a liability.

When Tante Irmgard dropped Leonora off at the festival site, the first person she saw was Tilo, getting out of his car. His eyes were bright behind the granny glasses as he came towards her.

"Leonora, thank goodness you're back." He pulled a face. "The understudy was all over the place. I know it was short notice but she'd heard you often enough. All she had to do was count."

Short notice – hardly. Leonora gave him a rueful smile.

"Not back until Sepp and Fisch approve."

Tilo shook his head. "Maestro Domenico wants you to sing. They'll have to have a good reason to say you can't."

Tilo's optimism was comforting but the test would be her ability to stand through Act One. And she'd still have Birgit behind her.

A shiver ran down her spine.

Fisch and Sepp were waiting in front of the lift, talking to an ASM.

"Leonora!" Fisch's face lit up. "The doctor faxed me your certificate. Everything's organized." She gestured to the ASM. "Gisela will come up in the lift with you and stay at the side where the audience can't see her. She'll also take you to and from your dressing room. And there's a chair for you in the prompt corner."

Sepp nodded. "Good to see you back, Leonora. Now let's get you up there and run through Act One. Tilo has come in to play it through on the piano so we can time it properly. Sing if you want to."

With Gisela on the platform Birgit could do nothing during the performance. But her failure to take over as High Priestess would rankle. Offstage Leonora was still vulnerable.

The lift rose smoothly. Leonora took her place behind the incense burner. Could she make it through the whole of Act One? And then do it all again in only a few hours' time?

- 21 -

It was a perfect evening, warm and still. The sun would be setting as the performance began; by the time Leonora appeared, darkness would have fallen. Opening the door to her dressing room, a prickle of nerves shivered across her skin.

Everything was in its place. Her costume was hanging on its rack and her wig was on its stand. All she had to do was set out her make-up, which Kim Ah had thoughtfully put away in her box and sent back to her with Carla. Nothing had been missing. It would be easy to believe that it never had been.

She released her breath in a long sigh. She could do this. This morning she had proved that.

A small package on her dressing table caught her eye. Was this another trick? She picked up the little parcel and turned it over. Whoever had wrapped it had taken care. She peeled back the paper, revealing a layer of soft white cloth, and beneath it the priestess doll, every detail perfect: the pleated linen shift, the colors on the bodice and the collar, the golden headdress. The tiny painted lips were smiling, as if about to sing.

Leonora felt the softness of the linen and the fine leather, and imagined the hours of patient stitching that had created this miniature version of herself. Silently she promised Frau Felder she would deserve it. Gently she propped the doll against the mirror. She would be her mascot for as long as she was on the stage.

Leonora began to make up her face, smoothing the pancake on quickly; if it streaked, she would have to wash it off and start again. In spite of her nerves, her hand was steady and her face was complete when Kim Ah knocked gently. He was all in black, his usual working clothes, but in honor of the opening night his shirt was silk and an embroidered silver dragon gleamed on one side of the high collar.

"You've found your present." Smiling, he lifted the doll's arms, palm opposite palm. "Now she really looks like you."

"How did you know the arms would move?" For a few seconds Leonora was puzzled, then the penny dropped. "Of course. I knew Frau Felder must have talked to someone. How else could she have got everything so exactly right?"

Kim Ah smiled, pleased that she had guessed. He took his place behind her chair and deftly pinned her wig into place, before attaching the headdress and microphone. Satisfied, he rested his hands lightly on her shoulders.

"You will be very beautiful tonight, Leonora." He gazed at her reflection in the mirror. "Birgit will not trouble you."

Startled, Leonora looked back at him; the nerves at the pit of her stomach clenched.

Kim Ah leaned towards her. "Do not worry, Leonora. I have not spoken to her." His lips curled in a mischievous smile. "But I reminded *all* the ladies of the Chorus to take extra care of their wigs as I have no spares. It would be so unfortunate if anyone's wig was misplaced, and she could not go onstage." Between half-closed lids, his eyes gleamed with amusement.

Leonora turned to face him. Subtlety could be lost on Birgit. "Do you think she understood?"

"Enough to be careful." Kim Ah smiled serenely. "No one wants to offend the wig master. Birgit will not take that risk." He picked up his comb and put it back in his box. "She will see me watching her, and behave. So do not worry."

Leonora gave him a rueful smile. "I'll always be on my guard when Birgit's around. But knowing you are looking out for me... it makes a difference." She broke off as the half hour call came over the intercom.

Kim Ah stood for a moment, smiling down at her. Then with a whispered *Toi toi toi* he left and Leonora was alone. It was only a matter of minutes until the 15 minute call.

She was standing in the middle of the room waiting for her dresser, when the knock on the door came. But the voice she heard was Tilo's.

He was more dressed-up than she had ever seen him, in a smart black suit and black silk polo, the outsized orchestral score tucked under his arm.

"No music notes, Leonora. Just the usual reminder from Maestro Domenico to watch his beat." Tilo pushed his glasses into place, as if to see her better. "You look amazing."

She nodded, pleased at the compliment. "So do you."

"Well, opening night…" He shifted the score to his other arm. "I'm doing the honors in the prompt box." He smiled and ran his fingers through his hair. "I'll be waiting for your entrance. It's pure magic seeing you floating up there. Toi toi toi, Leonora."

"And you, Tilo."

The door closed behind him. Outside a thrush sang.

Later Leonora would try to remember, step by step, the walk down to the stage, waiting with Birgit and Renata while the sound engineer checked their microphones, then the lift rising slowly in the darkness. But it was as if time had taken a great leap and brought her straight to the moment when they took their positions on the platform. Behind the scrim they would be invisible until the lights shone on them but if they dared look down, they could see the audience, a blur of faces shifting sideways along the rows.

A babble of sound drifted up from the orchestra warming up, until the leader gave the signal to tune and the instruments fused in a single note. Then huge applause as Maestro Domenico took his place.

With only the vast empty space in front of her, it took all Leonora's concentration to keep herself from swaying. Now there was nothing to do but wait.

Act One passed in a blur, punctuated by singing she would recall for the rest of her life; to think of it was to hear it again in her mind, every note as true as the first time she heard it. She would remember how Gianluca held on to the last note of *Celeste Aida* well over the bar line, dying away as Verdi had written, and the audience going wild. The applause went on so long that Maestro Domenico had to raise his baton to interrupt it by starting the trio. No-one begrudged Gianluca his glory but the longer the applause went on, the harder the next entry became.

At her sides Leonora's palms were clammy. The applause after Lily's *Ritorna vincitor* could be even longer. What if the applause drowned out the two bars before her entry and she couldn't get her note? She would have to keep the pitch in her mind throughout the applause and come in on the beat, whether she could hear or not.

Pins and needles were beginning to creep up her legs. She shifted her weight again, stretching each foot. On the stage, Walter's moment came and went and the war chorus began. No problems with the horse, then. A shiver of relief ran down her spine.

And now Lily was singing, the audience hushed, breathing in unison like one vast presence out there in the darkness. No-one colored a note or a phrase like Lily. Like Callas she took hold of her audience and made them believe. Her voice could turn your heart over.

Numi pietà... del mio soffrir... have pity oh gods... on my suffering

The last notes died away and the audience held its breath, as if no-one wanted to let go of the moment. And then the audience was on its feet, cheering and clapping. Leonora pitched the note of her entry, humming it as she watched the monitor. The applause went on and on.

At last the lights began to shine on the platform and there was a gasp from the audience as Leonora and the two priestesses were revealed, high above the stage. Maestro Domenico held up one hand to the orchestra, waiting for the audience to settle before cueing the harp. No time to think now, just sing, her voice floating away from her in a long pure line, the way the Maestro had taught her. There were no more nerves, only a sense of being suspended in the moment, an image, a sound, a small link in the chain of glorious music fulfilling its purpose.

By the time the priestesses were brought down to stage level everyone had dispersed and the Act Two set was being moved into place. Sepp whisked them quickly out of the way to the wings, where Birgit and Renata hurried off for their costume change. Leonora almost envied them. She would have nothing to do now until she reappeared at the end. It wouldn't be a solo line then; Birgit, Renata and the Chorus would be singing as well. Still, she was glad to be part of the ending. Everyone would be looking at Aida and Radames in their tomb, but she would be there above them in that final image.

"Good one, Leonora." Fisch moved briskly past her onto the stage, as Leonora made her way to the exit, where she found a beaming Tilo waiting for her.

"Spot on with the orchestra, well done. Did you hear the audience gasp when the lights came up on you?"

"It's strange, but it all happened so quickly that all I remember now is trying to hear the orchestra and watch the beat."

"Seriously, Leonora, Maestro Domenico is pleased. How you manage to sing so beautifully with all that light in your eyes, so high up…" He broke off, suddenly shy again, and looked at his watch. "I have to give some reminders to the handmaidens for the scene with Amneris. They should be just about ready. Will you be all right going up to your room in the dark?"

Leonora looked up at him, touched that he had taken the time to wait for her as she came off stage, understanding that she would be on her own, out of it, while the rest of the opera unfolded.

"I'll be fine. There'll be an ASM waiting to walk up with me."

He loped off, turning briefly to wave as Leonora called after him.

"Thank you, Tilo."

It was cold in the wings. Leonora was contemplating walking up on her own when Gisela arrived, her arms full of flowers, a telegram in her hand. Her face was flushed, as if she'd been running.

"I'm sorry, Leonora, you should have had these before curtain up but it's been so hectic. If it's not tea for one of the stars, it's a message to wardrobe, or the music staff." Shining her torch on the path ahead of them, she gave Leonora a cheerful grin. "Fisch needs me back as soon as I can make it. She'll have her stop watch on me, for sure."

Alone in her room, Leonora picked up the flowers. A perfect red rose from Walter; a posy from Carla and Tante Irmgard; a more formal bouquet of peonies from the Maestro and Frau Benedict. The florist had wrapped the stems in damp paper; they would stay fresh until she got home. She propped them in the tiny sink, leaving Walter's rose on her dressing table in pride of place. She would keep it in the theatre, leaving it in her water glass until she could bring in a vase. Her mother's simple telegram of love and luck she tucked behind the priestess doll. How she wished her mother could have been here tonight.

Carefully she unfastened her ornate collar and cuffs, and slipped out of her costume and into a wrap. Though it was hot and heavy to wear, she left her wig on; because of the microphone piece fastened into it, she'd need Kim Ah to help her take it off and put it back on again before the last scene. He'd offered but she didn't want to trouble him.

Over the intercom she could hear the orchestra tuning again. The woodwind had been affected by the weather and the orchestra had to take the A from them. It was still an A, but some people would hear the small difference in frequency from concert pitch. She wondered vaguely if Lily or Ilse Berg would complain. She smiled to herself. If they did, Carla was sure to find out.

She filled the electric jug with water and switched it on to make tea. It was going to be a lonely wait for the end of the opera.

No matter how many times Leonora heard it, the ending of *Aida* brought tears to her eyes, always at the same point, when Aida sees heaven opening: *già veggo il ciel dischiudersi...* Lily was painting each of the six consecutive notes on F with its own plangent color perfectly on pitch, followed by an exquisite octave leap to the top note. Like a great river, the audience was flowing with her. Everyone would remember what they felt when they heard her sing.

The last notes of the opera died away and there was silence, as if no-one could let go of the moment. Then the applause broke, rising and falling in great waves.

As an open air theatre, Hildeberg had no curtains. The lights came up and down as the cast took their bows, again and again, until at last the audience began to disperse.

VIP well-wishers crowded onto the stage, surrounding Lily, a sheaf of red roses in her arms, more flowers heaped at her feet, smiling like a triumphant Miss World about to receive her crown. Beside her, Ilse Berg looked as if she had bitten on something sour, though she had sung magnificently and had nearly as many bouquets as Lily. Had something been said? But Sepp and Fisch were already shepherding everyone from the stage, keen to avoid the crew going into overtime. Whatever drama had been in the making was averted.

Carla had taken trouble with her appearance. A strapless satin sheath in emerald green, a matching wrap draped across her elbows, her hair swept up to show off the green stones in her ears and round her neck. She had forgotten how dressed-up she was until she got to Leonora's dressing room and found her swathed in a towel, swirling cold cream on her face and body. All the nice things she'd meant to say went out of her head.

"Lord, Leonora, you look like a mud-wrestler."

She edged into the room, pulling the ends of her wrap close.

Leonora couldn't help laughing. "You should see your face. You look like a duchess trying not to touch the deserving poor." She squeezed out a wash cloth and began to wipe off her make-up. "Thank you for the flowers, Carla. For such a tiny role I feel very spoiled."

Carla looked on with a sensation new to her: she'd never thought she would admire modesty in a singer. She thought back to their first meeting, when she'd swept into the Maestro's studio determined to outshine the newcomer and put her in her place, jealous of every word of praise.

Still holding her wrap tightly, she picked her way cautiously back to the door. "Now I'd better go and find Kim Ah. I'm giving him a lift to Tante Irmgard's. She's gone ahead to put the champagne on ice."

Apart from a VIP reception held by the Mayor of Hildeberg, to which only the major principals were invited, there was no official opening night party for the rest of the cast and orchestra. There were so many people and nowhere nearby that could fit them all in. People might gather for drinks at a Gasthaus in the town but not everyone was staying there; many would be driving home and leaving straight after the performance.

Leonora dried herself off and put on her black jump suit. She was clean enough now; she could scrub off any missed patches in the bath later. Her foot had held up well but with no second cast to give her a night off, she was glad she could just have a quiet supper. Besides Carla and Tante Irmgard, it would just be Walter and Kim Ah, her closest friends.

Too late she realized no-one had said anything about Tilo. Why hadn't she thought to ask him?

But then Walter arrived, sweeping her into his arms and every other thought went out of her head.

- 22 -

Leonora opened her eyes, drifting up from a deep sleep. She had been dreaming of Walter. She half-expected to see him looking down at her. Instead it was Carla shaking her, already dressed, perfectly groomed in a cream silk shirt and black velvet trousers. Round her neck was a choker of antique pearls. Leonora brushed her hand over her eyes. There was something familiar about the pearls.

Following Leonora's gaze, Carla touched them lightly, a smile on her mouth. "They were Elisabeth-Lore's. She's wearing them in her portrait."

And in my dream, Leonora thought but didn't say. Every inch the aristocrat, wearing her great-aunt's pearls, the likeness was uncanny. Carla was sending a message that she intended to be Elisabeth-Lore's equal.

Shaking the sleep from her eyes, Leonora jumped out of bed. Today she would meet Carla's parents for the first time. Though Carla had assured her they were nothing like the Prussian aunts, Leonora was nervous.

"Why didn't you wake me before? I haven't even ironed my dress."

"Don't worry. Tante Irmgard has done it already. You didn't even move when she came in. That's how fast asleep you were." Carla tossed her head, sending her carefully-arranged hair flying. "Well, hurry up then."

For all her elegance, still the same Carla underneath. Leonora grabbed her dressing gown and headed for the bathroom.

Downstairs Tante Irmgard was as smart as her niece in a green linen dress with a white collar. Leonora could only wonder at this family who seemed to need so little sleep after drinking champagne and talking half the night.

She sat down gratefully at the place laid for her where a small pot of coffee was waiting. She poured herself a cup and took a sip. "I should have gone to bed earlier."

Tante Irmgard shook her head. "There's no point trying to sleep until you've unwound after a performance. You deserved to sleep in. We're all very proud of you."

"It went as well as I hoped, but for such a small part..."

"Small, maybe, but one that people remember." Her eyes twinkled. "And now you can say you've worked with all those famous names."

Carla leaned forward, her elbows on the table, resting her chin in her hands. "One day we'll be the famous names, Tante Irmgard, you'll see."

"That's in your hands, *Liebchen*. There's a lot more needed than the voice."

Carla gave her aunt a cheeky grin. "I know." Dropping her voice to a deep pitch, she rolled her Rs dramatically. "*Sacrrrifice, Worrk, and More Worrk.*"

Tante Irmgard took her niece's teasing in her stride. "You'll see. Now let me clear the table. Your parents will be here any minute."

Leonora was feeling nervous again. Last night she had given Tante Irmgard the flowers from the Maestro. Now she went over to where the flowers stood on a table in front of an oval mirror as if to admire them, while surreptitiously checking her appearance. And where was Walter? She could only hope he wouldn't be late the first time they met Graf and Gräfin von Kahl.

"Don't worry, Leonora. You look fine." Carla's face appeared in the mirror behind her. She never missed anything. "And here's Walter now."

He looked so handsome in his suit that Leonora wanted to rush into his arms and run away with him. He must have asked Carla last night what to wear, or did he know? Leonora knew that his family back home had connections to the local high society, regulars at opening nights, flying down to Melbourne for the Spring Racing and the traditional picnic in the members' car park. Meeting them if she ever did could be just as nerve-wracking. But they were far away and he was here smiling down at her in the way that made her heart turn over.

Immediately behind Walter were Carla's parents. Leonora didn't know what she'd expected but it wasn't these tall, slender people, sleek as thoroughbreds parading before a race.

Graf August von Kahl led the way and came straight to where Walter and Leonora were standing. With perfect European courtesy he waited to greet Carla until she had introduced them, and he in turn had introduced his wife.

Shyly Leonora offered her hand in the polite German custom. In his well-cut dark suit, plain white shirt and grey silk tie the Graf could be any successful businessman. Later Leonora would find it hard to say what made him look so distinguished. His bearing and quiet courtesy, perhaps. With the Gräfin, it was easier. In her simple cream suit, she reminded Leonora of Frau Benedict with her perfect manners and understated elegance.

As Carla came forward to be hugged and kissed Leonora had time to observe the Graf and Gräfin more closely. Carla was more like her father; they had the same coloring, the same energetic way of moving. Frau von Kahl smiled approvingly at her elegant daughter. Her influence was plain to see in Carla's sense of style."

"We have a surprise for you, Carlinchen. Ah, here she is."

"Bärchen!" Carla ran to hug her. "When did you arrive? Oh I

wish you had seen me do the rehearsal."

"Yesterday. And so do I, but there'll be another time. Now let me say hello to Leonora." Not standing on ceremony, she clasped Leonora in a hug that did credit to her name. "I just wish we could have seen more of you, Leonora. Such a beautiful voice. You too, Herr Saville."

"Walter, please." Carla and Leonora exchanged amused glances as Walter gave Bärchen his most dazzling smile, and she was instantly won over.

She was dressed-up for the occasion in a brown skirt and jacket with a crisp white shirt, beaming with pleasure at seeing all the family together.

Graf von Kahl smiled at Leonora. "I've booked a table at the Gasthaus zum Freischütz. It's the oldest inn in Hildeberg, even older than this house. I think you'll like it." He turned to his sister. "Why don't you lead the way, Irmgard? Elsa and I will walk with Leonora and Walter."

They fell into step along the street and Leonora found herself walking beside him. He smiled, setting her at ease. "It's only a few minutes to the inn."

Soon the footpath narrowed, forcing them to walk single file before turning into an old cobbled carriageway now blocked to traffic by a grey stone bollard pitted with age. Ahead of them lay a courtyard and beyond it the inn with its pointed gables, sloping walls and massive wooden door. A peaceful scene now but Leonora could picture how it once was, bustling with serving maids and stable boys, chickens pecking in the dirt for stray grains of corn.

Graf August stopped at the door, pointing out the date over the lintel: 1247 AD. Inside everything slanted with age, the timbered ceiling with its massive beams, the dark polished floor, the windows crisscrossed with lead. Half-curtains of stiff white lawn edged with lace hung in separate panels like flags. The table he had reserved was a massive slab of polished wood, worn to the grain with centuries of use. At each end was an ornate carved chair in the same wood; on the long sides were high-backed benches, like church pews.

Leonora caught her breath. This was the oldest house she had ever been in. Thinking of all the people who had lived and stayed here filled her with awe. She had felt the presence of the past sometimes at home, in the bush, unchanged for thousands of years, with its echoes of those who had lived there through millennia; but until now, never in a house. She wished her mother could be here too.

Australia seemed a world away. Nowhere could replace it as her home and she would always go back when she could. But she could be happy wherever her music took her, as long as she could sing. She knew that now. In the end, people were just people, even in Carla's aristocratic world.

She looked up and met Walter's eyes across the table. With a start she remembered she still hadn't told him about the audition.

A cool breeze was blowing as Leonora, Carla and Walter left the inn. Leonora walked back with Carla to pick up a jacket before spending the rest of the day with Walter. As they came close to Tante Irmgard's house, they heard the phone ringing. Carla ran ahead to answer. Leonora was half way up the stairs when Carla called her back.

"Leonora, the Maestro wants to speak to you."

"Maestro Domenico?"

"Of course not." Carla rolled her eyes and clamped her fingers over the mouthpiece. "It's *our* Maestro."

Leonora turned and ran back down, suddenly nervous. What was he going to say about her performance? It felt like her audition all over again.

"Maestro." Her voice came out in a squeak.

"*Complimenti*, Leonora. I am very satisfied."

"Thank you, Maestro." She let her breath out slowly, hoping he wouldn't hear she'd been holding it.

"Don't thank me. You were the one who performed so well. But now we must start to plan for bigger things. I am staying in Hildeberg for the whole of the festival to work with Lily – Frau Benjamin. That means I will also have time to work with you." He didn't wait for an answer. "There is an excellent music room in the Old Town Hall. I can see you there tomorrow at 11."

Leonora felt a surge of excitement followed by a stab of guilt. Walter was expecting to spend their free time together. But how could she refuse the Maestro? Even if she wanted to, and she didn't.

She drew in a deep breath.

"I'll be there, Maestro. What music shall I bring?"

"We'll discuss repertoire tomorrow. Rest well."

The line went quiet as he hung up. Slowly Leonora replaced the receiver. At the foot of the stairs Walter was waiting for her. The disappointment in his eyes was wounding.

"He wants you to work with him, doesn't he?"

She nodded. "But it won't be all day."

"It might as well be. By the time you've finished with the Maestro and eaten, it will be almost time to get ready for the performance." He looked at her accusingly. "We were supposed to spend our free time together."

"Wal, you know I can't turn the Maestro down." Impulsively Leonora put out her hands. "Don't make me feel bad about it. We've got all the rest of today for a start."

Walter shrugged. "Get your jacket, Lou. Then let's find somewhere we can talk."

In the Market Square the stalls were packing up.

Walter drew Leonora to a nearby bench. He'd held back, not

wanting his anger at what he saw as the Maestro's dominance of Leonora to get the better of him. But he needed to tell her how he felt.

"Lou, what's going on? Why suddenly all this extra time with the Maestro?"

"He wants me to audition for the opera program at Sankt Hubert." Leonora's cheeks burned; all her carefully planned words forgotten, she'd blurted it out so clumsily. "I've been trying to find the right time to tell you. Only there's always been someone else around."

"Then tell me now." Walter pinched his lips, frowning.

"They're doing *The Marriage of Figaro* in the young artists program and a season of *La Bohème* in the main theatre. It's only a small opera house but it has a good reputation. The Maestro thinks it would be a good start for me. It was a shock when he first told me but I know he's right. I can't just wait for things to happen."

"You don't have to do everything he says, Lou. Don't you want to go home? You could audition there just as easily. We could be together."

"Don't you see, Wal? My repertoire is Puccini, Mozart, the lyric soprano roles. I might get one role a year at home if I'm lucky, *if* any of the opera companies are putting on even one of those operas. Here they're in performance somewhere all the time. I know there'll be lots of competition, there are so many good singers, but at least the roles are there."

Most singers she knew wanted to build experience here. It hadn't occurred to her that Walter would be any different.

Walter shook his head. "It seems to me you'd have plenty of opportunity at home."

"And *you'd* have plenty here." Her eyes were shining as they always did when she talked about singing. "We could audition together."

He shrugged; he'd come here to talk about the present not the future. "Who knows?" He leaned across and touched her cheek. "But one thing's for sure. The Maestro isn't going to have you all to himself." His voice softened. "Leave some time for us, Lou. You promised."

"Don't worry, Wal." Leonora reached across and curled her fingers through his. "The Maestro's here to work with Lily on their concert and there are probably other people he wants to see. I'm not expecting more than an hour or two with him here and there." She squeezed his hand. "Look, the coffee stall's still open. I'll shout you."

Next morning Leonora was up early to warm up her voice. Opening her bedroom window, she leaned out, savoring the greenness in the air. Summer in Melbourne was dry and pungent, eucalyptus leaves and dust swirling in a hot north wind that unleashed storms and the deadly bush fires that paradoxically caused new growth to sprout.

She winced at the thought of home. It was there for Walter whenever he wanted it, a plane ticket away. For her it wasn't as simple as finding the money for an air fare, though that was hard enough. She had obligations to fulfil. She owed it to everyone who had helped her come this far to stay the course.

Dropping her hands, she closed her eyes, letting the breeze ripple over her face.

Yesterday they'd talked for a long time. In the end he'd agreed to think about auditioning with her. But had she made him understand why she needed to stay here? And if he did, would he stay with her? There were more questions than answers.

She turned away from the window. It was time to get ready for the Maestro.

The Old Town Hall was only a few minutes' walk away. Along the winding streets the lilac was in flower, cascading from the narrow spaces between the houses in clusters of white and purple, their scent drifting with the breeze like memories of lost gardens, blooming long after their owners had left to risk their lives for freedom beyond the Wall. The ancient town was coming back to life but reminders of those dark times remained.

Leonora's spirits lifted as she turned into the wide square with its timbered houses, freshly painted in terracotta, pale green and white. Tubs of flowers stood at intervals on the cobbles. She wondered how it must have looked hundreds of years before when the houses were first built and life was rough and ready.

The old wooden doors of the Town Hall stood open and she went up the steps straight into a spacious hall with staircases to the left and right, leading up to a gallery running round three sides. At the top of the stairs the Maestro stood waiting. Used to seeing him in a formal suit she was surprised to see him casually dressed in an open-necked shirt and linen slacks. Probably Armani, she thought; even in relaxed mode the Maestro was elegant.

"*Buon giorno*, Leonora." Smiling he pointed to the far end of the gallery. "The music room is at the other end. Did you sleep well?"

It so often felt as if the Maestro could read her mind. As if he somehow knew that she had stayed up late trying to make sense of what was happening with Walter. But he had already turned away and was walking quickly along the gallery. Perhaps his question was just out of politeness.

In its plainness the music room reminded Leonora of the Maestro's studio in Munich. A polished wooden floor, chairs stacked around the edges and a grand piano. Light streaming in from tall stained-glass windows depicting the town of Hildeberg with the abbey in the background; a great wooden ceiling arching above them. Leonora knew her ability to sing well could never depend on her surroundings. But how could she not be inspired, working in this room?

The Maestro sat down at the piano, and Leonora took her place in the bow of the piano, facing him. A shaft of light behind him was perfectly placed, adding to his already commanding presence. He seemed perfectly at ease and content, secure in his place in the world wherever he was.

He opened the lid of the piano and smiled up at her. "I have been engaged to work with Frau Benjamin while she is in Hildeberg, whenever and how much she wishes. So my time is at her disposal and my fee is already paid. But of course she cannot sing all day. It will be my pleasure to work with you between times. I have her consent. My reward will be to see you develop into the outstanding artist I know you can be."

Leonora was overwhelmed with a combination of gratitude and panic as she tried to find words to thank him. What an incredible gift, to have this extra time with the Maestro. If only Walter wasn't being so difficult about it.

The Maestro was looking at her intently, and again she had the feeling he saw more than she knew. "You have been given a special gift, Leonora. Work hard and do not let yourself be distracted." He struck a chord on the piano. "Now, let us sing. Today we will work only on exercises. I want your voice to be in perfect shape before we start to prepare your audition repertoire."

Leonora loved the precision of scales and arpeggios, the snaky colors of the chromatic scales running up and down in semitones, perfectly in tune, faster and faster until they flowed into a perfect *glissando*. Exercises to test how cleanly she could jump from one note to another then back again, perfectly in pitch. And finally her favorite *vocalise* by the great nineteenth century *bel canto* singing teacher Nicolo Vaccai, set to poetry by Metastasio, each one a song. By the time Leonora sang the last of the familiar phrases, the discipline of pure singing had done its work and she felt refreshed and strengthened.

As long as she could sing she could deal with whatever complications life threw at her.

At the house Leonora found Walter in the kitchen with Tante Irmgard.

"How did you go, Lou? Has he got you singing the Queen of the Night yet?"

"Very funny. Actually, we just worked on exercises. But tomorrow he wants to work on *The Marriage of Figaro*."

"Susanna?"

"No, the Countess." Leonora propped her music case against a chair and sat down at the table. "It surprised me too."

Tante Irmgard was watching them in her gentle way, sensing a tension between them. Like the Maestro, nothing seemed to escape her. She got up from the table to check the pots steaming on the stove. She'd insisted on making them a cooked lunch, knowing they wouldn't want to eat too close to that evening's performance.

She lifted the lid from the larger of the two pots and began to push noodle dough into the boiling water through a ridged board.

"Perhaps the role of the Countess is a new idea for you, Leonora, but if the Maestro suggests it, I'm sure there's a reason. She's young, beautiful, and the audience is always on her side. And it all comes right in the end. What more could you want?" Her smile lit up her face as she poured the steaming noodles into a colander and shook it gently.

But Leonora did want more: she wanted Walter. An uneasy thought came to her. What if the Maestro agreed with Walter and expected him to go home?

But now the steaming plates were on the table, and it was time to eat.

Sitting beside Walter as he drove them to the festival site, Leonora was well aware of the dangers of the second performance. After the emotion of an opening night it would be easy to relax and lose concentration. Exposed on her high platform, she couldn't afford to be complacent and Walter had the horse to deal with. Tonight they played no music in the car but stayed quiet, each with their own thoughts.

The car park was filling up. Walter stopped near the artists' entrance to let Leonora out.

"Don't wait for me, Lou. It's going to take a few minutes to find a place. I'll see you afterwards."

She took her bag from the back seat, grateful to escape the distraction of parking. "I don't know why, but I've got an uneasy feeling about the platform. What if it gets stuck half-way?"

Walter grinned. "Second night nerves. Everybody gets them."

Leonora pushed the car door shut and watched him drive away.

Everything was as usual, the sign on sheet, the stage crew going about their business. She couldn't expect to feel the excitement of an opening night at every performance but the audience should. And it was up to her to play her part in seeing that they did.

Alone with the familiar routine of make-up and costume, it was time to focus. But tonight her thoughts were dancing every which way and her hand twitched, splashing a blob of make-up onto her wrap.

She peered into her hand mirror. Close-up her eyebrows looked uneven. But there was no guarantee they would come out any better if she washed her make-up off and started again. She would ask Kim Ah to fix it when he came to check her wig.

In the end the scene flowed without mishap and Leonora received her share of applause. But she had learned something important. The performance could be just as good – had to be – even when she was feeling flat. To be transported to another sense of being was a gift.

- 23 -

Leonora's practice, her time with the Maestro and memorizing her music took several hours each day. She set her alarm early and was up as soon as it was light to do as much as she could before it was time to leave for her lesson. Even on the days off between performances, it was always voice first: don't talk too much, stay in smoky rooms or sit in a draught – the list went on. Walter still thought the Maestro was taking too much of her time.

There was no one she could talk to. Her mother would only worry about her and the time difference made a phone call difficult in any case. She had to work things out for herself.

The Town Hall clock struck ten as she came into the Music Room, punctual to the second. To her surprise Tilo was there too.

"*Buon giorno*, Leonora."

The Maestro came forward to meet her.

"You are wondering perhaps why Tilo is here." He paused, as if to give extra weight to his words. "He too is preparing for auditions as trainee conductor. You will do well to work on your repertoire together."

She would be happy to rehearse with Tilo. But first there was something she needed to ask.

"Maestro, you said I should learn the Countess in *Figaro*. Not Susanna?"

She felt awkward in front of Tilo, not wanting to challenge her teacher's opinion. But the Maestro seemed pleased with her question.

"Ah. You are thinking it is too soon. First should come the small role of Barbarina, so charming an appearance for a young singer; then Susanna. And only later the role of the Countess, when the voice is more mature. And perhaps when there is greater understanding of the pain of love betrayed." He gave her a keen look, then spread his hands as if to sweep the thought aside. "But in the opera studio it will be a young cast. In fact, in Mozart's time and that of Beaumarchais, who wrote the play on which the opera is based, such a countess may indeed have been very young. We have come to associate this role with a more mature singer but it may be more authentic this way. And there is no reason you should not sing it now. Vocally it is well within your scope."

He picked up one of the scores lying on top of the piano and handed it to Tilo. "We'll start with the recitative before the aria *Dove sono i bei momenti*. I'm sure you know it: *Deh Susanna non vien*." He beamed. "In Italian of course, as Mozart intended."

Tilo seated himself at the piano, quickly pushing his glasses into place before looking up at Leonora, and playing the opening chord of the recitative. As she began to sing, the Maestro walked deliberately to the end of the room and stood, arms folded, watching them. He was going to let them go through until the end, not missing a single point when he gave his verdict.

With Tilo at the piano, Leonora felt completely secure. She only had to glance at him for an entry and he would give her the cue under his breath. Like the Maestro, he knew every word of the score. From the way he played, she knew he was hearing the orchestra in his mind. His playing inspired her as she felt her way into the aria, Countess Almaviva's lament for lost love. At the end she thought Tilo looked pleased with their performance, but it would be the Maestro's opinion that counted.

He unfolded his arms and strode back to the piano. "For a first run-through, *non c'è male* – not bad. Now we shall begin to work." Time passed quickly in the repetition of phrases. When the

Maestro signaled the end of the session, it seemed to Leonora as if they had only just begun. He smiled in recognition as she checked her watch. "Yes, it is more than an hour already. But we shall meet again tomorrow. Work together as much as you can."

He lifted the lid of the grand piano and propped it open on the half stick. "Now *I* am going to practice before Miss Benjamin arrives." He smiled his satisfaction. "We are to give a *Lieder* recital in New York."

Tilo put his score into an old-fashioned black music case and followed Leonora to the door. The Maestro was already playing the accompaniment to Brahms' *Von Ewiger Liebe*. The sound drifted after them as they walked down the stairs until the heavy door leading to the street closed behind them.

Outside in the sunshine, the square was teeming with people.

"I enjoyed working with you today, Leonora," Tilo said quietly. "I'd really like to keep working with you when we go back to Munich." He cleared his throat. "It's not just because the Maestro asked me. It's a pleasure. I'll have to do a lot of coaching while I'm trying to get the chance to conduct. You'll be doing me a favor."

Leonora smiled up at him. "I think I'll be the one getting the favor." She held out her hand. "You've got a deal."

Her eyes were sparkling, as if the music was a light shining through her. He shook Leonora's hand, promising himself to watch out for her.

His glasses slipped again and he took them off. Leonora threw him an amused glance and laid her hand lightly on his arm. "Tilo, go and get those glasses fixed." Then she was gone into the crowd, calling over her shoulder, "I'll see you at the opera."

Once she was free of the crowds, Leonora felt so happy she wanted to skip along the street like a child. The rest of the day was hers. She couldn't wait to get back to Tante Irmgard's, where

Walter would be waiting for her. Running up the stairs, she paused in the kitchen doorway to catch her breath.

To her surprise, Lily was there too, dazzling in pale yellow, tiger scarf around her head, sitting at the table with Carla and Walter, smiling enigmatically. Surely not another shopping expedition.

"Well, Miss Leonora. That's quite an entrance." Lily threw back her head and laughed. "What have you been running from? I hope you left the Maestro in a good mood."

Demure as a schoolgirl in white shirt and black Alice band, Carla shook her head. "Don't you mean *who* is she running *to?*" Tucking back a stray lock of hair with a scarlet fingernail – more reminiscent of a screen siren than a schoolgirl, Leonora noted with amusement, as she took her place at the table – Carla turned to Lily, eyes dancing.

But instead of replying, Lily stretched out a hand and caught a strand of Carla's hair between her fingers, gazing at it as if lost in thought.

"Would you cut your hair and give it to me if I asked you? I've always wanted a wig this color."

Leonora and Walter sat transfixed, like spectators at a match. For once Carla didn't know what to say. Her face was a picture as she tried to work out if Lily meant it. Lily laughed uproariously and let go of Carla's hair.

"Don't look so upset, honey. As if I would."

Having put Carla neatly in her place, Lily slid out of her chair, revealing close-fitting jeans the same pale yellow as her sweater. "But now, it's time to work." Eyes sparkling with amusement, she rested her hand lightly on Leonora's shoulder, answering her unspoken question. "Carla is coming to fill in the mezzo for some duets I'm working on. But don't you worry, Miss Leonora, the Maestro and I will keep her in line."

Carla followed Lily meekly out of the room. Without them

the space seemed smaller. Like the end of an opera, Leonora thought, when everyone has gone and there's just the empty stage.

She gazed round the room, as if committing it to memory. "I'll miss being here, Wal. Carla and Tante Irmgard have been like family. Will you miss Hildeberg?"

"There's not much at Hildeberg outside the festival. As long as we're together, I won't mind that it's over." He took her hand and linked her fingers through his. "Come on, there's a place I want to show you." His face was so close she could feel the warmth of his skin. "It's our day off. We're going out."

"Where?"

With a teasing smile he pulled her to her feet. "Wait and see."

The beer garden was hidden at the end of a narrow lane. Walter led Leonora through the overgrown path, turning a corner into a patch of grass shaded by chestnut trees, their leaves like outstretched hands balancing the flower spikes on their palms. Wooden chairs and tables, faded to grey by long use, were brightened to silver here and there by splashes of sunlight.

The midday mealtime was over but a few tables were still occupied. An elderly couple had spread a white cloth under the picnic they'd brought. They looked up and smiled as Leonora and Walter went past, as if reminded of themselves when young.

Leonora looked round for a place to sit, but Walter crossed the grass to a gate that opened onto a smaller garden with high-backed benches and tables built into two corners; long wisps of blossom hung over them like curtains and trailed along the fences.

Leonora reached up and touched the silvery flowers. "A secret garden. It's perfect."

A gust of wind rustled the leaves as a waitress came in carrying a tray. Smiling she set two glasses of wine on the table with a platter of sandwiches, before leaving as quietly as she came.

"Surprised?" The look in Walter's eyes made Leonora's heart race.

He reached across and took her hands. "Lou, I'll have my own apartment when we get back. Move in with me."

Leonora's face clouded. "I can't, Wal." Her voice dropped to a whisper. "My scholarship...my room at Frau Felder's...it's paid for a year, until October." She broke off; she didn't want to talk to him about money, not here, not now.

A sparrow hopped along the table. The outside world no longer seemed so far away.

- 24 -

Signing the *Aida* call sheet for the last time, Leonora had mixed feelings. It was sad that the season was coming to an end but she was ready to leave the Priestess behind. More and more she found the music for her Sankt Hubert audition occupying her mind.

The final performance was to be filmed and the company had been called early to check the position of the television equipment and for notes from Kurt Stahl, who had returned to be interviewed in the intervals.

The half hour was up before she knew it and she was on the platform in the light, putting her heart and soul into her performance.

Back in her dressing room to wait for her final appearance at the end of the opera, Leonora began to pack. She picked up the priestess doll and placed her gently in her box. "Will you and I ever do this again?" she whispered.

There was a light knock and Kim Ah appeared in the doorway. "Talking to yourself, Leonora?"

"No." She held up the open box. "To her, actually. Is that worse?" She tucked a piece of tissue paper round the doll and reached for the lid. "With the film crew here I expected to be excited tonight. Instead it's that awful feeling of everything being for the last time. Staying with Tante Irmgard and Carla has been like being at home. Now it's all over and I have to go back to reality."

Kim Ah pulled up a chair and sat down. "The end of a production is always hard, if it's been a happy one. But the theatre really is like a family. You'll meet the same people again in other productions. And as for me, you are welcome to visit me any time you want, wherever I am. I mean it." His gentle face was solemn. "True friendship is never over, Leonora. As for the coming and going, that's life in the theatre. We learn to live with it. You will, too."

He paused, as if deciding whether to say more. "Perhaps something I have learned will help." He waited, to be certain she wanted him to go on. "I have found it useful only to do things I am really sure about. If I am not sure, I wait. Time usually brings an answer."

Leonora dabbed at a patch on her hand where the make-up had smudged. "I've got so many decisions to make when I get back to Munich. Auditions, what to sing." She looked up at Kim Ah. "And then there's Walter."

He came to stand behind her, his hands resting lightly on her shoulders. "The answer will come to you." He met her eyes in the mirror and bowed, so that she felt for a moment she had strayed into another, oriental world. From nowhere came the sudden conviction that one day she would sing Butterfly, and Kim Ah would be there.

Now he lifted his hands from her shoulders and adjusted her headdress. "Perfect. What good luck that this beautiful production will live on as a film." His teeth when he smiled were small and white like a child's. "So you see, for me you will never be far away." He tucked in another pin and smoothed the sides of her wig. "Whatever you felt, you sang beautifully again tonight. I think you know that." He held her gaze, as if seeking the answer in her eyes. "And now I must go and tidy up the Chorus. I'm going to miss them too."

Chin resting on her hands, Leonora watched him go. How simple and uncomplicated her friendship with him was. If only she could say the same about Walter.

The opera was over. Maestro Domenico, Kurt Stahl and the principals lined up again and again, with the full company behind them. The orchestra began to file out, but still the audience applauded, the cheers rising to a crescendo when Gianluca or Lily stepped forward. Behind Leonora, Renata was counting the curtain calls. "*Twenty-one*. Fisch will have to end it soon or they'll be bumping out the set all night."

She was right. This time the stage lights stayed down, a dull working light came on and the company was dismissed. For the last time the priestesses descended to the stage where Fisch was shooing everyone to the wings and the stage hands were already moving in, dismantling the opera like so many parts of a jigsaw puzzle, built up so slowly but broken apart in an instant.

Back in the dressing room the efficiency continued. Leonora was scarcely out of her costume and wig before one of the wardrobe staff came to collect them. In a few minutes all traces of the High Priestess would be gone and she would be her everyday self again.

She was wiping off the last of her make-up when there was a tap on the door and Carla bounded into the room, dramatic even in plain black jeans and sweater, looking extremely pleased with herself.

"Carla! How did you get here so quickly? Don't tell me you were backstage?"

Carla perched on the edge of Leonora's table and crossed her legs. The huge grin on her face made her look more like the Cheshire Cat than ever.

Leonora put two and two together. "You were, weren't you? How did you manage that?"

"Kurt Stahl. He was in the wings all evening except for his interviews. He said I could stand with him. Ilse Berg wasn't pleased." An idea Carla was clearly enjoying. "But she couldn't do a thing."

She uncrossed her legs, swinging them backwards and forwards like a little girl.

"Lou, I've had an idea." She waited until she had Leonora's full attention. "I'm going to New York."

"What?" About to step into her jeans, Leonora nearly lost her balance, hanging on to the back of her chair for support. "When? How long for?"

Eyes sparkling, Carla ignored the question. "Kurt Stahl told me a few companies over there are looking for a mezzo for their young artist programs. He thinks I'd have a good chance." Carla hopped off the table and pulled up a chair, exactly like Kim Ah, earlier.

Carla laughed. "Don't look so shocked, it's only for the auditions."

"I'm surprised, that's all." Leonora sat down to put on her shoes. "It's strange, only a few minutes ago I was talking to Kim Ah about getting used to moving on."

Carla put an arm round Leonora's shoulder in a hug. "You're part of our family now. Prussian aunts and all, we won't let you move on from us." Leaping to her feet Carla pushed the chair back against the wall. "Now hurry up. Walter is waiting for us downstairs."

The upstairs room of the Gasthaus was packed. Most of the cast had stayed for the traditional last drink together. There was a spattering of applause as each of the soloists arrived, then the hubbub began again. Soon Kurt Stahl would arrive to give his farewell speech, and then Leonora, Walter and Carla could go home to Tante Irmgard for supper.

Home. Leonora had been thinking about it all day. Where would it be for her from now on? She would have to go wherever the work was, a modern-day nomad, living out of a suitcase. But she hadn't expected the life she had begun to establish in

Munich to break up so quickly. If she was successful in Sankt Hubert, she could be leaving in only a few weeks and her time in the Maestro's studio would come to an end. She had barely begun to put down roots only to have them torn up again.

She felt Walter's arm around her and leaned back against him. Suddenly it seemed obvious. Home was with Walter. Somehow they would make it work.

But she wouldn't move in with him, not yet. First she needed him to audition with her for Sankt Hubert.

- 25 -

Munich, August1991

Leonora was smiling as she turned into Lindenstrasse. The trees dazzled lime green and gold in the sunlight. She had let go of all her doubts and tumbled headlong into love. Why had she waited so long? Surely she had known Walter was the one at Christmas, months ago.

She blushed at the memory of their lovemaking, the curve of Walter's back against her palm, the wine and salt taste of his mouth, their bodies skin on skin. Walter was her first and last thought every day. Until she saw him again she danced on air; poetry and music filled her head.

She hugged her world with Walter close and rejoiced in it.

Frau Felder saw Leonora come through the garden gate and look up to the Madonna and Child over the front door, as she always did. The late afternoon sun spilled over the entrance onto Leonora's upturned face, glowing in the pool of light.

Lying on her bed in her attic room Leonora gazed at the stars through the skylight. The Sankt Hubert audition letter had arrived. She would audition in Vienna too; if they both wanted her, she would go to Vienna after a year in Sankt Hubert. She had no doubt they would want Walter. Tenors were sought after everywhere.

Whatever happened she'd be with Walter all the time. She was the happiest girl in the world.

A memory stirred; she'd heard those words before.

...sono la fanciulla più lieta...del mondo...

Butterfly? But before she could make the connection, she fell asleep.

- 26 -

Sankt Hubert, August 1991

The apartment was half-way along Richard Wagner Strasse in what must once have been the elegant town house of a wealthy family. Leonora's hand shook with excitement as she turned the key and stepped into the hall with its floor of small black and white diamond-shaped tiles. Ahead was a wide stone staircase with an elaborate wrought-iron hand rail. She would find her apartment on the first floor.

A hand-written card in the slot beside the door read simply *L. Ford, Sankt Hubert Opera Studio.* Nothing to say that this would be hers only for the audition period. To anyone else it might look as though she had already been accepted. Leonora crossed her fingers. She hadn't written it herself, so no one could say she was tempting fate. Taking it as a good omen for her audition, she unlocked the door and went in.

In the main room, perhaps once a drawing room, arched windows overlooked the street and the coming and goings of visitors. The furniture was simple: a polished wooden table and four chairs, two armchairs, a sofa bed with a plain brown cover. But some of the room's former glory remained in a low-hanging central lamp, its pleated silk and velvet shade in faded purple and dusty green like an enormous old-fashioned hat. A ruffle of matching green velvet covered the chain suspending it, and three green tassels hung from the dish-shaped brass fitting against the high ceiling.

Leonora was enchanted. This, or somewhere like it, was where she wanted to live, if her audition was successful. There was no piano but she could arrange that.

Dropping her luggage on the sofa bed she went out into the passage. The small bathroom had seen better days and the kitchen was no bigger than a cupboard. The only bedroom was just big enough for the double bed, a bentwood chair and a small chest of drawers. Whoever lived here would have to make do with an old-fashioned wardrobe in the hall, and a curtained alcove beside it for storage. She wouldn't mind that, neither would Walter.

But she was getting ahead of herself. They would both have to get a place in the Opera Studio, the Sankt Hubert opera company's development program, before they could start thinking about where they would live. For now she had the apartment to herself. Walter had been allocated his own lodgings and they had agreed not to meet until after the first audition. She half-regretted the decision. But she was already edgy and the adrenalin was beginning to run. She was never good company before a performance.

Leonora roamed through the apartment. What if they didn't ask to hear anything from her carefully-prepared list? And there would be no opportunity to rehearse with the pianist. You sang and they followed, if you were lucky.

But that's how it was; there was no point dwelling on it.

The bus at the end of the street took Leonora straight to the rear of the opera house and the stage door, where rows of bicycles were parked on each side like a guard of honor. This was a city where singers cycled to work.

"Name?" An elderly man at the entrance checked his list and handed her a clipboard with a form to fill out. "Please take a seat. You will be called."

Leonora scanned the form. All the usual questions: voice type, repertoire, teacher, experience. She was glad to have something to do while she waited.

Five minutes later she was in the wings at the prompt corner, next to the stage manager's work space, dark and empty now. She could see the brightly lit stage ahead, bare except for an upright piano. The ASM who had brought her here had disappeared and she was alone.

"Thank you Frau Ford, we are ready for you." Leonora walked onto the stage, handed her music to the pianist, and stood waiting. The house was in darkness except for a shaded light in the center of a row half way back, where three figures were seated behind a production desk.

"Guten Morgen, Frau Ford." A woman's voice with a slight American accent. "We will hear the Cilea, please."

"*Io son l'umile ancella del genio creator – I am the humble servant of the creative spirit*," from *Adriana Lecouvreur*. For a second Leonora held her breath.

Loosely based on the life of an actress at the Comédie Française in the eighteenth century, Francesco Cilea's opera had one of the most unlikely plots ever written: a love triangle where the heroine Adriana is poisoned by a bunch of violets sent to her by her rival. But singers and public alike loved the music – Caruso had sung the role of Maurizio, Adriana's lover, at the première in 1902. The opera had stayed in the repertoire.

The Maestro had chosen this aria, where Adriana sings passionately of her dedication to her art, to show the quality of Leonora's voice and her ability to move the listener. She hadn't expected to sing it first up. Its dynamic range from dramatic forte to softest pianissimo would reveal any flaws in her technique immediately. These people knew what they were about. They were not going to waste any time finding out.

It was the first time Leonora had sung in a traditional theatre since arriving in Germany. Above her the white and gold tiers of the balconies glimmered in the semi-darkness; she imagined them full of people leaning forward to hear her, immersed in the music she was creating. Gathering all her concentration, she began to sing, projecting her voice out into the auditorium as she had been taught. In some places the acoustic was so dense it gave nothing back, like singing into a blanket. Here it was perfect; she could hear every note floating away, clear and undistorted by any echo. Soon the thrill of standing on the stage in this exquisite small theatre outweighed the tension that inevitably came with an audition. She was enjoying herself.

The words of the aria had meaning for her:

...del verso io son l'accento, l'eco del dramma uman

...I am the sound of poetry, echo of human drama...

As she came to the last almost whispered phrase everything was flowing, through the smooth octave leaps to the final controlled crescendo from pianissimo to forte: *...un soffio e la mia voce che al nuovo di morra*

...my voice is a sigh that dies away with the new day...

When the notes sat as securely in her voice as they did today, she could feel nothing but happiness.

The aria at an end, there was a murmured consultation in the stalls.

"Frau Ford, it's not on your list but we'd like to hear you sing *Come scoglio* from *Così fan tutte*. Do you know it?" This time it was a man's voice.

"Yes." Leonora moved a little further downstage. "But I don't have the music with me." She turned to the pianist, a slim woman with dark sleeked-back hair like a ballerina; she shook her head. Leonora waited. Perhaps she was off the hook and they'd choose something else. It was a huge leap of style from Cilea to Mozart, and from the singer's perspective, surely the wrong way round. She loved *Così fan tutte* – *That's how women are* – another opera with an unlikely plot, where two women swear undying faithfulness to their lovers, who test them by returning in disguise to woo them – successfully – and prove how fickle they really are. *Come scoglio – Like a rock –* where Fiordiligi swears that her love will withstand tempests, was full of long runs up and down the scale and wide leaps between notes, all to be sung at speed. Then there were the repetitions, never exactly the same. And more of them than there seemed to be enough breath to get through. You'd always want to sing an aria like this before the more dramatic *Io son l'umile ancella.* Too late to do anything about that now.

She was aware of movement behind the production desk and a shadowy figure heading for the pass door. Seconds later a distinguished-looking man arrived on stage, replaced the pianist at the piano and began to play.

Praying she would remember it all, Leonora launched into the aria. Mozart was said to have written many of his arias with his wife Constanze in mind. What a voice she must have had. But there were also stories that if a soprano gave the composer too much trouble, he might work in some extra difficult passages. Navigating the wide leaps between notes that the aria began with, Leonora could believe it. But she had to show that she would cope with whatever was thrown at her. The pianist, whoever he was, was going with her tempi; she managed the tricky triplet section without having to rush and made it to the last high notes without running out of breath. Whatever happened, she could tell the Maestro truthfully she hadn't disgraced herself – or him.

"Thank you, Frau Ford. That is all." The woman's voice again. With a friendly nod, the unknown pianist disappeared back into the wings and the first pianist sat down at the piano again, ready for the next audition. With a murmur of thanks, Leonora left the stage. It was over.

If the audition had been a surprise, an even greater one awaited her at the stage door: her old thorn in the flesh, Birgit, in a full length purple concert dress.

"Leonora, how wonderful to see you. How was it?"

The ferrety smile belied the gushing words.

"Oh, you know, auditions." Leonora made a vague gesture. Did she really imagine Leonora would be pleased to see her after what she did at Hildeberg? More likely she was staging a scene for the benefit of the stage door keeper. Remembering the Maestro's axiom to be polite to *everyone*, Leonora wished her luck and escaped into the sunshine to find Walter.

At the front of the opera house, Walter was gazing into the small marble fountain in the forecourt. Leonora stood and watched him for a moment. In his audition suit, with the sun shining on his hair, surely none of the other tenors would match him for looks. And he could sing.

He looked up as she came towards him, with a smile that made her catch her breath.

"How did you go?"

She put her arms round him, careful not to crease his suit. "Okay, I think. You know what it's like, now it's over it's all a bit of a blank." Leonora dropped her arms and looked back at the opera house, trying to visualize herself on the stage. Should she tell him they'd asked for an aria that wasn't even on her list? Not the world's best musician, it might throw him and it might not happen anyway. She changed the subject.

"You'll never guess who's in there, auditioning now. It's Birgit, dressed up like Adèle going to the ball in *Fledermaus*."

"At 10.30 in the morning?" Walter's lips twitched. "What color?"

"Purple of course. Maybe they should name that color after her. *Three balls of pale Birgit lambswool, please. No, make that dark Birgit merino.*" She sighed. "What I can't work out is why she was so friendly to me. It was all put on, of course."

Walter put his arm round her. "Don't worry about her, Lou. She's not important." He looked at his watch. "Now I'd better go in and get this audition over with. Don't wait for me. I'll go home to change afterwards and come over later. I don't want to stay in this suit all day."

Leonora stopped off at the main railway station to pick up a map. They should see some of the sights and get to know the city while they were here. The map showed the tram running through the oldest part, the *Altstadt*; she could take the tram as far as the river, and pick up her bus from there.

The sleek red and white tram swayed through the narrow streets, so close to the ornate façades of the buildings on either side that she could almost lean out and touch them. Like Hildeberg, arched carriage entries gave tantalizing glimpses of café tables and old-fashioned shop fronts in the dim courtyards beyond. The tram rattled on over a bridge and there was the river below, the tiny ripples in the steel grey water shining like fish scales.

On the far side a row of colorful market umbrellas lined the bank, above them a steep cliff and the remains of an old castle outlined against the sky.

Here the tram had its final stop. Already there was a queue of shoppers laden with purchases from the market, waiting to make the return journey to the city.

Leonora joined the crowd getting off. She could see the first stalls – fruit, vegetables; it must be a farmers' market. With luck there would be bread, ham and cheese as well.

But first she wanted to stand in the sunshine and look at the river. It reminded her of Melbourne. She loved the way the Yarra changed its mood: upstream meandering gently with eucalypts thronging the banks; then straightening out as it entered the city's heart, busy with rowing boats and the ferries that took you out into Port Phillip Bay.

She closed her eyes. It was good to have a river. But this one was so far from the sea, and home.

Late that afternoon Leonora and Walter climbed up the steep path to the square in front of the old castle. Below them the tiled roofs of the old city deepened from terracotta to wine-red. In the distance the hills were a dark line against the horizon.

"Look, Wal. It's just like the paintings and photographs I've been seeing in books all my life. It couldn't be anywhere but Europe. I know I could live here." Leonora looked up at Walter. "Couldn't you?"

"Maybe for a year or two. But I'll always want to go back home." He put his hand across his eyes to shield them from the low-slanting sun and gazed into the distance. "I'm used to wide open spaces, the ocean, the *surf*. Everything here seems so small."

Leonora leaned back against his shoulder. "I don't want to live away from Australia forever either. But we'll have to go where the work is, and for me that's more likely to be here." She sighed. "There are too many good sopranos in the world. Sometimes I wish *I* was a tenor."

Walter laughed and put his arm around her. "Well I certainly don't."

To Leonora the old town was even more enchanting at night. Lights twinkled in the courtyards, and above them a new moon was rising. It seemed another good omen. This first round of auditions was the start of a new life; they would make it work, whatever it took to be together.

They were following the sound of jazz in a nearby courtyard when she heard her name. She turned her head and there was Birgit.

"Leonora." Birgit's smile held a hint of malice. "What a piece of luck to run into you." Her eyes slid past Leonora to Walter, standing back in the shadows. "I've just had a message they want to hear me again."

She struck a pose, arms lifted, like a pop star pulling off a high note, her purple nails black in the twilight. "Of course, they'll have called you two back already. *You're* both used to being at the top of the list." She fluttered her eyelashes, still looking at Walter. "I'm so pleased I ran into you." Slowly she dropped her arms and made a show of looking at her watch. "Must run. *Ciao ciao.*"

Leonora flung herself into Walter's arms.

"She *knows* something, Wal. I wouldn't put it past her to follow us just to have her moment of spite. Why?"

"Because she hasn't got a tenth of your talent." Walter stroked her hair back from her face. "Or your looks."

"I *want* this, Wal. At last being able to sing full-time and not always having to worry about money."

"Come on, Lou. She's bluffing. We only auditioned this morning. And we don't know what the call-back is for. It could be to sort out the ones they *don't* want."

"You're such an optimist, Wal." Leonora blinked back her tears and smiled. "I think I just got my appetite back."

Propped on one elbow, Leonora gazed at Walter, as if the sight of him beside her was a dream. She reached out and touched his hair; could she feel its softness so acutely if she too were still sleeping? She let her hand rest lightly on his head, resisting the temptation to wake him.

Watching him, it seemed to Leonora more desirable than ever that they should make their début together here in Sankt Hubert, just far enough away from the critics in Vienna and Munich to spread their wings without fear of a mistake or two. And both places close enough for lessons and to see and hear great singers. But the thought that Birgit might be preferred had shaken her.

Leonora lay back on her pillow and tried to relax, her mind spinning. She thought of Carla in New York, where the competition would be even fiercer. But Carla would just toss her head and take it in her stride. She would take no more notice of Birgit than she would a fly. Leonora smiled at the thought.

Whatever happened, she had work to do, a list of roles to memorize. So many singers had their first big chance because they were ready to step in when someone canceled. If that happened to her, she'd be prepared.

Quietly she slipped out of bed and tiptoed to the kitchen. She would work on Liu from *Turandot*. She was in the mood for those defiant words to the ice-cold Turandot:

Tu, che di gel sei cinta...l'amerai anche tu
You, girdled with ice, you too will love him

Poor Liu, sacrificing her life for unrequited love.

What was it about Puccini and his tragic heroines? If this was truly her voice, was she ever going to sing a cheerful role?

"Lou, babe, will you never stop working?" Walter's head appeared round the sitting room door.

"Sorry, Wal. Did I wake you up? I thought you could sleep through anything."

He smiled and came over to the table under the velvet shade where Leonora was sitting in front of an open score. His breath was warm against her cheek as he put his arms round her.

"I thought I heard the phone. Didn't you?"

Leonora shook her head. She'd been too absorbed in the score.

"If it rings again, you should go down and answer it. It might be the opera company."

Leonora was instantly on edge. "Already? Isn't it too soon?"

Walter sat down and leaned his elbows on the table. "Maybe you should go and see if there's a message for you."

With visiting artists coming and going all the time, none of the apartments in the building had its own phone. Instead there was an old-fashioned payphone in the entrance hall and a small whiteboard. Whoever answered a call for someone else had the choice of writing down the message or calling them to the phone if they were in. Most people took a message.

Leonora hesitated. Walter took the pencil she was still holding and put it on the table. "Come on, Lou. I'll come with you."

He took her hand and they went down the stairs together. Her face was pale; he could feel her fingers trembling. He marveled at how she felt everything so intensely; it was part of what made her special.

In two strides he was at the board. "It *is* for you, Lou. There's a number to ring the opera company back."

Seeing her uncertainty, he dialed the number and held out the phone. She came over and took it, her eyes wide, her voice husky with emotion as she announced herself. Walter stood back and waited.

Leonora's sudden gasp and radiant smile left him in no doubt. The news was good. She hung up and turned to him, shaking with excitement.

"It's yes, Wal. They've offered me a place. They're sending a letter. But I won't accept until we know about you. We have to go to your apartment now and see if there's a message." She seized his arm. "If only they hadn't put you so far away."

Walter shrugged. "They probably just went down a list. Even if they'd known we knew each other, it wouldn't have changed anything."

Walter had been billeted with another singer, a bass-baritone who was just finishing the first year of a two-year contract with the Sankt Hubert Opera. He came out of his room as soon as he heard the front door open. "There's a message for you, Walter." His cheeky smile reminded Leonora of Carla when she was first on the scene with some exciting news. "You're in." He tapped his hand against his head in a comical gesture. "Don't ask me how I know and don't tell them I told you."

Dizzy with relief, Leonora fell into Walter's arms.

- 27 -

Munich, August 1991

The linden trees in front of the house were turning an astonishing yellow, their thick honey scent clouding the air like mist. Leonora stepped onto the path and looked up at the Madonna. She would soon be leaving. It would be a wrench. Everything she did now was tinged with a sense of farewell. How many more times would she run up the stairs to the Maestro's studio or sing with Carla before she left? Thinking like this was giving her a headache; she had to stop. Nothing would be for the last time. She would be coming back, often.

She quickened her pace. Walter would be waiting for her at the student hostel where they were rehearsing a farewell concert with Carla and Tilo.

She opened the common room door to the cheerful sound of Tilo playing arpeggios on the piano. He looked up as Leonora came in and segued into a few bars of *Mi chiamano Mimi* from *La Bohème* with a pianistic flourish. "Our heroine appears. What does Carla think about such a soprano-centric program?"

"She suggested it." Carla swept into the room behind Leonora in a swirl of black and scarlet on heels so high she was almost on tip-toe. "Mutti and Vati asked for it specially. The great Elisabeth-Lore's repertoire, you know." She dropped her music onto the piano top. "I'll be doing all my party pieces too, *of course*."

"Don't tell me, let me guess." Walter took in Carla's sleek black top, her scarlet gypsy skirt and the red scarf holding back her hair. "Not *Carmen*, then."

Carla clicked an imaginary castanet under his nose. "What

else?" She drummed her heels on the floor, swirling her skirt like a flamenco dancer. "It's all arranged. We can have the concert at Starnberg. Mutti and Bärchen are dying to do it. It will be like having their own music festival and all the Prussian aunts can come and wear their jewels." Her eyes danced. "*I don't* think." She leaned against the piano and nodded to Tilo. "Let's start with Carmen."

"*Butterfly* and *Bohème* first. We'll do the solos later."

Round one to Tilo. He was making Carla sing Suzuki, Butterfly's maid, dressed up as Carmen. Walter and Leonora could hardly keep a straight face but Tilo played on serenely. Carla just laughed. She enjoyed meeting her match from an unexpected quarter. But when she started to sing, she created the illusion so well that if Leonora turned her head to look, she half-expected to see a kimono.

A week later they were driving to Starnberg in Tilo's battered VW station wagon. On Leonora's last visit, everything had been covered with snow. Now the autumn sunshine was lighting up the blue-green of the spruce trees along the drive and the pale yellow wash of the stucco on the villa's façade.

Carla bounded through the door and twirled in the entrance hall for sheer delight at being home, ending up at the foot of the stair as if she had just swept down in a grand entrance. She was dressed simply today in jeans and sweatshirt, for once playing only herself. She gestured for the others to follow her.

"Come on, I'll show you your rooms. We have the house to ourselves tonight. Mutti and Vati won't be here until tomorrow. "

On the landing she turned towards them with her Cheshire Cat smile.

"Tilo and Walter, you are together on this floor. Leonora and I are sharing the tower room." She left a theatrical pause. "Sorry."

The guest bedroom on the first floor was arranged as a

comfortable sitting room, with its own bathroom. Divan beds were pushed against two of the walls to serve as couches during the day and a large writing table and two upholstered chairs were arranged in the middle of the room.

Carla watched with a smile as Tilo took out his music and spread it on the table, while Walter pulled out his washing gear and went to stow it in the bathroom.

"Look, Leonora. See what you can tell from the way people unpack. Tilo goes straight to work, very German. And Walter…"

"Checks out the shower, very Australian!" They both laughed.

Upstairs in the tower room, the bamboo bookcase had been moved to one side and a trundle bed set up beside it. Carla tossed her overnight bag onto the extra bed and turned to Leonora. "I'm not being selfish, wanting to share this room with you. I *know* you saw Elisabeth-Lore, whatever you say. That makes you part of the family."

Somewhere in the house a clock struck, then another. Carla listened until the chimes died away, as if in this room her mercurial personality could rest.

"And I couldn't have put you and Walter together." The glint was back in her eyes. "Bärchen would be shocked!"

Downstairs Tilo was still at the table perusing his score. Walter was lying on his bed reading. Leonora wanted nothing more than to stretch out beside him, to run her fingers through his hair, still damp from the shower, and make love. She sighed. It was going to be a long few days.

Carla darted across the room and placed a hand on Tilo's score.

"*Kaffee* time, Maestro. Bärchen won't believe she's looking after you properly unless she can fill you up with food at least four times a day. I'll show you the music room and the rest of the house afterwards."

Kaffee was a simple affair. The table in the kitchen was set with the blue pottery from Leonora's previous visit and a platter of large jam doughnuts – *Berliner Pfannkuchen*.

Bärchen beamed with pleasure as the doughnuts began to disappear. "Eat up, *Kinder*. You can't do your best on an empty stomach." She smiled at Tilo, waiting modestly for the platter to come his way again. "You too, Herr Konrad. You mustn't let these singers eat them all."

He looked up at her, returning her smile. "Actually, Frau Bär, it's not good for them to eat too much just before a performance. Luckily, we pianists do need feeding up before we work."

Bärchen patted him on the shoulder, almost purring. "*Guten Appetit, Kinder*. Now I have some things to do in the village."

Carla looked on fondly as Bärchen went off to get her hat and coat. "You've found the way to Bärchen's heart, Tilo. Just *eat*." As if to illustrate her point, she took a large bite from the doughnut in her hand. "Who would have thought our quiet Tilo could be such a flatterer."

Tilo grinned. "Must be the company I keep."

Leonora followed Carla up the stairs. The portrait of Elisabeth-Lore at the top of the first flight looked down on them as they came towards her, a slight smile on her lips. When Leonora looked back from the upper landing, the portrait still seemed to be watching them, as if the eyes were alive.

Carla caught Leonora's glance and took her arm.

"Come on, we're going up to the attic to try on dresses."

The next flight of stairs was very narrow, the treads plain wood. At the top Carla opened a small door leading into a long room with tiny windows on one side. It smelled of the pine roof beams, warm and dusty. Suitcases and boxes were stored along the walls; at the end of the room were a table and a row of bentwood chairs stacked on top of each other, and what appeared to be a tall cupboard covered in a dust sheet.

Carla stopped and looked around, as if checking that nothing had changed.

"In Elisabeth-Lore's time, the maids' rooms were up here, but Vati had the partitions taken out so that I could play here when it was raining."

She led the way to the end of the room and pulled off the dust sheet, revealing a large wardrobe painted with a faded pattern of roses. "When I have a house of my own, this will be in it. It's a traditional wedding cupboard for a bride to store her trousseau. Elisabeth-Lore had it made." Carla watched out of the corner of her eye to see if Leonora reacted at the name. "But that's not why I want you to see it. Look inside."

She opened the door. Long calico bags hung from a central rail. She picked out a bag and lifted it carefully. A dress glimmered in the dim light of the attic, pale green lace over a silk underdress. Carla touched the dress reverently, her eyes shining.

"My grandmother's dresses. She left them to me in her will, and now I know what I'm going to do with them. We're going to wear them for our concert."

She let the bag fall again and hung the dress carefully back on the rail before pulling out another one. "Here's one for you. Don't worry, it'll fit you; we're the same size and I've tried every dress in this cupboard."

Crystals glittered on a dress of silver net and on a hair band looped over the hanger. Carla laid her cheek against the fabric and closed her eyes.

"*Arpège*. My grandmother always wore it." She opened her eyes and held out the dress. "Do you like it?"

"Carla, it's beautiful. But if you're wearing the green one, shouldn't I wear a paler color?"

The mischievous gleam was back in Carla's eyes. "I wasn't thinking of wearing that for the concert." She lifted another cover revealing a sleeveless dress of rose gold gauze scattered with rhinestones, its matching scarf draped around the shoulders. Carla felt inside and pulled up a little silk bag. "There's a rhinestone hair clip too."

Holding the two dresses side by side, she waltzed round the attic.

"Gold and silver, Lou. That's what the Maestro said about our voices, remember?"

She twirled back to Leonora, and held out the silver dress. "Well, what do you think?"

"It's perfect, Carla. I've never worn anything so beautiful."

"It's settled, then. Come on, let's take them downstairs and try them on."

Leonora slipped the cover from her dress, amazed at the freshness of the delicate fabric after so long. She lifted her arms for Carla to slide the dress over her head and then held up the gold dress for her. Side by side they looked at themselves in the mirror, a strange feeling, like looking back in time.

"See, they fit us perfectly. Grandmother would be very happy if she could see us now." Carla leaned closer, her eyes teasing. "Perhaps she can."

"Don't tell me. Not *another* ghost."

Carla looked over her shoulder, as if watching for someone behind her. "You'll have to wait and see," she whispered. "But I'm right about the dresses." She picked up the gauze shawl that matched her dress and draped it over her shoulder. "We're going to look sensational."

She gave a last twirl in front of the mirror.

The next morning Carla led Leonora, Walter and Tilo down to the shore of the lake. The air was sharp with the scent of resin from the larch firs beside the path; the early morning mist had lifted and the water glistened, its surface hardly moving. Carla took a key from her pocket and unlocked the door of an unpretentious timber building, its boards weathered silver grey. Instead of the boat shed they were expecting, they found themselves in a hall with a small stage and proscenium arch at the far end. Folding chairs were stacked against the walls on each side.

Carla switched on the lights. "My great-great-grandfather had it built for Elisabeth-Lore. They used to have concerts here, afternoon tea dances, all sorts of things. Anyone from the village could use it. They still can." She went to the middle of the hall and sang a scale. "It's a good place to practice when it's not cold."

Leonora looked up at the timbered ceiling and sang a sustained high note. It came back to her, clear and true. "What's it like when the hall is full?"

"Not so much resonance but still good." Carla ran up the steps at the side of the stage and came downstage center, between deep blue curtains held back with tasseled cords that must once have been silver. "Come up and try it from here."

The others followed her onto the stage, where Tilo made straight for the piano, opened the lid and ran his fingers up and down the keys. "An upright grand. And it's in tune." Beaming, he sat down and began to play the introduction to the flower duet from Butterfly; on cue, Leonora and Carla joined in, while Walter went down into the hall to listen.

…mammole e tuberose, corolle di verbene, petali d'ogni fior
…violets, tuberoses, branches of verbena, petals of every flower

Looking up at them, Walter saw what the Maestro had known from the start. Leonora was born for this. His own future he could not see so clearly. Briefly the thought stung him. But it could be years before Leonora was ready to sing Butterfly in a major production. Time was on his side.

The duet came to an end and there was a burst of clapping from the doorway. Gräfin Elsa had come in while they were singing and now made her way down the hall to where Walter was standing. She was dressed for the country in a dark green Loden coat with a colorful woolen scarf tied under her chin.

She slipped her arm through Walter's and gestured to the stage, where the others had come forward to greet her.

"It's so exciting to have a concert here again." She gave Walter's arm a small squeeze. "Come up to the house when you've finished." Her eyes sparkled green as Carla's, gentler but full of fun. "Bärchen is dying to talk to you about the cakes."

It was to be a late afternoon *Kaffeekonzert*, like those popular in the nineteen twenties and thirties. Bärchen was in her element and had roped in her friends to join her in baking the cakes. Small tables had been borrowed from friends and neighbors, and were to be delivered during the day. Like a big family party at home, Leonora thought. She often felt she needed to pinch herself to make sure the world she found herself in, so different from her life in suburban Melbourne, was real. Finding these small similarities was reassuring. Generosity was to be found everywhere.

The morning's rehearsal completed, they gathered in the dining room for sandwiches and fruit, Bärchen having declared the kitchen off limits until all the baking was done.

Carla helped herself to a pear and cut it in quarters. "You know, Mutti, I think we should start on the stage then come down and do our solos wandering round the tables. It's a pity we didn't think of doing some cabaret."

Gräfin Elsa smiled at her daughter. "They'll love the opera pieces, Carlinchen. Everyone here knows that's where your career will be."

Carla nodded. "If only we had some of Elisabeth-Lore's dresses too."

Gräfin Elsa looked thoughtful. "Elisabeth-Lore would never have sung at a *Kaffeekonzert*. I don't suppose she ever went to one. They weren't so much the fashion then. But your grandmother... she adored dressing up and going out to a *Kaffeekonzert* or a tea dance. *Her* dresses will be perfect."

Carla and Leonora dressed for the concert in the tower room. Gräfin Elsa had been at pains to find matching evening bags and shoes big enough for modern feet, sizes larger than Carla's grandmother. For Leonora a pair of silver sandals with a low heel, for Carla satin pumps once bronze, faded now to the color of her dress. Cream-colored stockings and long satin gloves were laid out beside the dresses.

Carla held a stocking up to the light and tested the stretch of the lace band that would hold it in place, before laying it back on the bed and picking up the beaded satin evening bag. "There's something inside." Eagerly she opened the gilt clasp and pulled out a tiny bottle of *Arpège* and a lace handkerchief, a minute square of lawn with a wide border of hand-made lace. "Mutti thinks of everything." She picked up the bag laid out for Leonora. "See what Mutti has found for you."

Leonora was touched that so much care had been taken for her too. Her bag was made of silver mesh gathered into a frame etched with a pattern of flowers and leaves. A silvered cord with a small tassel at each end formed the handle. Carefully she pushed the tiny knobs on the frame apart, and looked inside. Her handkerchief was silk, its only ornament a small blue flower in one corner; her perfume, *Mitsouko*."

Carla held out her hand for the little bottle. "I wonder why Mutti picked this for you. She has perfect taste in these things. There's bound to be a story." She handed it back and Leonora put it away in her bag. It was an unwritten rule that no one wore perfume when they were performing. It had never bothered her but it gave some singers hay fever.

"We'll try it on you afterwards. Come on, let's get ready. We can warm up in the music room before we go down to the lake house."

They dressed quickly. Slipping the silver dress over her head, Leonora imagined the excitement of a bride being fitted for her trousseau: the calico *toile* made to measure before the fragile material was cut; the perfect stitching and the crystal beading; the first outing on a romantic evening. Standing next to Carla in front of the mirror, she thought of the grandmother whose dress she was now wearing and felt her happiness like an echo from long ago.

Carla and Leonora were not the only ones who had dressed up. Downstairs Gräfin Elsa appeared in a black cloche hat with a bunch of violets on the side, and a long black coat with a high fur collar. Graf August was dapper in a pin-stripe suit and broad-brimmed hat.

"Mutti, Vati, you're perfect." Carla leaped over the last two steps, comically out of character with her costume.

Gräfin Elsa smiled her satisfaction. "I think we may say the same about both of you."

Leonora opened her evening bag and took out the small perfume bottle, ready to say her thanks, but Carla was ahead of her.

"Mutti, why did you choose Mitsouko for Leonora? There must be a story. We're dying to know."

Gräfin Elsa smiled. "It had to be a perfume that was already in existence when the dresses were made, and there is a story. Like Butterfly, Mitsouko fell in love with a foreigner." She touched Leonora's cheek lightly as she often did with Carla. "Leonora will be a perfect Cio-cio San. I hope we can be there when the time comes. Now wrap up well, *Kinder*. It's time to go."

At the lake house, Walter and Tilo were already on the stage warming up, handsome in their borrowed white tie and tails. The café scene was complete with tablecloths and tea-lights in glass shades on every table.

Carla danced up the stairs. "Will we do?" Her eyes sparkled as she took Walter's arm. "What do you think of your gorgeous Butterfly now?" He laughed and gently shook her off. "I wouldn't have left her, that's for sure." He kissed Leonora lightly on the lips. "You look wonderful, Lou. You both do."

They stood together on the stage, heads close, like a team of players gathering energy before a game. All at once, Leonora was overwhelmed with a sense of impending loss. Only Tilo saw the shadow pass over her face and guessed its cause.

"Don't worry, Leonora. We'll keep meeting up again, you'll see. You won't find it so easy to get rid of us. Now, you'd better sing a few scales to put it out of your mind and loosen up. Come on, Carla, you too."

He went back to the piano and struck a chord for them to begin. Soon they were running up and down the scales trying to match each other. Leonora could sing higher than Carla but Carla could sing lower. Gradually they were closing the gap at their favored end of the range and it was only the color of their sound that told them apart.

"All right." Tilo stood up. "That's enough. I can see Bärchen wanting to let the people in. Toi toi toi."

"And *chookas*." Carla laughed. "I even remember what it means: a full house and there'll be chicken for dinner!" She laughed again. "But today you'll have to make do with cake!"

- 28 -

The concert had been an even greater success than they could have hoped. After the opera pieces, the three singers had wandered among the tables singing encores – even a few pop songs. The performance had left Leonora, Walter and Carla too full of energy to sleep. Only Tilo was sensible and went to bed.

They'd sat in the kitchen with an ecstatic Bärchen, then at Carla's insistence made their way to the tower room to drink champagne, stretching out the excitement of the day. Not knowing when they might all be together again, they were reluctant to bring it to a close. They had relived the concert, teasing each other about who had the most applause. And when they could no longer keep their eyes open, they had finally gone to bed, after promising they would find a way to meet again, wherever they were.

Now Walter and Leonora were on their way back to Munich. On the autobahn the roar of the passing cars had kept them from talking much. Leonora was feeling her usual after-a-concert let-down and was glad to sit back and doze. This companiable silence was one of the things Leonora loved about Walter. As they pulled up in front of Frau Felder's house, he reached for her hand.

"Lou, now I've finally got you to myself you're coming home with me tonight."

"But what about Frau Felder? She's expecting me back today. And I'm supposed to phone the Maestro."

"Just tell Frau Felder you'll be away overnight. You can ring the Maestro later from my place. Come on, Lou. He won't want to see you before tomorrow anyway."

Inside the house everything was quiet: Frau Felder was not at home. Instead there was a note for Leonora on the hall table. "Is anything wrong?" Walter put his arm round her as she read.

"No, Frau Felder's gone to her daughter's. She'll be back tomorrow afternoon."

"Then it's all sorted. You're coming with me."

A whole day to themselves. Leonora felt her spirits rise as she followed Walter out of the house.

Leonora reached for her watch. Walter had left her to sleep in. She sprang out of bed, threw on her jeans and a tee shirt, and hurried into the kitchen, where she found Walter sitting at the table drinking coffee.

"Wal, you should have woken me. You know I'm supposed to ring the Maestro."

He looked up with a mischievous smile that reminded her of Carla. "A few hours won't make any difference. We'll be gone soon enough anyway."

Sliding into the chair beside him, Leonora wasn't convinced. "That's just why I should be seeing him as much as I can. Don't you feel the same?"

"I don't know. Sometimes I think I've learned all I can from him. Honestly, Lou, I don't think he's that interested in me."

Leonora was shocked. "Wal, you're a *tenor, a tall good-looking tenor*. How could he *not* be interested in you?"

"You're biased. Have I told you how gorgeous you look when you've just woken up?" He leaned across and kissed her. "It's true, though, Lou. He's not as interested in me as he is in you. He thinks I don't take it seriously enough."

"But why? You got into Sankt Hubert, you work just as hard as I do."

Walter laughed. "Now I know you're biased. You know I don't." He refilled his coffee mug and took a long swallow. "The Maestro's pretty smart. I think he's worked out I'll most likely end up going home."

"Of course we'll go home. But we have to make it here before we do. Sankt Hubert is just the first step."

Was it her imagination or had Walter begun to talk about going home more often since they'd been accepted into the opera studio? A trickle of doubt ran through Leonora like a shiver.

"Don't look so worried, Lou. It will all work out, you'll see."

She nodded, wanting to believe him.

"Come on, I'll make you some toast. And then we're going back to bed." He hammed a wheedling expression and she started to laugh.

"Wal, we should never talk about singing at home. It always ends up with me wanting to go and practice and you wanting to go to bed."

"Well, let's combine the two. Madam Butterfly, anyone?"

"You're hopeless. Just make the toast and I'll let you know."

With Walter's eyes on her she knew she would end up staying longer than she intended.

It was late afternoon when Leonora got back to Frau Felder's. The lights were on and the familiar smell of baking was in the air. Leonora dropped her things on the hall table and picked up the phone. As she dialed the Maestro's number, she braced herself for a reproof that she hadn't rung sooner.

She was lucky. Frau Meyer answered the phone.

"Maestro Mazzone's not here, Leonora. Did you get his message?"

Leonora swallowed. She hadn't even checked.

"Frau Felder's been away and I've only just got home." Her cheeks felt hot with embarrassment, like a child caught out in a misdemeanor. "I knew I should have rung before."

"Don't worry. He said to tell you he's kept tomorrow morning free for you. Can you come at 8.30?"

Leonora gave a wry smile at the early start, perhaps the Maestro's way of making a point about her lateness. "Of course. I need to do something to get back into his good books."

Frau Meyer laughed. "You're always in his good books, Leonora. He's just testing your priorities. I'll let him know you'll be there."

Leonora hung up the phone and tapped on Frau Felder's door. She came to open it so quickly, she must have been waiting for Leonora's knock.

"There you are, Mädele. I'm sorry I wasn't here when you got back from Starnberg. Now come in and tell me all about it." She took Leonora's arm and drew her into the familiar room, where the table was already laid for the evening meal. Leonora was touched. How she was going to miss her.

The next morning Leonora left the house early. The train was full and she stood all the way to Odeonsplatz. Outside the early coolness caught her throat; hurriedly she pulled up the collar of her jacket. The last thing she wanted was to turn up in Sankt Hubert with a cold.

She jogged across the road, past the National Theater, where the banners were already advertising the winter season. How naïve she had been when she first came, imagining her name there.

At the Maestro's studio, Frau Meyer was already at work, neat as always in her grey suit. She looked up and smiled as Leonora greeted her. Another familiar face Leonora would miss.

In the studio the Maestro was seated at the piano, warming up his hands.

"*Buon Giorno*, Leonora. I have much to tell you today. But

first we shall work. Are you ready to sing?"

"Yes, Maestro."

"Then I shall put you through your paces." He gave her a searching look. "You must be ready to sing anything, no matter the time of day. Let us see if you are."

Without offering her a single scale to warm up, the Maestro began to play the introduction to *Come scoglio*, Fiordiligi's aria from *Così fan tutte*. He knew she'd been asked to sing it at her audition. It had been challenging enough then. With its octave-and-a-half leaps and fiendishly long phrases, it was even more of a test at 8.30 in the morning.

He was playing very fast. When she got to the triplets on *e una barbara speranza* that went on for six bars, she hardly had time to sing the notes, let alone keep the beat exactly the same, each triplet equal, each repeated note perfectly in pitch. The Maestro played on, only the slightest twitch of an eyebrow responding to the unevenness of her phrasing. By the end Leonora was ready to gasp for breath but she hadn't spent nearly a year working with the Maestro for nothing. He set the rules and his students had to follow.

He played the final two chords with a flourish and looked up at her. Even at this early hour he was immaculately dressed in a dark suit, white shirt and elegant silk tie. In professionalism he asked nothing he did not exemplify himself.

"That surprised you, I think."

"It was very fast, Maestro."

He smiled. "Indeed. But that is the fashion. To me it is against the natural flow of this glorious music. But you must be prepared for it, practice for it. I do not need to tell you that your triplets were uneven. Work on them. Sing them in your practice until you can control everything, whatever the tempo. In a moment we will go through the aria again. But first I have something to tell you."

He got up from the piano, went across to the table and poured them each a glass of water. "A reminder to keep well-hydrated. The voice needs that."

Leonora sipped her water and waited for the Maestro to continue. He seemed in no hurry.

At last he put down his glass and went back to the piano. His hands resting lightly on the keys, he looked across at her.

"And now to the news. Frau Benedict is to be head of a new young artists program in Vienna. She would like you to audition. You will have to satisfy an audition panel in the usual way. Frau Benedict will not be involved; there can be no preferential treatment. If you are successful, you would join her program when your contract in Sankt Hubert is at an end." His voice softened. "What an opportunity that would be: working with Frau Benedict on repertoire, performing in Vienna." He paused, as if gazing at the city in his mind's eye. "Now tell me what you think."

Leonora's head was whirling. She could hardly think at all. She was aware of the Maestro smiling at her, waiting for an answer, as she struggled for words.

"Will you be there, Maestro?"

He laughed. "I see you are ahead of me. I will be joining Frau Benedict in Vienna a few days every month. We can arrange to have lessons there while you are in Sankt Hubert." He nodded. "So, we are agreed. Now, *La Bohème*. Act Four, the final duet with Rodolfo. From memory."

The news had disturbed Leonora's concentration and the Maestro had to correct her more than once. But she soon settled into her stride and by the end of her lesson he seemed pleased.

He stood up and closed the lid of the piano. "*Bene*, Leonora. *Molto bene*." He came forward to where she was standing in the bow of the grand piano.

"It will be an important time for you in Sankt Hubert. Another step on your way to becoming – one day – a true *prima donna*."

He smiled. "We Italians know what that means. Not someone who has foolish tantrums, but a first lady of the lyric theatre." He held out his hand. "I know you have it in you, Leonora."

They shook hands, and Leonora stood there for a moment, hesitating. Suddenly Sankt Hubert seemed so far away. How would she manage on her own?

As if he understood, the Maestro was reassuring. "We shall see each other again soon. Frau Meyer has a copy of my schedule for you." He smiled. "Your times are marked. I shall expect you."

Leonora nodded, not trusting herself to speak. The clatter of her footsteps on the wooden floor as she left seemed an echo of her first day in the studio, when the walk across the room seemed endless.

At the door she turned back. "Thank you, Maestro. Thank you for everything."

- 29 -

Sankt Hubert, September 1991

Dropping the suitcases he was carrying, Walter swept Leonora off her feet and swung her round. They'd arrived in Sankt Hubert late in the afternoon after a long drive from Munich. She'd got her wish. The apartment she'd fallen in love with at her audition had been empty and they could afford the rent. Now all they had to do was move in and unpack. She looked up at the ceiling with its intricate plaster molding. "I love these old rooms. And the address, Wal. Richard Wagner Strasse. How perfect is that?"

"You know me, Lou. All I need is somewhere to eat and somewhere to sleep, close enough to the studio to let me get up late." He held her gaze. "And you."

Leonora looked into his eyes and saw herself, a tiny reflection in their center. Reluctantly she pushed him away. "Come on, Wal, there's work to do. I want to unpack and get my music ready tonight. Then we should eat some of that food Frau Felder gave us."

Walter grinned. "Dumplings. And goulash. I think she wants to keep us fed until Christmas."

"Christmas in Austria." Leonora's face lit up. "Our second together. We'll be able to have our own celebration, a tree, everything." She let her gaze wander round the room. "Look, Wal. We can put the tree in the window. It's perfect. Do you think that's why so many houses have a bay window overlooking the street? So that people can see each other's trees at Christmas?"

Putting his arms round her Walter shook his head, smiling. "Now how would I know that?"

Then he was looking at her in the way that made her heart

turn over and all thought of unpacking was put aside.

There was no-one around the stage door of the opera house when they arrived the next morning, only rows of bicycles.

The glass window of the stage door office was open. An elderly man in the local costume of grey flannel jacket trimmed with green got up from his chair and handed them a clipboard.

"*Opernstudio?*"

Walter scanned the list and pointed out their names. "Leonora Ford and Walter Saville."

The old man's face crinkled into a smile. "Welcome to the opera house. You must sign in every time you enter or leave so that we always know who is here." He nodded cheerfully. "Security and fire regulations. Today you are meeting Frau Fischer in the front foyer."

Frau Fischer? Could it really be Fisch?

They hurried back the way they had come. People were already gathered in the foyer. Leonora relaxed. There was no sign of Birgit. And it really was Fisch, in her regulation overalls with a Che Guevara cap on her head. She bustled over to greet them, a huge smile on her face.

"*Surprise!* For me too. I only found out last week I'd got the job here as head of production staff." She checked her watch, the gesture they knew so well from Hildeberg. "The Herr Direktor will be here in a few minutes to welcome you."

On the dot of ten, Günter Meinhardt came into the foyer. He kept his welcome brief, a man who wasted no time on unnecessary words. After wishing them good luck, he handed over to Fisch, who began to distribute a pile of spiral-bound booklets.

"Welcome, everyone. I am Barbara Fischer, the studio production manager, better known as Fisch." She paused, letting her glance rest briefly on each singer. "Please take your booklet home and read it carefully. It contains everything you need to know about the opera studio. I know you are all aware that this is a wonderful opportunity for you." There was a low murmur of assent as Fisch held up her copy of the booklet.

"I have just two words to add. *Preparation and punctuality.*" The p-sound popped from her lips with relish, like a child discovering it for the first time. "Please check your schedules and come ready to start work, *on time.*"

Leonora caught a sideways glance from Walter and pressed her lips together to suppress a grin. They'd both had the same thought: *Disziplin und Professionalismus.* Fisch loved a slogan.

"As you know," Fisch continued, "we will be working on The *Marriage of Figaro* in the studio. Some of you will be covering roles in *La Bohème* in the opera house. You may be called to stand in at any time. *Be ready.* And always ring in if for a very good reason you can't be at rehearsal. Believe me, there is a waiting list for your places."

No-one moved but the atmosphere in the room was intense, as if they had all stood to attention.

Fisch nodded and slipped her copy of the booklet into a folder. "Now, please introduce yourselves before we take a quick tour of the theatre. After that, you're free for practice and study to prepare for tomorrow."

Obediently everyone shook hands, trying to remember each other's names, before following Fisch up the marble staircase. At the top she turned.

"By the way, another piece of advice: there's a very good cake shop behind the opera house. You won't be popular if wardrobe has to alter your costumes because you've eaten too much Sachertorte. Believe me, it happens." She laughed. "That's enough lecture for the day. Come and see where you will be performing."

It was the first time Leonora and Walter had seen the

auditorium in full light. The wine-red seating and the gold-fringed drapes on the stage curtain reflected the late nineteenth-century love of plush and velvet. Balconies and boxes curved in a half-circle around a central dome; crystal chandeliers added brilliance to the effect of warmth and opulence.

"I can't wait to sing in here." It was a light voice, a soprano. Whoever it was had spoken for them all.

Fisch nodded. "Work hard and I'm sure you will. Don't forget to sign out at the stage door before you leave."

As they went out through the main doors and round the back of the theatre, people were already flipping through the booklet to check the cast lists. Leonora thought she'd wait until they were on their own but Walter had already found the page.

He frowned and pulled a face. Puzzled, Leonora looked over his shoulder. "What is it?"

"*Figaro.* They've got me down for Basilio and Don Curzio, the music teacher and the judge: character roles, *bit parts*. I thought I'd at least get the understudy of Rodolfo in *Bohème*." His cheeks were burning. "If I'm typecast as a comic tenor in an opera studio what hope have I got in an opera house?"

Leonora was shocked. If they'd done this to Walter, what was in store for her?

She read through the list twice to be sure. They'd given her the Countess in *Figaro* and Mimi in the *Bohème* second cast in the main theatre. That meant she was Mimi's understudy and would get the chance to sing the role at a matinée, as well as going on if the main Mimi was ill. Two major roles that fitted perfectly with the Maestro's plans for her. Walter had been overlooked while she'd been given everything she'd hoped for. She felt terrible.

She took his hand. She wanted to say that plenty of up-and-coming tenors got their start with the character parts in *Figaro* and went on to starring roles but that would be cold comfort. Then an idea came to her. "Why don't you work on Rodolfo with me anyway, Wal? We can practice together. Then you'll be ready if you get the chance."

He shrugged. "Don't you think they'd have offered me the understudy already if they wanted me?"

Later that day, their unpacking finished, Leonora was sitting in the window seat immersed in *La Bohème* when Walter burst into the room.

"Have you read the production notes for *Figaro*?"

Leonora looked up. "Not yet. Why?"

He flung himself down beside her. "They've only set it on a *cruise ship*. Basilio is supposed to be a DJ. Can you believe it?"

He tossed his booklet onto the table, misjudging the distance and sending it skidding across the floor. "We'll hardly see each other in rehearsal. The only time we'll be on stage together is right at the end." His face was white with anger. "So much for everyone loves a tenor. I might as well not be in it."

Leonora had never seen him so upset about what he sang.

"I know it seems like a mad idea but it could be hilarious, everyone running between decks and in and out of cabins. We weren't on stage together in Hildeberg either and we made it work."

Walter shook his head. "I came here for you, Lou. I've done everything you want. But this..." Seeing her stricken face, he broke off and stood up. "I need some air."

At the door he turned. "It's not your fault, Lou. I'll see you later."

Leonora looked down at the score of *Bohème* still open on her knee. The notes blurred though her tears and her hands shook. This wasn't how it was supposed to be.

- 30 -

Leonora was in turmoil. Everything Walter had said was true. He'd never have come to Sankt Hubert on his own. He had every right to be upset about his casting. He'd trained with the Maestro as a lyric tenor: Rodolfo in *La Bohème*, Don José in *Carmen*, Pinkerton in *Butterfly*. In the comic parts in *Figaro* he'd be expected to sing in character, distorting the natural beauty of his voice.

When Walter came back from his run she was still in the window seat where he'd left her. Normally so full of light, her face was clouded.

He sat down beside her.

"I shouldn't have taken it out on you, Lou."

She shook her head, her eyes bright with indignation. "No. You're right. It isn't fair. I'd be the same."

Her face was cool against his cheek. Breathing in the scent of her skin, it touched him that she took his side. Somehow he'd make the best of it.

The *Figaro* set was a so-called black box without scenery. Its three black canvas walls could fit neatly in front of the *Bohème* set and pack flat to go on tour. Furniture and props were carried on and off by the cast. Running around the stage trying not to bump into each other turned into an intricate choreography. Like falling dominos, it only took one person to make a wrong turn for the whole process to collapse. The cast's biggest problem was trying not to laugh. Fred, the director, a wiry American working on his first opera, was just as likely to join in.

At the first production rehearsal, perched bird-like on a bar stool, Fred brimmed with nervous energy, as if he might at any moment grow wings and leap into the air.

"I expect you know this opera is based on a play by Beaumarchais. But did you know the full title was *La Folle Journée ou Le Mariage de Figaro*? A day of madness – I've been thinking about that a lot. You can take it in so many ways."

Bouncing off his stool, he looked into the expectant faces in front of him.

"It is a mad day with all the characters running around trying to outwit each other. It's really funny. But there's a darker kind of madness going on as well." He paused and shook his head. "*Le droit du seigneur* – the right of the lord of the manor to the first night with a servant's bride. Unthinkable, repugnant to us today, an obscene misuse of power. But Beaumarchais was smart enough to know people weren't interested in moralizing or a lecture. Instead, he held up a mirror to society by making his audience laugh."

He folded his arms, resting his gaze briefly on each of them, pressing home his point.

"We *should* laugh at all the goings on, so familiar to Beaumarchais' audience. But we need to bring out the contrast of the darker side too. Figaro's antics to prevent his master the Count from claiming his "right" may be amusing but there's desperation behind it. And the Countess – she knows exactly what is going on." He turned to where Leonora was standing with Walter. "What intrigues me, is how she forgives her husband at the end. Is that really possible? Or do we have the eighteenth century version of a Hollywood executive demanding a happy ending to the movie?" He nodded at Leonora. "We'll work it out. But we can't take ourselves too seriously or we'll end up with a tragedy. The audience has to have fun. I hope you will too."

Leonora glanced up at Walter. Fred was holding his attention; it was a good start.

By the second week of rehearsal they had established a routine, going in and coming home together, sometimes going for a meal afterwards with Fred and the cast.

Fred was giving Walter plenty of scope to build his character as the music teacher Basilio. And as the lawyer Don Curzio he was in one of the funniest scenes of the opera, when the character of Marcellina, an older woman trying to trap Figaro into marriage, turns out to be his mother.

Fred was in stitches the first time they ran through the scene. "Brilliant, everyone. All I need now is for you to stop giggling. Let the audience do the laughing. *You* are supposed to be serious."

Walter gave a cheeky grin. "Should that apply to the director too?"

When the break was called he went straight to Leonora. "You were right, Lou. I didn't realize Mozart could be so funny. Now I just need to work out how to keep a straight face."

The rehearsal room was filling up as the *Bohème* Chorus drifted in. Leonora took her place in the group of chairs reserved for the understudies. She had come in this morning to observe Act One, only to find that the director had decided not to work on Mimi's first scene with Rodolfo. And he didn't seem to have made up his mind yet when he would.

Leonora gripped the edges of her score. This was some of the most famous music ever written: even people who didn't go to the opera knew *Your tiny hand is frozen* and *They call me Mimi*. What was the use of a rehearsal plan if the director didn't stick to it? And how was she supposed to find out when he did want to rehearse the scene?

Bohème was turning out to be the complete opposite of *Figaro*. No one seemed to be responsible for telling the understudies anything. They were expected to sit in on rehearsals, watch the main cast and make their own notes. Getting time with one of the busy pianists to go through their music felt like trying to win a lottery.

When Leonora asked the stage manager about an understudy rehearsal, she'd been told in no uncertain terms that any extra time – supposing there was any – would be used for more important things. She would have a walk through on stage in the morning of her matinée and that would be it.

As she sat debating whether to stay on the off chance the director might change his mind and rehearse the scene after all, the stage manager's voice broke into her thoughts.

"Ladies and gentlemen, this morning's rehearsal has been changed to a Chorus music call. Everyone else is released."

Trying to leave her frustration behind her, Leonora was heading for the door when a familiar color caught her eye.

Purple... Surely not... But there she was, lips drawn back in an ingratiating smile.

Birgit.

If Leonora had needed anything else to make this a morning to forget, seeing Birgit was it.

- 31 -

The days were getting shorter; by the afternoon the light indoors was subdued. Not bothering to take off her coat, Leonora switched on the lamp above the table and sat down, resting her elbows in the pool of light, chin on her hands. She looked up at the velvet shade suspended above her. She'd wanted to come back to Sankt Hubert and she'd got her wish. But she hadn't expected to find herself caught between two stools: the elation of performing the Countess and the confusion of where she fitted in as the understudy to Mimi. She hadn't been able to speak to Fisch and was still none the wiser. And now there would be Birgit to watch out for.

But there was some good news. The opera studio had lent her a small upright piano. In return Leonora would play for coaching sessions when they were a pianist short and pay for tuning herself.

The piano had arrived the day before. It had taken four men to maneuver it up the stairs into the apartment; it felt like Christmas morning when it was finally in place. Its walnut veneer glowed; if you looked closely, the patterns in the panel above the music rack formed a kindly face, eyes shut, listening. It was an old instrument; she liked to think of all the hands that had played it.

With a decisive gesture she got up and took off her coat. Crossing to the piano she sat down and began to play the slow first movement of the Moonlight Sonata – *Adagio sostenuto*.

Beethoven had called it *Sonata quasi una fantasia*; it was the poet Ludwig Rellstab who said it made him think of moonlight on Lake Lucerne. Losing herself in the music, Leonora let her imagination take her home: the moon dappling the pale bark of ghost gums and etching their blossom with silver; the deep gold of an autumn moon rising behind roof tops, impossibly round and close.

As the sound of the last notes died away, she let her hands rest on the keys, perfectly still and composed, as if the music flowing through her had washed all her frustration away.

"Wake up, Wal." Leonora shook him gently, then again, harder. Eyes closed, Walter lifted his head from the pillow and let it fall back again.

"Come *on*, Wal. I need to talk to you *now*."

He half-opened his eyes, widening them as he took in the sight of Leonora dressed and wearing her coat, a paper bag clutched in her hand.

"What's happened?" He looked from Leonora's face to the bag then back again, his expression a picture of bewilderment.

"I've just spoken to Fisch."

Walter sat up and ran his fingers through his hair.

"What, this early? On Saturday?"

"It's not that early, Wal. When I woke up you were still asleep so I thought I'd go to the bakery and get something for breakfast." Moving the paper bag to her other hand, Leonora began to unbutton her coat. "There was a message on the board downstairs to ring Fisch any time after 8 this morning. So I did."

She shook her head in disbelief.

"There's been a change of cast in *Bohème*. There's a new Mimi arriving on Monday. Fisch wanted to make sure I heard before anyone else." Leonora shrugged. "I won't be doing the matinée. It's been moved to the evening, with the new singer."

Walter's face flushed. "You mean they've taken away your performance?"

"Not just that, the understudy too." Her voice shook. "Fisch said there were so many problems coordinating the *Figaro* and *Bohème* schedules that no one can be in both."

"What?" Walter reached for the clothes he'd left lying on the floor. "I don't get it. They gave you the part, you've done nothing wrong, but now they've changed their minds? Can they do that?"

Leonora pressed her lips together to stop them trembling. "All our performances come under our training with the opera studio. They can change as much as they like."

She looked down at the paper bag in her hand, as if surprised to see it there. Dropping it on the bed, she slipped out of her coat and sat down.

"Fisch told me in confidence that there won't be another understudy. They'll cancel or bring in an outside replacement if the new singer can't perform."

"Ilse Berg all over again." Walter rolled his eyes. "Except she wasn't a soprano. Did Fisch say who the new Mimi is?"

Leonora shook her head. "Only that she'll announce it at the next *Bohème* rehearsal."

Walter reached up and stroked her hair. He wanted to comfort her but privately he thought it was better this way. The studio had given her too much to do. Now they had fixed it.

He took the bag from her and opened it, releasing a waft of sugar and cinnamon. "Doughnuts?" He pursed his lips, trying to sound like Fisch. "What did I say about not eating too much cake?"

He'd meant to make her smile but Leonora's eyes brimmed with tears. "I thought you at least would understand after missing out on Rodolfo." Her voice broke on a sob. "And whatever Fisch says, everyone will think I've been sacked. Birgit will see to that."

"No they won't. Because no one will believe her. And I do understand." He pulled a face. "I thought if I could make you laugh it would cheer you up."

Her woebegone expression cut him to the heart.

"Let's go out, Lou. Let's take the day off and drive up to the hills. We're both free and you need a break."

Leonora gave him a bleak look but she didn't say no.

They walked the hiking trail to the hilltop lookout at the highest point. On cue the clouds had rolled away to reveal the Alps beyond, precision cut and gleaming against a postcard blue sky.

Leonora had only seen mountains like these in photographs, so sparkling and radiant they must surely have been touched up. Yet there they were in all their glory, taking her breath away. It put her troubles in perspective.

Walter saw the color come back into her cheeks.

The velvet lampshade was casting its light over the remains of their simple dinner, cold meats, rye bread and a bottle of wine they had bought on their way home. Walter leaned across the table and refilled Leonora's glass.

"Lou, I've been thinking. Now that you're not doing *Bohème* there won't be anything to keep us here between Christmas and New Year. We could easily stretch it to ten days, two weeks even." He paused, as if she might already have guessed what was on his mind. "Come with me to Sydney, Lou."

Leonora didn't know what to say. By next July she might have saved enough to go home for a month in the annual theatre break; any sooner was impossible. Then there was her Vienna audition to prepare for. Putting off the Maestro was unthinkable.

Her heart sank. With her release from *Bohème* a burden had lifted only to be replaced by another: going with Walter or staying for the Maestro. That's how Walter would see it. Unless she could make him understand it wasn't about either of them. She wanted to go home with him when they had more time, not in a rush like this. And when she could afford it. He'd probably offer to pay for her or lend her the money but she didn't want that. It wouldn't feel right.

Looking into his glowing face it pained her to disappoint him.

"I only heard about *Bohème* this morning, Wal. I haven't had time to get used to it." She got up from the table and began to clear the dishes. "I can't answer you now. But I promise to think about it."

- 32 -

Figaro opening night. Leonora stood in front of the long mirror in her dressing room, checking her costume. In her shift dress, white knee high boots and blonde bouffant wig she was Dusty Springfield to the life, exactly the look the designer wanted. What would the audience make of it?

She leaned forward and peered at her false eyelashes; the designer had insisted on a full set, top and bottom. Satisfied that they wouldn't come unstuck and that the heavy black eyeliner was dry and wouldn't smudge, Leonora went back to her dressing table and put on the long string of plastic beads the wardrobe department had found in a junk shop. Plastic seemed unlikely for a countess but sixties fashion had thrown out the image of twinsets and pearls. She loved her costume.

Over the loudspeaker in her room, the first act was coming to an end. After the interval she would appear for the first time. Alone on stage she would sing the beautiful and poignant aria *Porgi Amor*, pleading with the god of Love to bring her husband back to her. It was a beloved role for many great sopranos and the standard Leonora would be measured against was daunting.

Leonora had tried to understand the Countess. If she had lived in the freedom of today, would she have been so forbearing to her straying husband, however much she loved him? Leonora wasn't sure. She'd even asked herself what she would do if she found out Walter was seeing someone else, and come to no conclusion; she couldn't imagine ever needing to answer that. She had decided to accept the Countess as she found her in the music: playful, loving and in the end forgiving; and tried to make her real. Tonight she would find out if she had.

The 15 minute call came over the loudspeaker. Her dresser would arrive any moment to accompany her down to the stage. With this costume she really didn't need any help but who knew how long it would be before she would be entitled to a personal dresser again. She would enjoy every moment.

Two days after Figaro opening night, Leonora was alone in the apartment preparing for her second performance; Walter had gone out to get a paper to see if there was a review. Hearing a knock on the door Leonora thought he must have forgotten to take his key. Instead it was their downstairs neighbor, Herr Martin, out of breath from dashing up the stairs.

"Frau Ford, there's a phone call for you. It's Maestro Mazzone."

Before Leonora could speak he had turned and was hurrying back down again. She ran down behind him murmuring her thanks, thinking it was almost like a scene from the opera where the cast was forever running up and down between the upper and lower decks of the set.

"Maestro, it's Leonora – I'm sorry you had to wait."

"*Buon giorno*, Leonora. It is not a problem. If my students will spread themselves so far away, what can I do? Perhaps we should acquire one of those portable phones I see people carrying around. But what use are they if not everyone has one?"

Leonora could hear the smile in his voice; whatever he had heard about *Figaro* must have been all right.

"That is not why I am calling you. I have had a very good report of your performance from one of the Vienna music critics. It will not be reviewed in his paper but he has told me that I can be very satisfied. *Brava*, Leonora."

"And the production? Did he like it?"

"Ah, the *production*." The smile was still in his voice. "In fact he found it amusing. He is always happy to consider something new, though you should not be surprised if others do not agree. But it is your audition for Vienna that I wish to discuss. If you will arrange to come to Munich for a few days in January, we shall make a very good start."

He paused, waiting for Leonora's answer.

Her throat felt dry; she had to make her decision now.

"Yes, Maestro. Thank you."

There was nothing else she could have said.

"*Bene*. January then, after New Year. Frau Meyer will arrange it."

Leonora walked slowly back upstairs; now the decision was made it seemed so obvious. Walter could go home while she was working with the Maestro. They could go to Australia together in July or August in the break between theatre seasons. It would be simpler that way.

With a mingled sense of relief and excitement Leonora went back into the apartment. She would ring Frau Felder later to tell her she was coming back for a visit and ask if she could stay. It would be carnival time again in Munich, *Fasching*. The city would be one big party, people out on the street in their costumes, lights sparkling against the snow.

It would be like coming home – not her real home, nothing would replace that – but her musical home, where she would always return to study and reflect, and one day, if she deserved it, see her name on the banners in front of the opera house.

When Walter came in with the newspaper Leonora was already immersed in the score of *Così fan tutte*. She'd done well with *Come scoglio* in her audition for Sankt Hubert. It would be good for Vienna too. She looked up smiling as Walter came over.

He tossed the paper onto the table and bent down to kiss her cheek.

"Page six. It's a dud review of the production but you get a good mention and the photos are good." He opened the paper to the page and handed it to her. "I don't know if you'll still be smiling after you've read this."

Leonora took the paper and began to read aloud. '*When the Countess was revealed on stage in her 1960s dolly bird dress I was almost expecting a rendition of Send in the Clowns.*'

She looked up at Walter. "I wonder if this man has ever seen *A Little Night Music*. If he means to be sarcastic he's got it wrong. *Figaro* and *Night Music* have a lot in common, aristocrats running around, mixed up love affairs. I bet Mozart would have loved it." She put the paper down. "I can't be bothered with the rest of it. I don't want to be thinking about it tonight. You know what second performances can be like."

Walter shrugged. "Maybe it's best not to read the crits at all."

Leonora wasn't sure.

"It depends who it is. If it's someone whose opinion you respect, maybe it's useful. But in the end that's all it is, someone's personal taste. It's what people like the Maestro think that matters."

She took a deep breath. There was never going to be a good moment for what she needed to say next.

"Wal… about Sydney…"

She stopped, taken aback by the sudden flash of anger in his eyes.

"You're not coming with me, are you." It wasn't a question.

"The Maestro phoned while you were out. He wants me to go to Munich in January to work on repertoire for an audition in Vienna. He…"

"What is it with you and him?" Interrupting her, Walter's voice was bitter. "Why do you let him run your life, Lou? What difference does it make anyway where you are? You could prepare just as well in Sydney."

"I *can't*, Wal. I *need* to work with him." She was near tears. "We can go home together in the summer break when there's more time. And you can audition in Vienna too. The Maestro…"

Glaring at her, Walter took a step back.

"I thought when we came to Sankt Hubert you'd get yourself out from under his thumb. Well, I've had enough. It's him or me. Make your choice."

Turning on his heel, he stormed out of the apartment leaving Leonora numb with shock. He hadn't even taken off his coat.

All day Leonora waited at home, hoping Walter would come back. She made herself eat a sandwich, worked through her breathing exercises, warmed up her voice. The time dragged on. She made her way to the theatre without him.

Alone in her dressing room, she went through her routine. She felt like a shell, burned out and empty.

She wouldn't see Walter until the curtain call and then her solo bows would give him the perfect opportunity to leave the stage and avoid her. If he didn't wait for her afterwards she didn't know what she would do.

By the time Leonora was ready to go on stage she had seen no one except her dresser. She thought back to Hildeberg when Kim Ah and Tilo had always been at hand to help her. She had taken it all for granted.

Technique and concentration would see her through her performance but wouldn't cancel the raw emotion that made her throat ache.

Head bowed she took her place on the darkened stage, letting the sound of the orchestra draw her in as the curtain rose and she began to sing *Porgi Amor*.

Lifting her head she almost stopped singing. Above her in the box closest to the stage was Birgit, leaning forward on her elbows, mouthing the words of the aria at her:

O mi rendi il mio tesoro – Oh return my beloved to me...

The last thing Leonora could have imagined was to look up and see Birgit. That would have been shock enough. But what was she doing, so obviously mirroring every word?

It was Hildeberg all over again: still seeing Leonora as an interloper taking the roles she'd wanted for herself, and trying to make her stumble.

Silently thanking Mozart for the bar-and-a-half rest before her next line, Leonora turned her head away until there was no more than a purple blur at the corner of her eye.

Birgit was the least of her worries.

The curtain calls went on longer than usual. While the principal singers took their last bows in front of the curtain, the stage crew were already packing up behind it. When Leonora could finally leave the stage, there was no sign of Walter.

It was a weeknight and few people had come backstage. In her dressing room Leonora was alone again. With a lump in her throat she packed up and was just about to leave when she heard a knock. Thinking it was one of the assistant stage managers, she picked up her bag and went to open the door.

It was Walter, drawn and tired, the light shining behind him making a halo of his hair and casting his face in shadow.

"Lou, I'm sorry…" His voice trailed off.

In an instant Leonora was in his arms.

The words tumbled out as they both spoke at once.

"I'll stay, I won't go, I don't have to go…"

Relief swept through her.

"Take me home, Wal, we can talk later. Let's just go home."

- 33 -

Sankt Hubert, December 1991

The air was thick with snow as Leonora and Walter made their way towards the station. The third day of Christmas marked the end of the public holiday and people were on the move again. Leonora clung to Walter's arm; in a few minutes he would be on the train to Vienna to connect with his flight to Sydney.

Inside the station *Glühwein* spices mingled with the scent of fresh-baked bread and wafts of *bratwurst*. Leonora could never smell the peppery-sweet aroma of the wine without remembering the Christmas market in Munich when she had slipped and fallen into Walter's arms. Now they'd had their second Christmas together.

The wintry European weather was a far cry from the warmth and light of Australia but they had made their celebration as much like home as they could. They had decorated a small tree with colored lights and given it pride of place in the apartment window overlooking the street.

On Christmas Eve they had walked through the snowy streets under a clear frosty sky, faint stars like fireflies coming and going against the darkness, the crunch of the snow under their feet the only sound.

Back in the apartment they had switched on the lights on the tree and opened a bottle of wine. Curled up on the couch together they had listened to the tapes Walter had brought in from the car before falling into bed and each other's arms.

On Christmas Day they had made bacon sandwiches and opened their parcels from home – practical gifts: warm scarves, jars of salty vegemite spread, biscuits and chocolate. Leonora had saved up to buy Walter a watch and he had surprised her with a leather-bound score of Madam Butterfly, the initials LF printed in gold on the spine.

Later they had gone to a small Gasthaus for a traditional local meal of goose and spicy red cabbage – the nearest thing to the roast turkey they would have had at home, however hot the day. They hadn't been the only ones. Sitting at the long communal table was a group of players from the opera orchestra who had stayed in Sankt Hubert to play in a performance of Bach's *Christmas Oratorio*. Over glasses of beer and wine it had soon turned into a party, reminding Leonora so much of Christmas at home that she'd begun to wish she was going with Walter after all.

And now he was about to leave, it was harder than she'd ever imagined to let him go.

Ahead of them the huge timetable rolled round. Leonora looked up, willing Walter's train to be delayed. Implacably the numbers rolled again; his train was on time.

He turned to Leonora and put his arms around her, holding her close.

"It's all right if you don't want to come onto the platform, Lou."

She sensed the tension in his body, the traveler's impatience to be gone now that the journey was to start; like waiting in the wings before you made your entrance, keyed up for the first step on stage.

"No, I'll come." She linked her arm in his and hung onto him, as if to print the warmth of him into her memory.

"Come in with me, Lou. There's still 10 minutes."

Leonora followed him into a carriage marked *Wien* and waited while he looked for a seat and propped his suitcase on it to claim it.

"*Fünf Minuten, meine Damen und Herren.*"

"Five minutes. I have to go, Wal."

They held each other close as long as they dared – the train would leave without further warning – and then Leonora was back on the platform looking up at Walter at the open window. Impulsively as the train started to move he snatched off his scarf and tossed it to her.

"Keep warm, Lou. Don't worry, I'll be back before you know it."

Holding the scarf against her cheek Leonora stood and watched until the train had snaked its way out of sight. Slowly she retraced her steps, letting the stream of people carry her along.

Outside the station the snow had all but stopped, a few stray snowflakes here and there drifting like minuscule feathers. Tomorrow she would be back to catch the train to Munich, Frau Felder and the Maestro.

Tucking the scarf into her pocket, Leonora stepped out into the frosty air.

- 34 -

Munich, New Year's Eve 1991

Silvester Abend, St Silvester's Eve, the last day of the old year. On walls and pathways snow had banked up; icicles hung like ghostly fingers from roofs and letterboxes. Minus five, minus eight overnight and not much more during the day. Leaving the house was a shock, the icy air stinging eyes and lungs. Leonora kept Walter's scarf tucked round her throat and longed for his warmth.

Looking out into the frozen garden, she half wished she'd given in and gone with him. But he would be with his family at their beach house, friends coming and going, no one she knew. It was better to wait.

She loosened the scarf and held it to her lips; there was no phone at the beach house, he'd call her when he could. It wouldn't be tonight.

Sighing she turned back into the room, sat down at the table and smoothed open a blue air letter to write to her mother. Later she would go down and drink a glass of *Sekt* with Frau Felder. Perhaps Carla would call from New York or Kim Ah from Paris.

But it was Walter she longed for.

Two days into the New Year the extreme cold had passed. Leonora made her way into the city under a sky the blue of a renaissance painting. Light glinted on frost and snow, revelers in fancy dress from the night before mingled with the crowds hurrying to work.

It seemed no time at all since she had last run up the stairs to the Maestro's studio. In the waiting room Frau Meyer's typewriter was under its green canvas cover and the files on her desk were tidied away. The office was still closed for the holiday. Slipping out of her boots into her indoor shoes, the same *Hausschuhe* she had worn for her rehearsal with Carla at Frau Benedict's, Leonora smiled at the memory. Everyone changed their shoes in this weather. People even carried their evening shoes in a bag to the opera and left their boots at the cloakroom. She hadn't known that then.

With a smile full of good humor, the Maestro stood up from the piano and came towards her. Eyes twinkling he gave a small bow as he shook her hand.

"*Contessa, buon anno!*"

"*Buon anno, Maestro!*"

Happy as a child home for the holidays, Leonora put her music case on the table. Behind her the swish of the studio door made her turn.

"Tilo!"

The Maestro chuckled. "He has come from Salzburg for a few weeks. A welcome surprise for you, I think."

Leonora nodded. Without Walter and her friends Munich was lonely.

"*Ciao* Tilo." She gave him an appraising look. "I'm trying to work out what's different about you." She laughed. "You're not wearing black."

"*Ciao* Leonora." His expression was warm, less shy. "The Maestro's been telling me about the Sankt Hubert *Figaro*. I have so many questions."

"But first we work." The Maestro clapped his hands. "To the pianoforte, if you please. Let us start with some of the beautiful Vaccai *vocalise*. And then we shall work through Leonora's audition pieces. I shall observe."

Before Leonora could hand him her music, Tilo began to play.

It was one of her favorites, an exercise to practice the long grace note, the *appoggiatura.*

Senza l'amabile dio di Citera, i di non tornano di primavera…

Without the gentle god of love, the days of spring would not return…

The words reminded her of Walter. Surely she would hear from him soon.

"Mädele, Herr Saville am Telefon!"

Leonora sped down the stairs, anxious not to lose a minute.

"Wal, it's Lou. Can you hear me?" Her words repeated in a strange echo as if she had said them twice.

"Just. It's a bit noisy here. I've had to come to the pub to phone." The echo was at his end too.

Leonora was puzzled. "Are you still at the beach?"

"Yes. My father wants to keep the family…" A crash in the background cut him off. He tried again. "He wants to keep the family together a bit longer…" A burst of laughter drowned him out. "…wants me to stay…couple of weeks."

Between the echo and the noise Leonora could barely make out the words. Had Walter said he wasn't coming back yet? Her stomach lurched.

"Wal?"

Another gust of laughter. Someone was telling jokes at the bar.

"Wal, just tell me when you're coming back."

"Sorry, Lou. I can hardly hear you. I'll call you when I get back to Sydney…" Then his words were lost in the clamor. All she heard was "Keep warm, Lou". And the click as the call ended.

Try as she might, Leonora could think of little else but Walter's call. Was he staying two more weeks at the beach and then going to Sydney or coming back to Sankt Hubert in two weeks? She was desperate to talk to him again.

In her lessons she could escape for an hour or two. With Tilo at the piano the Maestro took her through her repertoire, walking around, listening, giving instructions: "Now *Come scoglio!*" or "Let me hear *Adriana!*" There was no time to think of anything else.

Away from the studio the questions came back to plague her. Even rehearsing with Tilo didn't shut them out. Twice this morning already he'd had to correct her at the same spot.

"It's a dotted quaver there, Leonora." He stopped playing and looked up at her. "Did you mark it in your score?"

She nodded. "I don't know where my mind is this morning."

Tilo knew exactly where it was. "Have you heard from Walter?"

The concern in his voice broke her reserve and her pent-up feelings spilled out; her hands were shaking as she grasped her music stand to steady herself.

"I might as well not have. He rang me from the local pub and we could hardly hear each other speak."

"*The pub?*" Tilo peered at her over his glasses.

"He's at his family's beach house and there's no phone. New Year in the pub, you can imagine the noise. We won't be able to talk properly until he gets back to Sydney, maybe in a few days, maybe not for another two weeks." Leonora bit her lip in frustration. "I couldn't understand what he meant." She shook her head. "I'm sorry Tilo. I shouldn't have let this get in the way of our rehearsal."

He smiled up at her. "It hasn't. Shall we start again at the bar with the dotted quaver?"

Looking into Tilo's kind face, Leonora was comforted.

A week after the call from the pub, Leonora was in the hall putting on her coat when the phone rang. It was after midnight in Australia. It wouldn't be Walter. It was probably someone for Frau Felder, who was out. Leonora hesitated. Should she answer or leave whoever it was to call back? She decided to take a message; it might be urgent.

"*Leonora Ford. Guten Tag.*"

"Lou! It's Walter."

"Wal!" Her heart raced. "Where are you?"

"Sydney. It's pretty late. Everyone else has gone to bed. We won't be disturbed."

The line was so clear this time he could have been in the next room. Leonora cradled the phone against her cheek. "I've missed you, Wal. I can't wait to see you. When are you coming back?"

"That's what I want to talk to you about." He took a slow breath. "My father… he wants me to stay on here."

A shock of adrenalin hit Leonora like icy water.

"What do you mean?" The words were choking her. "Are you saying you're not coming back?"

"I was trying to tell you when I rang before. My father's feeling his age a bit. He doesn't want me so far away."

The line had no echo; there was no mistaking what Walter had said. Leonora's fingers clenched white on the phone. "What about us?"

"Come to Sydney, Lou." His voice was eager. "I've thought it all through. The opera auditions are on in March. If you come now we can audition together."

"Wal, we've talked about this. We agreed I'd come for a visit in July." Leonora was trying to make sense of what she was hearing. "It's only a few months until we finish in Sankt Hubert."

There was a long silence at the end of the phone.

"I've promised my father I'd stay, Lou. I can't go back to Sankt Hubert. I've canceled my place at the opera studio. It's up to you now. It's time to choose."

- 35 -

Munich, January 1992

Leonora stared at her reflection. Three sleepless nights, three more phone calls that had resolved nothing had left their mark on her pale face and swollen eyes. Her throat was raw. Adding to her misery, she'd canceled her lesson with the Maestro. In this state she could no more sing than fly.

Leonora didn't blame Walter for wanting to stay close to his father. What troubled her was his assumption that he could decide without her. As if she could drop her scholarship just like that, disappointing everyone who had helped her. How could he put aside everything that was important to her? She'd thought he understood.

Her mind was numb from too much thinking.

In ten days she was due in Vienna. She had to pull herself together. She had no idea how.

"Mädele, you have a visitor."

Leonora jumped up from her bed where she'd been lying with a cold face cloth on her eyes, and went to open the door.

"Come quickly, Mädele." Frau Felder's face was rosy with excitement. Whoever it was, she was enjoying the mystery. With a swish of her apron she was already hurrying away.

In Frau Felder's sitting room Lily Benjamin was gazing at the dolls. She looked round as Leonora came in. In a white velvet maxi-dress with a silver scarf at the neck she glittered like the Snow Queen.

"Leonora, honey. I guess you're surprised to see me." A

mischievous smile lit up her face. "Don't worry, I'm not here to take you shopping." She took in Leonora's wan face and her expression softened. "Come and sit down, honey. Frau Felder's gone to make us some tea."

"Lily…" Leonora struggled for words as she joined Lily at the table. "I didn't know you were in Munich."

"Sshh." Lily raised a silver-tipped finger to her lips. "Officially I'm on my way to Milan. I'm playing truant for a couple of days. I'm thinking of doing *Salome* but I want to work through it with the Maestro before I decide." Her eyes gleamed. "The dance of the seven veils…such a scandal at the première… I'm tempted." She paused, as if she saw the scene playing out before her. "But there's a mighty standard to live up to, so many great sopranos before me. I have to be sure."

Salome, Oscar Wilde's play written in French, translated into German, set to music by Richard Strauss; an opera as exotic as Lily. A spark of excitement warmed Leonora. Only a few people would know Lily was considering the role.

"*Salome*, Lily!" Leonora's face lit up. "You'll be a sensation."

Lily gave Leonora a shrewd look.

Frau Felder set two of her best flowery cups on the table and placed the matching teapot in front of Lily.

She beamed at Leonora. "Frau Benjamin is staying for lunch. *Sauerbraten* stew with dumplings. I'm going to show her how to make them. Come into the kitchen when you've had your tea."

"Soul food, Leonora. It's what you need. You're looking very peaky." Lily reached for the teapot and poured the tea. "Now why don't you tell me what's the matter? Canceling the Maestro, that's a big step."

Leonora shivered. Sooner or later she'd have to face him. She was dreading it. "Did he send you, Lily?"

"No." Lily dropped a slice of lemon into her tea. "You should know by now he never interferes. You can ask his advice but he won't try to influence you. Your decisions must be your own." She looked up. "I saw Tilo at the studio and I asked about you. He seemed concerned. So here I am." She took a few sips of tea. "When Tilo tells me you're too upset to sing, it doesn't seem right. And I think, perhaps talking about it will help."

She put down her cup and leaned forward.

"Leonora, honey, the Maestro believes in you, you've performed for Beata Benedict. You've got the voice, you proved that in *Aida.*" She reached across the table and laid her hand gently on Leonora's arm. "So what's the matter?"

"It's Walter." Tears prickled at the corners of Leonora's eyes. "He was only supposed to be away for a few weeks but now he's not coming back." Her mouth twisted as she tried to hold back the tears. "He's canceled his place in Sankt Hubert." Her voice broke. "He wants me to give up everything here and go to Sydney." She swallowed and took a deep breath.

"And if you don't go?"

Leonora bowed her head. "Then it's over, I suppose." She looked up at Lily. "His father asked him to stay. Wal says he can't refuse him."

"What do *you* want, honey?" Lily's voice was gentle.

"That's just it. I want to be with him but I want to be here too." Leonora shook her head. "I'm not ready to go back, it's too soon. I want to have time to plan the future."

"Then take your time, honey." Lily gazed at Leonora's tear-stained face with compassion. "Wait until you're sure what's right for you. One thing I can tell you. Music chooses us as much as we choose it. If it's your true calling, it won't be denied."

She smiled. "Now, how about those dumplings? The sooner we make them, the sooner we can eat."

Leonora folded Walter's scarf and put it away in her suitcase. Would she ever wear it again? In a few days she would go to

Vienna for her audition and then to Sankt Hubert to wait for the result. Then she would make her decision.

Whatever that was, she would take her time.

- 36 -

Sankt Hubert, February 1992

Leonora pushed open the door. A glimmer of green drew her eye to the piano; the score Walter had given her for Christmas lay on the closed lid where she had left it. She hesitated on the threshold, as if to defer the proof that he had gone.

Wearily she closed the door behind her. The room was tidy, all trace of Walter gone. What else had she expected? Before she left for Munich she had put away the few things he hadn't taken with him.

In the bedroom everything was in its place, neat as the day they'd moved in. Leonora took the doona and a pillow into the sitting room. She could not bear to sleep in their bed alone.

"*Hallo*, Leonora. Thank goodness you're back. We're doing *Figaro* again." Fisch stood up from her desk and bustled round to shake Leonora's hand. "But what's happened with Walter? Are you all right? How was Vienna?"

Typical Fisch, firing off one question after another. Always straight to the point. Leonora managed a smile. In her workaday overalls Fisch was a reassuring sight.

"It's a long story, yes, and I think the audition was ok." She caught her breath as Fisch's words sank in. "What do you mean, we're doing *Figaro* again?"

"Ah…" Fisch tapped a finger against the tiny fish-shaped stud in her nose. "We haven't announced it yet but we're bringing it back for the Sankt Hubert festival in July, in the grounds of the castle. Under the stars, like Hildeberg. The night will be our black box."

Leonora froze. *July.* She'd all but decided to stay in Sankt Hubert until the theatre break when her place at the studio would end. Then she could go home for the holiday knowing she hadn't let anyone down, and work things out with Walter. The news about *Figaro* was throwing this up in the air; she might not even be able to wait to hear back from Vienna before deciding about the festival.

"Leonora, what is it? You're white as a ghost." Fisch gestured towards the chairs in front of her desk. "Come and sit down."

Leonora took the glass of water Fisch held out to her and swallowed a mouthful. "It's a surprise, that's all. I was planning to go home to Australia for the July break."

"You wouldn't give up a chance like this, surely?" Fisch was serious. "It's a popular festival. There'll be a lot of influential people there to hear you."

Leonora put the glass back on Fisch's desk.

"If I'm asked." She let the question slip past.

"You will be. Until then, just keep it to yourself." Fisch bustled back to the other side of the desk and flicked through a pile of papers. "Now where's that call sheet...we're a pianist short this week. Can you fill in? I've checked your rehearsals and marked the sessions you could do. It's mostly note-bashing I'm afraid, helping people memorize." She pulled out a paper and handed it to Leonora with a thoughtful look. Between rehearsals, practice and piano coaching she'd have little time left to brood.

Leonora ran her eyes over the call sheet. The studio end of year gala was to be scenes from *Carmen.* She'd been cast as the village maiden Micaëla in one scene and the gypsy Frasquita in two others: the trio with Carmen and the smugglers' sextet. If only Walter had stayed he could have sung Don José.

Fisch's voice broke into her thoughts. "Leonora? Will you do it?"

Leonora nodded. She needed to get back to work.

"I will. Can you give me the score?"

Fisch's lips twitched into a satisfied grin.

Beating the tambourine in the gypsy dance, Leonora was beginning to feel like herself again. She'd been worried about facing her friends at the studio who had known her and Walter as a couple but they were all too busy to make much of his absence.

Her days were full. The only time she could speak to Walter was early in the morning or late at night. If he called her, it would disturb the other residents. If she called him, she couldn't be sure he would be at home. After several missed attempts, they had agreed to take it in turns to call each other on Sundays.

When she left in the morning or came back at night, she hurried past the phone and the blank message board, silent reminders of her dilemma.

They were still at an impasse. He'd promised to wait for her until July but that was all.

-37-

Sankt Hubert, March 1992

The letters arrived on the same day. Leonora sat at the table beneath the lampshade, the two envelopes before her, each with its distinctive logo.

She opened the Sankt Hubert letter first. It was the offer Fisch had told her to expect. The fee was generous, more than she had earned at Hildeberg; the Countess was a much bigger role.

She picked up the other envelope, holding it in both hands. She was at a crossroad; this letter had power over her future.

She eased the envelope open and drew out the single sheet of paper.

One year contract as a Young Artist.

Lily's words came back to her: if music was your calling, it would not let you go. In that moment she made her decision. It was a gift she could not refuse.

Tomorrow she would send her acceptance letters. But first she would write to Walter. Her heart still ached for him but her future was here.

She was going to Vienna.

ACT THREE

-38-

Melbourne, November 2000

No one was in the rehearsal room when Leonora arrived. She stood in the doorway, taking in the familiar smell of dust and old paint that lingered like a memory that wouldn't fade.

Day in day out, the stage managers would fight the dust like an ancient enemy, sweeping and spraying water. The dust always came back. But if the spraying was missed, the singers noticed. They came in sniffing the air; if it felt too dry they began to cough, one after the other, like an audience at the sight of dry ice smoke.

Crossing the floor, over the outline of the set marked in tape, Leonora took a shallow breath through her nose. Not a hint of dust; technology had won the day. Yet the room still exuded its familiar scent, nostalgic as wood smoke on a frosty evening.

The piano was already open, its lid propped on the half-stick. Leonora leaned over and struck a chord, testing the resonance; it was a good room to sing in.

She was deliberately early today, wanting time to steady herself. Though it was only a music rehearsal, the verdict would soon get out. She needed to be at her best.

Her eye caught the movement of leaves outside the window, shadows behind the opaque glass, a far cry from the spiky winter branches standing sentinel outside her apartment in New York. She shivered as if she could still feel the cold. Winter was never a singer's friend.

She had come home without a care in the world from a season of *Madam Butterfly* at The Met. The Melbourne season of *Butterfly* was a co-production, with Leonora and her Met costar Mario Mancini joining a local cast. Then a slip on an icy path and a broken ankle had left Mario on crutches, unable to follow her, and her Butterfly without a Lieutenant Pinkerton. It was too late to replace him; star tenors were booked up for years. The understudy would have to go on.

But then she'd seen who it was.

Walter.

She could have refused to work with him – she was a big enough name now. But it wasn't the way she wanted to begin what was supposed to be her triumphant return.

The window darkened as a cloud passed and the leaves ceased their dance. Leonora turned away. The others would be here soon.

In the curve of the piano two music stands waited side by side. She took one and moved it away. There would be no hiding: they would look each other in the eye and sing face to face.

She glanced at her watch. It was almost time. She was ready.

He arrived at the last minute as the rehearsal room clock ticked onto the hour, delaying as long as he could. He'd known for months he'd have to face her, but he'd never imagined performing with her.

She was standing at the piano with the rehearsal pianist, one hand on the open score as if to emphasize a point. She looked no different from when he'd last seen her. More sure of herself, more poised, but still with that air of fragility, that candid expression that made you believe every emotion it reflected.

He stood there unable to move. Later he wouldn't remember how he made it to the piano, only his confusion at the sight of her.

Now she was riffling the pages of the score.

"We're starting with the duet, Wal." The diminutive slipped easily from her lips.

The love duet. The wedding night. Was she setting him up?
He was in no position to refuse; there was no other understudy. Without a Pinkerton the opera would be canceled. He'd be responsible for too much loss of work.
He looked up as she began to sing.
Non piango più...I'll weep no more...
At the production rehearsal he'd have to take Leonora in his arms, act the passionate lover. He didn't know how he was going to do it.

The clock had ticked to the hour again, the pianist had closed his score and left quickly for his next rehearsal, Walter close behind him. Leonora watched them go. She had pushed Walter enough with the scene she had chosen. But it had told her what she needed to know. His voice was equal to the role. Now she would see if he could perform it.

Her music was still open on the stand, the notes the Maestro had given her penciled above the stave. Butterfly had been his vision for her from the start. What would he say to her now? She rested her fingertips lightly on the words, as if to wish them back to life and hear his voice again.

- 39 -

The late spring morning was balmy as Leonora walked through the botanical gardens to the theatre, past joggers and families strolling along the pathways. She delighted in the birds she'd known since childhood, the sulphur-crested cockatoos screeching overhead, the whistles and squawks of the rainbow lorikeets, the magpies warbling out their coloratura. She walked on, past the white tower of Government House behind its imposing gates, past the Shrine, the war memorial, with its eternal flame.

She caught the scent of eucalyptus on the breeze and stopped for a moment to inhale and savor it, oily, pungent, reassuring her she was home.

Yesterday had gone well enough; there was no point dwelling on how her next rehearsal with Walter would unfold.

It was almost nine years since she'd watched his train pull out of the station. His face was leaner now, the bone structure more pronounced, his grey-green eyes and his hair – bleached by the sun – a sharper contrast against the tan of his skin, but still the Walter she remembered. Only the look in his eyes was different.

She wondered briefly what he'd thought of her, what changes he might have seen, but he'd barely lifted his eyes from his score. So much for looking each other in the eye and singing face to face. But until they did, their performance would never come to life. Sooner or later it had to happen.

The day passed in solo music calls and meetings with the wardrobe staff to check her costumes which had been sent over from New York. Her wigs would be fitted when Kim Ah arrived in time for the first dress rehearsal. She had exercised her diva's privilege and asked for him. Now in demand throughout the opera world, it was a tribute to their enduring friendship that he always found time for her.

What would Kim Ah make of Walter when they met again, she wondered.

The next morning Leonora entered the rehearsal room with the sense of anticipation she always felt at the start of a new season. Today she would meet the little girl who would be her stage child, Butterfly's son, Trouble. Girls were thought easier to manage; dressed in a sailor suit, who was to know? The child would be crucial to Leonora's performance at the end of the opera. They had to be comfortable with each other.

She needn't have worried. When the company chaperone arrived holding the little girl by the hand, Leonora was enchanted. With her short dark curls and big blue eyes, the small figure was like a tiny version of herself. Taking her hand, Leonora knelt beside her. "I'm Leonora," she said. "What's your name?"

"Lulu. I'm four." The child stood there smiling at her with such confidence, an endearing dimple in each cheek, that Leonora knew she was the one. She didn't need to audition anyone else.

"Well, Lulu. I'm very pleased to meet you. I'm Butterfly, your mother in the story we're going to tell."

It had always been the plan to work on the scenes between Butterfly and Trouble first, to give them all the time possible to become used to each other. But from the moment she saw her, Leonora took Lulu to her heart. There was something about this child that drew her, the way she understood when to lie quietly in Leonora's arms, or how to react to the dramatic outpouring of Butterfly's sorrow. She knew the music and would hum the melody in her high treble. When she arrived with her chaperone at the start of each rehearsal, she came forward and announced herself, like a miniature diva: "Lulu is here."

She took to prefixing everyone's name with "my". The pianist became "my Adam", the director "My D'rector". Leonora she simply referred to as She or Her, as if there could be no mistaking who she meant. And when they were on stage, "My Butterfly". Only later did Leonora realize Lulu never once said "my Kate" to Kate Pinkerton, the American wife who had come to take Trouble away from Butterfly.

At first Leonora and Lulu worked alone, one of the assistant stage managers standing in for the other principals, and the pianist singing in their lines. Then came the day when the rest of the cast arrived to join them.

The director knelt in front of Lulu, his hands on her shoulders.

"Lulu, do you remember what we talked about in this scene? Suzuki will bring you in and you will run to Leonora. She will be Butterfly then."

Lulu nodded, solemn as a tiny sphinx.

"She will be singing about how much she loves you. Just look at her. You know what to do."

This was the test. Would Lulu be distracted by the first part of the scene where Sharpless, the American Consul, urges Butterfly to give up her child and marry a Japanese suitor?

In this first run-through, Leonora could have held back and marked through the music. Instead she chose to sing full-voice and put everything she could into the scene. She needed to know that Lulu would react in front of others just as she had when they had rehearsed alone.

The warmth of the small body in her arms touched a maternal instinct in her; as she sang, Leonora sensed Butterfly's despair more deeply than ever. When the humming chorus began, soothing Trouble to sleep, Leonora's eyes were wet with tears. At the end, there was silence in the room. She stroked the curls from Lulu's face, holding the moment. Lulu had played her part to perfection.

The emotion of the scene stayed with Leonora. She hadn't expected to be so moved but she would draw on her feelings as she built her performance in rehearsal, until she could stand back from them. She couldn't afford to choke on tears on stage.

But something else lingered. With Lulu there was a bond Leonora had never felt before. She was still thinking about it as she took her usual path through the gardens later that day and made her way to the theatre for her wig fitting. Smiling at the thought of seeing Kim Ah, she quickened her pace. She could talk to him about anything; he would listen and never judge.

She pushed open the door of the wardrobe department and stood in the doorway. There he was, slim and immaculate in his black working clothes, his face shining at her, radiating kindness and affection. He held out his hands and she went towards him.

"Kim Ah, you never change." They exchanged a kiss on each cheek in the French way. "Is that wig for me?" She gestured towards the wig block on a nearby table.

He nodded, adjusting an ornament, a cluster of trailing blossoms. "This is your wig for the whole opera. You're on stage so much I wanted to make it easy for you. We'll only have to change the ornaments. This one is for your wedding. We'll make it simpler for Act Two and leave it completely plain for the last scene." He smiled. "What do you think?"

But Leonora's attention had been caught by a small blond wig on the same table. "Is that for Trouble?" Eyes shining, she didn't wait for an answer. "I can't tell you how wonderful Lulu is, Kim Ah. There's something special about her. She's born to be on the stage."

Kim Ah picked up the wig and adjusted a curl. "I suppose she gets that from her father."

"Her father?' She looked at Kim Ah, nonplussed.

"You didn't know?" Kim Ah's face was serious. "I'm sorry, Leonora, I had no idea." He placed the wig back on its block and turned towards her. "It's Walter. Lulu is Walter's daughter."

The walk back through the gardens passed Leonora by as she struggled with her emotions. She scarcely noticed the people around her, too deep in thought to look up at the lorikeets darting between the trees. She'd come to sing Butterfly to her home audience, family and friends, not to reopen old wounds. She couldn't understand why she should feel so deeply after so long that Walter had a child.

But it wasn't a child, it was Lulu. The child who could have been hers.

She tapped in the security code at the entrance to her apartment and the gate swung open. A cool evening breeze touched the nape of her neck as she turned and walked up the path.

She had to think of Lulu as Walter's child, nothing more.

Walter steeled himself as he approached the rehearsal room. In a way it was a relief to be facing Leonora at last. Lulu had done nothing but talk about Her, stirring memories he'd forgotten or thought long behind him.

He couldn't remember the last time he'd felt so nervous in rehearsal. Before a performance sometimes, but never this stomach-churning tension.

Leonora was already there, chatting with the director. They seemed relaxed: the morning session must have gone well. Catching sight of Walter, the director beckoned him over, smiling.

"You've worked with each other before, I hear." Walter nodded, wondering how much he knew. But it seemed the director was intent only on saving time. "No need for introductions then. We can get started straight away. Ah, here's Lulu."

As soon as she saw them, Lulu ran across, gazing up at them with satisfaction. "My Butterfly," she said, taking Leonora's hand. "My Daddy, my D'rector."

The director laughed. "It seems introductions have been made after all." He looked round the room. "Suzuki, Sharpless, Kate

Pinkerton. Good, everyone is here. We'll start with the lullaby, number 11 in your scores. After seeing Pinkerton's ship in the harbor, Butterfly has been waiting for him all night but he has not come. Suzuki and Trouble are asleep."

Leonora and Frannie, the mezzo singing Suzuki, took their places. Walter stood at the side, ready for his entrance. A lump came to his throat as he watched Lulu being lifted onto Trouble's little bed.

The piano began to play. Leonora turned, woke Suzuki and went to pick up Lulu. Carrying Lulu in her arms, she began the lullaby:

Dormi amor mio, dormi sul mio cor, tu sei con Dio ed io con mio dolor...

Sleep my beloved, sleep against my heart; you are with God, and I with my sorrow...

He'd rehearsed the trio with Sharpless and Suzuki well. But seeing his own child in Butterfly's arms, the pathos struck at his heart. Pinkerton's cowardice in sending his American wife to take the child shocked Walter to the core. It was as if he had shed his skin – Pinkerton was alive for him.

He struggled to calm his breathing. His throat closed, he barely got out the words.

...mi struggo dal rimorso...

...I am consumed with remorse...

He stumbled through to his exit. He'd touched a deeper level of awareness as if until now he had been merely mouthing words and following stage directions. He felt raw. Was this how every rehearsal was going to be? He slumped into a chair, oblivious to the rest of the scene happening in front of him.

No one took any notice – strong emotion often surfaced in *Butterfly*.

It was warm in the studio, but he felt cold. It was as if something had shifted in his mind that could never be put back:

memories long pushed aside were crowding in.

He had to pull himself together. He wasn't Pinkerton, the American naval officer who'd light-heartedly taken a local wife for convenience in nineteenth century Japan and left her, returning only to take their child away from her.

And Leonora wasn't Butterfly. What he thought of as his affair with her was long in the past. And he'd hardly abandoned her. He'd waited for her in Sydney long enough.

Yet here they were in a twist of fate acting the story of a man who promised to return and didn't, and Leonora was holding his child in her arms. At least he hadn't left her with that problem.

His stomach lurched. Would she have told him?

Surely he would have known.

To Walter's relief, the director postponed the final scene, Butterfly's suicide. On top of what he was already feeling, it would have been too much. When they did rehearse it he wouldn't be needed. He would be offstage until just before the final curtain.

Unless he wanted to, he would never need to see it.

He wondered whether he should speak to Leonora but she had gone over to Kim Ah. Before he could make up his mind, the chaperone brought Lulu to him. She put her hand in his and looked up at him.

"Poor Butterfly." Her little face was serious. Then she smiled. "Daddy, *gelato*. You promised."

So he had. He looked across to where Kim Ah was standing with Leonora and held up his hand to say goodbye. Kim Ah gazed back at him intently. The others might not have noticed his emotion but Kim Ah had seen and understood.

Holding his daughter's hand, Walter felt a moment's wonder that this small being should be his. Then he picked her up and swung her onto his shoulder. "Come on then," he said. "I know just the place."

Along the river the city lights threw long streaks of color in the water. To Leonora, the high rise office towers seemed as if dropped from another world. She looked across to the old station with its red brick and yellow facings, squatting on the far bank like a Victorian relic. A visiting architect once said it was a building only a mother could love. But people did love it. They would never allow it to be pulled down.

She turned to Kim Ah, sitting companionably at her side.

"When we went our separate ways in Munich, I was afraid I'd never see any of you again, but you were right, our paths kept crossing. You, Tilo, Carla. All except Walter. Even though I came home whenever I could to see my mother."

She stopped, and turned her gaze back to the shimmering light-play on the river.

Kim Ah waited.

"Walter was my first love. I thought we'd be together for ever. It broke my heart when he told me he wasn't coming back. He wouldn't even discuss it. That was the hardest part. Realizing we were too different to have a future. And we were so far away from each other. We didn't have mobile phones to talk whenever we wanted to." She stood up and rested her hands lightly on the balustrade at the river's edge. "Imagine, these days people break up on their mobiles." She shook her head in disbelief.

"And Lulu?"

Leonora let her hands fall to her side. "That he would have a child never entered my head." She shrugged. "Perhaps if I'd had longer to think about it…" She met Kim Ah's eyes. "I've already found myself wishing she was mine. But she's not." She lowered her gaze. "It's not too late to think about a child of my own. She's made me realize that."

Walter's relief at not being called for the rehearsal of the final scene wasn't to last long. The director had decided he should be there after all in case Lulu was upset by the story. She would witness Kate Pinkerton asking Butterfly to give up her child. Then she would be blindfolded and seated on a stool with a doll and a little American flag, until the end, when Sharpless would come to pick her up. And they were to stay in position because the curtain would come up for the audience to see the last image again.

The director had explained it carefully to Lulu and she had repeated his words to Walter. "It's just a story, Daddy. It's not true." Then she had looked up at him, wide-eyed and solemn. "It's a very sad story. It is."

Walter marveled at the transformation that came over Leonora as she began the scene. The wardrobe department had given her a simple cotton *yukata* to rehearse in, to get used to kneeling and standing up in the traditional Japanese way for women. But it was her demeanor that created the illusion. As the meeting between Butterfly and Kate Pinkerton unfolded, he found himself living it, as if witnessing something real. *How can they do this to her?* He almost spoke the words aloud. As Butterfly began to sing of death, he was filled with the horror of it.

Then Lulu came in. Kim Ah had put on her little blond wig, so that she could get used to wearing it. She was Lulu and yet not Lulu. The magic of theatre was taking over.

Later he was astonished at how the scene had moved him. Apart from the sound of Leonora's voice and the piano, there was complete stillness in the room. He could hear the indrawn breath of those around him as Butterfly took the sacred knife from the ancestral shrine. It was only a packing case, doing duty for the altar, but Leonora made him see it. Knowing what was to come sharpened his sense of dread. He was shocked to feel tears in his eyes as Leonora tied on the blindfold and placed Lulu on the stool. He wasn't alone. Behind the production desk, the director was brushing his hand across his eyes. When Leonora came from behind the screen and fell to the ground, reaching for her child with her last strength, Walter was still sitting in his chair, transfixed. It was only when the rehearsal pianist sang Pinkerton's final anguished three cries of "*Butterfly...Butterfly... Butterfly...*" that he realized he had missed his entrance.

Oblivious to the coming and going around him, Walter leaned against the back of the bench, closed his eyes and lifted his head to feel the sun on his face. At the end of the rehearsal he'd escaped as soon as he could; he could still feel his cheeks burning. He'd seen Lulu off on an outing with her chaperone to a nearby children's playground, and had made his way to the river. The feeling he'd had when he first saw Leonora was overwhelming him again. He had only a day or two's respite before he had to face the scene he dreaded most. He knew this director. The love scene would go as far as he thought he could get away with.

Walter let his head drop, eyes still closed. He'd already made a fool of himself with the missed entry. What lay ahead in his scenes with Leonora he couldn't imagine. Groaning inwardly, his breath escaped in a long sigh.

He felt a shadow across his face.

"It's all right, Wal."

Leonora. He opened his eyes to see her standing in front of him.

"Nobody cares about a missed entrance in rehearsal. I took it as a compliment. Not a dry eye in the house."

He felt himself naked and flayed under her gaze, helpless as a trapped animal.

Conscious of his discomfort Leonora sat down beside him, a clear space between them. "But that's not what it's about, is it? It's the love scene, isn't it?"

"Lou, I'm so sorry..." His voice trailed off. It was the first time he'd spoken her name.

"Wal, it was years ago." Her voice was gentle. "We wanted – needed – different things. We would have split up sooner or later and perhaps more damage would have been done."

She waited for him to speak but he was silent.

"It was a shock for me too when I heard the understudy was you. But we can get over it, use it even."

He gave her a puzzled look.

"I mean it. We just have to break the ice. I'm going to ask for a closed rehearsal."

He didn't answer and she tried again.

"It *will* be all right, Wal. If you only knew some of the tenors I've worked with; you'll be a gift from heaven."

He shook his head. "Why did it have to be *Butterfly*? It's brought it all back, how I left you. I didn't even come back to pack up. The coward's way out, like Pinkerton. And then seeing you with Lulu..." He broke off.

Leonora stood up. "Lulu's very special, Wal." It was on the tip of her tongue to ask about her mother but she held back. She had a brief, unpleasant vision of a woman in purple – surely that couldn't be – before Walter spoke again.

"Her mother's a dancer. She had to stay in Sydney for the ballet she's doing."

She laid a hand on Walter's arm. His skin felt warm beneath her fingers, nothing more.

"Come on then, Wal. Time to face the music."

- 40 -

On the day he was to rehearse the wedding scene with Leonora, only the need to look after Lulu got Walter out of bed. If she noticed his distraction, she didn't show it. Or perhaps she did, he thought, watching her put the cereal bowls on the table and insisting on pouring milk for him. He knew he could never put into words the depth of his love for that wise little face glowing back at him across the table. Kim Ah would have called her an old soul.

Walter pushed the hair back from his eyes. He wished he had made more of an effort to keep in touch. Once he could have talked to Kim Ah about anything. Now, he wasn't sure.

His emotional response to the suicide scene had thrown him. He hadn't always seen eye to eye with the Maestro but he'd absorbed more than he'd realized at the time. He was professional in his work: he studied his roles well, he was punctual, audiences liked him. But Leonora was showing him there was more. And mixed in with everything was the sense that he'd lost control.

Lulu scraped her spoon across the bottom of her bowl, drawing his attention back to her. Her chaperone would be picking her up soon and taking her out to play. Then, for him, it really would be time to face the music.

Driving to rehearsal Walter wanted nothing more than to take Lulu and fly back to Sydney. If he did, the comfortable career he'd built for himself as resident tenor would probably be over. But even if it wouldn't – people always forgot in time – could he do that to Leonora and the rest of the cast? He'd been the only option to step into the role. If he backed out now, the opera would have to be canceled. The argument went back and forth in his head like a child counting, yes – no – yes – no. Finally he switched on the radio and turned up the volume, driving down the road with the bass beat thumping, anything to drown out his thoughts. Weary of himself, he parked his car and went to face the day.

True to her word, Leonora had arranged for the rehearsal to be closed. Apart from Leonora, only the director, the stage manager and the rehearsal pianist were present. They would just be blocking the moves at first, not usually a process to be nervous about. But this director was known for his realism. Walter dreaded what he would be called on to do.

It seemed so casual at first: catching a glimpse of Butterfly changing into her simple white robe behind a screen, neither of them singing out, so that he could gloss over some of the words that worried him, though he had argued with himself over and over that there was no reason why they should.

…ancor non m'hai detto che m'ami…

Pinkerton's words to Butterfly – *you have not said you love me* – slipped out safely under his breath. If they kept on marking through the music without singing in full voice, he could distance himself from those words – and Butterfly's reply that she feared she would die of love.

The director called a halt while Leonora slipped on a cotton robe, cut like the one she would wear on stage. Then he explained the next moves. But instead of giving them detail, he asked them to improvise; he wanted to see the tension build, through Butterfly's fears and Pinkerton calming her, until the final scene when Butterfly would be in his arms. The last image for the audience would be Pinkerton slipping the white robe from Butterfly's shoulders to reveal her unclothed body.

Walter froze, his mind blank. Why couldn't they have been given specific moves, told what to do. He was honest enough to admit to himself that in other circumstances he would have welcomed the freedom to improvise. Directors who dictated every tiny point were never popular.

They took their places again and Leonora emerged from behind the screen. And she was singing in full voice.

He should have been warned by the scene he had witnessed between Leonora and Lulu. The real Pinkerton needed no defenses against Butterfly. Walter did. He'd had no time to prepare himself. And the words were out in the open.

He knew Leonora wasn't thinking of him when she sang, but he wasn't there with her in Butterfly's world. He was still Walter, struggling not to lose control of his emotions again.

He felt stiff and wooden as he tried to respond to the music. He knew it was in the score but it took him aback when Leonora threw herself into his arms as he sang *sei mia – you are mine*, her response *si, per la vita – yes, for ever.*

Blindly he followed her lead as she whispered to him to draw her down onto the blanket that served as the tatami mat they would have on stage. As Butterfly sang of the ecstasy of love and Pinkerton of his possession of her, Walter froze again. On their last high C together it was Leonora who took his hands and guided them to slip the robe from her shoulders and let it fall to the ground.

Kim Ah timed his arrival at the end of the rehearsal perfectly. Officially he was there to discuss whether in this traditional production Walter should have a beard. The director and designer had yet to make up their minds. Personally, Kim Ah was against it. The audience needed to see all of Walter's face, historically accurate or not.

Unofficially, Kim Ah was there to see his old friend. He'd

realized Walter was struggling when he heard the director urging Leonora to break the ice, thinking that Walter's wooden performance was due to shyness with such an established star. Leonora hadn't enlightened him. Kim Ah's face softened: still so loyal, always so professional. But something had to give between Walter and Leonora.

The rehearsal broke up and Kim Ah seized his chance.

"Walter, can you stay a minute?" He smiled at Leonora, who was coming over to speak to him. "Beard business." He was counting on her reading the situation and leaving him alone with Walter. As if he'd spoken his intention aloud, she nodded and left the room with the director. His voice carried back to Kim Ah and Walter, his exasperation dropping like stones into the silence.

"That extraordinary child, born to perform. And her father, the proverbial stunned mullet on stage. If only there were someone else…"

His voice trailed off but there was no glossing over what they had heard.

Walter grimaced. "He's right. If only he knew how close I've been to giving up. But they keep telling me there isn't anyone else."

Kim Ah looked at his old friend. Was there too much distance between them now for him to speak the truth?

"What is it, Wal? What is it really?"

"It's Lou." The old name, the first time Kim Ah had heard Walter use it since the two had met again. "I just can't face her." Walter shook his head. "If I'd just met her socially there would have been other people there. I could have managed. But meeting her again like this…" He broke off, his face flushed. "And now the director wants a nude scene. I can't do it."

It seemed simple enough to Kim Ah. Leonora would be wearing a body stocking, covered to wrist and ankle to keep her warm on the draughty set. But it wouldn't matter what she was wearing. Something had triggered this reaction in Walter. It happened sometimes to Kim Ah, when he would wake from a nightmare of bombs falling. He never knew what had brought the bad dream. But Walter knew.

"You've never really talked to Leonora about what happened, have you?"

Walter brushed his hand across his eyes.

"I tried. I begged her to come to Sydney." He shook his head. "We only had the old dial up phone for international calls. It wasn't easy."

Kim Ah flinched. If the truth was to come out, he would say his piece too. "Wal, I sometimes wonder if you understood how hard it was for Leonora." He stopped himself from adding, *how you broke her heart*. "You should have gone back to talk to her. You made a decision and expected her to follow. You weren't really giving her a choice. I think you know that. Perhaps you've been hiding it from yourself all this time. It's not too late to make your peace."

Walter frowned. "Does it matter now? It's all in the past for her, she told me so herself."

Kim Ah's usually gentle face was stern.

"It mattered then and it matters now. This isn't about Leonora. It's about you. You're the one who has to get over what happened."

Walter felt the adrenalin punch through his veins as panic took hold of him. "But how am I going to do that?"

Kim Ah smiled. "You will talk to her. I shall arrange it." He stretched out his hand and tapped Walter lightly on the chest. "Don't even think of not turning up. Now, about that beard."

It was warm in the courtyard behind the house Kim Ah had rented for his time in Melbourne. The high drone of cicadas throbbed in the air, the familiar sound of summer.

He raised his glass. "To friendship." He took a sip of wine. "Leonora, Walter. Friendship is precious. It is to be treasured. I have given myself the task to clear the air between you. Not just for you but for myself also."

He turned to Walter. "All this time Leonora, Carla and I have stayed in touch. But you have been missing. Perhaps of your own choice, perhaps because there was a barrier you were not able to cross." He paused; the sky was darkening, the buzz of the cicadas hypnotic, a scent of a night-blooming flower drifting from somewhere unseen. If the air could be cleared, what better moment than this?

"What happened, Wal? Why didn't you keep your promise to go back?"

Sensing that Leonora was about to speak, Kim Ah made a small gesture for her to wait. Walter should have all the time he needed to say what he had to say first.

As if releasing a long-pent up breath, Walter let out a sigh. "It was coming home to Sydney that did it. The sunshine and... *openness*. It made Sankt Hubert seem so small, like squeezing myself into something that didn't fit, was never going to fit. And my father...there was a lot of pressure on me to stay. It was easy to give in."

He turned to face Leonora. "I was convinced you'd come in the end, even if I had to wait until you finished at the opera studio." He shook his head. "I'm so sorry, Lou. I can't believe how selfish I was, even leaving you to pack up my things. I don't think I'll ever forgive myself for that."

He sensed rather than saw Leonora's smile as she leaned towards him.

"You were forgiven a long time ago, Wal."

The sky was dark now; small solar lights began to glow around the edge of the courtyard; the cicadas sang on.

Kim Ah stood up, his lips curved in a satisfied smile; it was time to put on the steam boat and lighten the mood.

Two days later the full company assembled for the first full run of Act One. There was an air of excitement in the room, a sense that the company was heading for a success. Everyone was there, the designers, wardrobe and music staff, watching expectantly. Many of them were happy to see Walter get this chance; they had no idea of the struggle that had been taking place.

The first scenes ran smoothly, the marriage contract and Butterfly's entrance with her ladies, her rejection by the high priest – the Bonze – and her family: no one put a foot wrong. Trooping off after delivering their curses in splendid voice, the Chorus were astonished to see the director frowning. Everyone had done their part, all the voices were well-balanced – in their view it was a great cast. He'd been so positive in their rehearsals. Surely he wasn't going to turn temperamental on them now.

He didn't know himself what he would do if there was a repeat of what he regarded as a disastrous mismatch between Leonora and Walter in the love scene. True, Walter had carried off his first entry well but it hadn't been with Leonora. He shifted in his chair, leaned his elbows on the production desk and rested his chin on his hands, bracing himself. He would let the scene run, however woodenly Walter Saville played it.

And then a weight fell from his shoulders. A different Walter was emerging before his eyes, credible, tender, supporting Leonora in his arms and gently taking her hands from her face.

Bimba, bimba, non piangere…

Little one, do not cry…

The director began to relax. So it was shyness after all. Sitting quietly next to him, Kim Ah allowed himself the gentlest of smiles.

- 41 -

Leonora pushed open the door of her dressing room; her senses sharpened as she took in the smell of ironing and newly cleaned costumes. Leaving the rest of the room in darkness, she settled herself in the bright pool of light around the mirror, secure in her own private space. Her personal things were laid out on a towel as she'd left them after the dress rehearsal: her make-up still in the old fishing box that was all she could afford in her student days, the compartments meant for hooks and trout flies filled with color sticks, safety pins, bits of elastic, needle and thread, a couple of old stockings. Her lucky piece. She had never wanted to replace it.

Opening her bag she took out a tissue-wrapped package: the exquisite *Butterfly* doll that was Frau Felder's last gift to her. Gently Leonora stood the small figure on the table, its benign gaze reminding her of the dolls in Frau Felder's sitting room. How she wished her old friend had lived to see this day. There had been so much kindness from so many people; she sat quietly, remembering them all.

A big card was propped against the mirror: a child's drawing of a wobbly figure holding a smaller one, *buterfly and trubble* in uneven letters at the bottom, with an *o* and *x* hug and kiss. Beside it a pile of cards and faxes and a simple bunch of roses her mother had picked for her from their garden. As she filled a glass with water for the flowers, Leonora sang softly under her breath. *Tutta la primavera, seminiamo april...*

Whenever she sang the flower duet it was the Maestro's garden in his beloved Toscana that she saw. He would be thinking of her now, as he did for every première. But it would be winter that he was seeing through his window, the pencil pines dark against the early snow. How she wished he could be here. He would be proud of her. He'd seen her in New York but he had never seen Walter perform. He would be proud of him too, surprised perhaps, but proud nonetheless.

After the quiet conversation with Walter in the courtyard, they had reminisced over the steam boat. There had been no drama, only a gradual thawing until Walter had met Leonora's eyes and she had just said, "I know. It's going to be all right." They'd even managed to talk about Butterfly and make a joke of the famous nude moment; in New York, the "was she or wasn't she?" question was still being hotly disputed.

But Walter hadn't spoken about his wife and Leonora hadn't told him about Tilo – quiet reliable Tilo, who had waited so long for her to see more in him than music. Her relationship with Walter belonged to the past. It had no place in the future. Perhaps they would meet again as colleagues, hear news of each other from time to time, but they would not keep in touch. It was enough to know that they could now part as friends.

Rummaging in the fishing box for a piece of stocking, Leonora stretched it over her head. Once Kim Ah had designed her make-up she still liked to put it on herself. With a practiced hand she swept the foundation over her face and neck, blotting out her features until all she saw was an ivory mask. A touch of ochre on her eye-lids, eyebrows smudged upwards like small black wings; a single line below her eyes to match the curve of the brow; deep red lips in a precise cupid's bow.

Fifteen years old.

A soft knock at the door: her dresser Vi, wheeling in a clothes rack. The focus of the room shifted as the overhead light came on, spilling Leonora out of her cocoon, bringing closer the moment of truth. She let her gaze linger on the kimonos hanging in order on the rack. All made to measure and labeled with her name, the opera, the role, the scene. She'd dreamed of this when she was first on stage, a novice wearing someone else's costume reworked to fit her. Even now, she felt the same excitement. Ample as the Venus of Willendorf, Vi patted the costumes into place, spacing the hangers along the rail like a mother lining up her children. She could be in her twenties or her forties but a quiet authority belied her youth. In the short time she had known her, Leonora had come to trust her completely.

"Everything's here." Vi spoke quietly, acknowledging Leonora's need to concentrate. "Are you ready to get dressed?"

Leonora smiled up at her. "After Kim Ah does my wig. It will only take a few minutes to slip on the first kimono. There's nothing I need to put over my head."

As Vi left, Kim Ah arrived, elegant in black silk tunic and narrow pants. Leonora caught the faint scent of cinnamon and bergamot as he moved.

"How's my favorite geisha this evening?"

"Just make me look as beautiful as you."

They both laughed. Leonora felt her opening night tension relax as Kim Ah took off the stocking and brushed her hair, putting in a few pin curls to anchor the wig, before stretching the stocking over her head again.

Watching him in the mirror tweak the wig deftly into place reminded her of the first time they'd worked together.

"Do you remember my first season in *La Bohème* in Paris, how you used to stand in the wings every night? At first I thought you were checking up on your wigs. Then I realized it was because you loved the music so much."

"It's as close as I can get to singing opera myself. I'll be in the wings again tonight." He smiled at her reflection. "We've both come a long way since then."

Leonora was thoughtful. "And yet, seeing Wal again, it feels like coming full circle."

Kim Ah gazed back at her, his face Buddha-like in the mirror. "It was time. I think in the West you call it closure."

She made a small face. "Do you think his wife knows about me?"

"Perhaps." He tucked the last pin into the wig. "Would you mind?"

Leonora shook her head. "No. Not any more, not for a long time."

"Look, it's a butterfly orchid." Vi placed the pot with its cascade of white flowers beside the mirror. Leonora reached for the card. If only the Maestro and Frau Benedict could have been here tonight. But they hadn't felt up to the long flight. Leonora understood. Carefully she propped the card next to Lulu's. Behind it, Butterfly's face looked back at her from the mirror.

"Only fifteen years old, getting ready to have her heart broken." She looked up at Vi. "But she doesn't know that yet. She's happy. She's given up everything to be with her American husband."

Vi didn't speak; Leonora was talking herself into character and wouldn't expect an answer. Understanding these things was part of her job. Quietly she handed Leonora her white socks, divided at the toe for the Japanese sandals she would step into when she was fully dressed.

One by one Vi took the wedding garments from the rack.

First the white inner kimono; next a pale green under kimono, and last, the bridal kimono, hand painted in delicate pastel colors – each one carefully crossed left over right in what they both thought of as the masculine way. But the graceful Japanese lady who came to help Leonora with her movement said that the kimono was only crossed right over left in death.

Finally Vi fastened on the obi, already folded and tied to fit, and handed Leonora Butterfly's little bag of treasures to tuck into her sleeve.

All that remained was for Leonora to slip her feet into her sandals before she left for the stage.

Right from the start the audience will know that Pinkerton never intended to be faithful; for him the marriage is a temporary convenience. He will pursue his butterfly even if he breaks her fragile wings. His last words before her entrance will be a toast to the day he will find a real American wife. And then he will leave her.

But she doesn't know that. Leonora must put everything that is to come from her mind.

Alone with her thoughts, she began to walk round the dressing room, feeling the kimonos' weight, sinking herself into the person of Butterfly. For her, today is only full of happiness.

As she walked, she hummed the opening bars of her entrance, feeling the words, the joyful breath of spring on the sea and the earth, the glorious rising music.

The luckiest girl in Japan…in the world…

Leonora's call to the stage has come early, as she had asked. With Vi holding up the train of her kimono, they take the short cut under the stage, through the passage behind the orchestra to prompt side, where Butterfly's friends wait in the dimness of the wings, figures from a Japanese woodcut come to life. Together they move gracefully into the scene and Leonora sings her first notes as Butterfly, full of rapture at the beauty of the day.

Her joy is short-lived: relations vie for position and Pinkerton is impatient for the wedding to be over, even when she shows him her most sacred possession, the knife her father used to end his life at the Emperor's command.

Now, to the sound of a great gong in the wings, the high priest comes raging over the ramp at the back of the stage in his flapping robes: Butterfly has been to the mission to adopt her husband's religion. Howling their rejection, her wedding guests desert her, their shrieks echoing in the distance. And Pinkerton watches with amusement as Suzuki helps Butterfly prepare for the night, until at last she is alone with him.

The audience is a dark, breathing presence that has waited for this moment. Around them is pure stillness. There is no sound from the wings. No one coughs.

Walter looks down at Leonora. All through rehearsals he has wondered at her capacity to transform herself; beneath her white robe she is trembling, the blossoms in her hair quivering. It is as if he has become an observer, watching her performance draw him deep into the scene. He is in an enchanted place, ready to promise her anything. He will never hurt this fragile creature.

Leonora senses the change in him: even after he had begun to relax in rehearsal, it had never felt as if his performance had fully come to life. Now at last Walter is giving her everything in return. The love duet unfolds, the orchestra rising and falling with their voices, every note true. Time stops, the audience holds its breath.

Ah dolce notte...tutto estatico d'amore...

Vieni, vieni, sei mia..ah vien...

The final top C is in perfect unison as Walter takes her in his arms. The curtain comes down as he slips her kimono from her shoulders to a gasp from the audience. A burst of applause rolls towards them and then they are back in the organized chaos of the scene change with the stage manager hurrying them away like children who will be late for school.

Back in her dressing room, Leonora allows herself a few minutes to change out of her costume and drink the cup of tea Vi has waiting for her. This small rest is precious. She has to sing with intensity, almost without pause, until the end of the opera. The second act cannot start without her; some singers give in to the temptation to add a few extra minutes to the interval. For

Leonora it is a point of honor to be ready on time as the Maestro had taught her. "If a singer needs these tricks", he had told her, "perhaps she is not ready to sing this role."

In a few moments Kim Ah will arrive to remove the wedding flowers from her wig and smooth it down. Until then she can close her eyes and relax. Like Vi, he will respect her need for silence.

Perfectly on time as always, she hears his gentle knock. His hands are so light on her head she barely feels them. Then it is time to gather her strength for the demanding second act.

Swallowing the last of her tea, Leonora signals to Vi that she is ready. Her kimonos for this act are simple and easy to put on. Pinkerton has been gone for three years and times are hard for Butterfly.

In the corridor outside the dressing room, Frannie, her Suzuki, is waiting for her. Arms linked like sisters, they make their way to the stage, where they take their places in the semi-darkness. Tense with the drama still to come, they wait in silence.

As if from a great distance, Leonora hears the applause as the conductor makes his entry, and the stage manager's voice, low into the microphone: *house curtain – go!* The curtain rises, lights come up on stage. She is in Butterfly's house in far-away Japan, in another century.

In the shadows Suzuki rings her bell and begins to pray.

…fate che Butterfly non pianga più…

…let Butterfly grieve no more…

And Butterfly waits…

Then it is over, the curtain is down. Beyond it the applause is tremendous as they hold their position: Butterfly dead, Pinkerton kneeling beside her, Sharpless, the American Consul, holding the child. The curtain rises again on the final tableau to silence, then the audience is on its feet, clapping wildly.

Later, Leonora will look back on this night as one of her

greatest performances. Holding Lulu in her arms for the final farewell, she has felt the parting with an intensity she will recall for the rest of her life.

The curtain drops again and the cast lines up on stage. Full Company bows then the principals one by one, the applause increasing each time; bravos and cheers for Walter, but the loudest of all for Leonora, drained and fragile from her performance as she comes down to center stage, first alone then leading Lulu by the hand.

At last the curtain stays down, everyone hugging and congratulating each other. Side by side in the midst of the throng, Walter puts his arm round Leonora's shoulder, the emotion of the last scene still on his face. "I'll never forget this, Lou. I owe it all to you."

Outside Leonora's dressing room, well-wishers were already gathering to congratulate her. There would be a reception later but first Leonora needed a few minutes alone to wind down. She was grateful when Vi intervened in her gentle way, reminding Leonora that she needed to take the costumes back to the wardrobe. Quietly she helped Leonora change, replacing everything neatly on the rack, then left as unobtrusively as she had come.

Alone, Leonora began to take out the pins from her wig, taking care not to disarrange it as she lifted it off and set it back on its stand. Wiping off her make-up, she saw her own face again. Butterfly was slipping away from her.

Now it was time to put on fresh make-up for the inevitable photographs – she didn't begrudge them: she knew what she owed her audience – to brush out her hair and put on the peony-red shift and matching high-heeled sandals that looked so simple but had been hand-made for her in Paris. She nodded to her reflection in the mirror, satisfied with what she saw.

She was just getting ready to leave and wondering why Kim Ah hadn't been round to collect her wig, when she heard his knock and his face appeared round the door, eyes sparkling, as if enjoying a private joke.

"Leonora, you have a visitor. I'm so sorry but I couldn't stop her, she insisted."

She...Leonora's heart sank; surely not Walter's wife. Didn't she have her own performance in Sydney? Not that it really mattered. She braced herself and put on her best diva smile. She would tell Kim Ah what she thought later.

But now Kim Ah had flung open the door and there was Carla, magnificent in emerald green, her hair falling in dramatic waves to her shoulders. For a few seconds she held her pose, enjoying Leonora's amazement, before sweeping into the room, arms outstretched.

"Lou, I was in tears all through the second act. You're the only singer in the world apart from Lily who can do that to me." She perched on the visitor's chair, took a gold compact out of her bag, and checked her eye make-up. "You were completely wonderful. And Walter..." She examined Leonora shrewdly. "I always thought he might have it in him but I'd say you brought it out of him." She snapped her compact shut and put it back in her bag. "When I heard you'd be singing together, I was determined to be at the première, come what may. And here I am."

Leonora contemplated her friend with affection. "It's a wonderful surprise, Carla. It's almost like old times, you, me, Kim Ah..." She hesitated. "And Walter. We're only missing Lily."

"And Tilo." Carla jumped in to finish the sentence. Her eyes sparkled with the mischievous glint Leonora knew so well. "I'm not supposed to tell you really, it's not official yet. There's talk of Lily directing *Tosca* in New York."

"Lily? Directing?"

"Why not? She's not the only singer doing it. Look at Brigitte

Fassbaender in Innsbruck. Anyway, she wants you."

"Me?" The Maestro's words came back to Leonora: she would know when she was ready to sing Tosca. Perhaps it was time.

"And wait till you hear who she wants to conduct."

Leonora couldn't help laughing. "You look as if you're about to pull a rabbit out of a hat."

Carla smiled her Cheshire Cat smile. "Perhaps I am. Anyway, it's Tilo."

"*Tilo?* But he would have told me."

"It's still being discussed and nothing's official yet. But as if either of you are going to turn it down when it is." She pointed a scarlet-tipped finger at Leonora. "Now we'd better go and meet your public. I promise not to get in the way."

"Some hope." Leonora linked her arm through Carla's. "But I'll overlook it just this once."

Still too full of performance energy to sleep, Leonora stood at her apartment window gazing into the darkness. The streets were empty and silent; only the chirruping of the possums in the trees and the call now and then of a night-flying bird gave any sign of life.

She would try to come home to perform more often, establish a base in Melbourne between engagements to spend more time with her mother. At the reception she had watched her with amusement taking Carla in her stride until they were chatting like old friends.

Kim Ah was right. The theatre was a family whose members came and went, paths crossing and recrossing, never lost to each other. Even Walter had come back.

She turned and saw the message light flashing on her phone. She pressed the answer button – a few short rings and she heard his voice.

"Leonora."

"Tilo." It was as if he was there in the room. "It's done, my first performance of Butterfly at home."

"More than done, I hear. Carla says it was a triumph." He paused, as if weighing his words. "For Walter too. And she told you about *Tosca*. Will you do it?"

Leonora didn't hesitate. "I will. I'll be home soon, there's so much to tell you."

She was aware of a movement at the end of the phone; he was pushing his glasses back into place, an echo of his younger self.

"But will you be coming home to me or *Tosca*?"

It had been a journey but finally she had arrived. Love and music: she could stretch out her hands and take them both.

"To you *and* Tosca, Tilo. But above all to you."

ACKNOWLEDGEMENTS

The late much-loved Louise Zaetta, who encouraged me to write this book.

Iresha, Brigid, Amanda, Kim and Ian, from our Cortona writers group, who have been there until I finally made it to the end of this project, and Kevin, opera tenor and playwright, always ready to burst into song, sadly no longer with us.

Jürgen Zielinski, make-up artist, wig master and opera guru, for his friendship and wisdom. Any mistakes are my own.

Peter Bishop at Varuna, the National Writers' House, during my two residences there, and the staff and volunteers who made it all possible.

Laurel Cohn at Pathways to Publication for her editorial advice and believing I could bring this work to completion.

Julie Postance at iinspire media for guiding me through the publishing process.

My family, for being the best thing in my life.

Thank you.

Patricia Ryan acknowledges the Boonwurrung people of the Kulin Nation as the Traditional Owners and Custodians of the land on which this book was written. She pays her respects to their Elders, past, present and emerging, and acknowledges and upholds their continuing relationship to this land.

ABOUT THE AUTHOR

Patricia Ryan was born in Oxford in the United Kingdom, grew up in London and studied languages and singing in London and Munich. Since her first visit outside the UK to France as a schoolgirl, she has travelled to many parts of the world and believes that the more we interact with other cultures the more we find we have in common, and that music can unite us all.

Patricia Ryan lives in Melbourne, Australia. This is her first novel.

Made in the USA
Middletown, DE
28 December 2022

20580995R00172